David,
From one Burroughs fan
To Another —

[signature]

Copyright © 2005. Joel Jenkins

1st printing 2005. CyberPulp Press
2nd printing 2006. RageMachine Press
3rd printing 2007. PulpWork Press, New York.

ISBN 978-0-9797329-4-2

Cover illustration by Mats Minnhagen
Additonal back cover illustrations by Noel Tuazon

All rights reserved. No part of this book may be used or reproduced in any manner whatsoever without written permission from the publisher except in the case of brief quotations embodied in critical articles or reviews.

Dire Planet

Joel Jenkins

Table of Contents

Introduction:	5
Chapter I: The Stasis Loop	7
Chapter II: Lana Shar	11
Chapter III: Wings in the Mist	17
Chapter IV: The Caves of Ledgrim	25
Chapter Five: Attack on Ledgrim	33
Chapter Six: The Mind Master	41
Chapter Seven: Lair of the Galbran	47
Chapter Eight: Escape from the Galbran	61
Chapter Nine: Captive of the Sinthral	69
Chapter Ten: Escape From the Sinthral	79
Chapter Eleven: Return of the Sinthral	89
Chapter Twelve: Caladrex	99
Chapter Thirteen: The Ghost of Caladrex	119
Chapter Fourteen: The Death Trap	135
Chapter Fifteen: Temple of the Vackri	149
Chapter Sixteen: Defense of Gredgehold	169
Chapter Seventeen: Fugitives of Braxenridge	183
Chapter Eighteen: The Laboratory of Sar Savaht	197
Chapter Nineteen: Through the Portals of Time	215
Chapter Twenty: At the Gates of Ledgrim	231

Introduction:

The promotion of this book will no doubt include the phrase "in the tradition of Edgar Rice Burroughs". It is both true and a kind of short-hand for customers. If you liked Burroughs' Barsoom novels and wish there were more, then this book will please. And it does please in spades.

I've thought long on why that should be. It's not a pastiche of Burroughs. You won't find John Carter or the egg-laying Dejah Thoris here. Joel Jenkins has obviously grown up on the same books I did—tales of interplanetary romance written for the early Pulps like Blue Book and Argosy-All-Story. But it's not pastiche.

Some may wonder at my distinction. A pastiche is by definition an author trying to copy another. It's a fake. Like a bad Frazetta copy it shows off where the pasticher fails in the master's shadow. I don't as a rule like pastiches.

What is better—and Joel Jenkins has succeeded at this—is when an author takes the spirit of another and lets their own imagination, their own sensibilities, their own time and place in reality, filtered through that excitement, tell a great story. This is the difference between another tiresome Lovecraft copy and a great new Cthulhu Mythos story. One you meet with a groan of "not again!" and the other makes you so excited that you want to go back and re-read all the books in your library. "Sticks" by Karl Edward Wagner was one such story. Written in Wagner's own voice, it is stunningly creepy, wonderfully Lovecraftian.

Dire Planet is also such a tale. Filled with daring escapes and long, spectacular punch-ups, (Garvey Dire's battle with the Galbrans is epically entertaining. You wonder "how can they ever survive?" but you know they will and you will not feel the writer has pressed too hard on your credibility.) Dire Planet is a love-song to scientific romance. But it is also couched in our own time. There are no fainting beauties or head-smacking stupidities for plot sake.

Edgar Rice Burroughs was truly great, but his tools are not the tools of today. Joel Jenkins is a writer of 21st Century as well as a fan of the 20th. What he does here will bring a familiar smile to your face, even if you haven't smiled it for decades.

Let's hope he has as many sequels in him as Burroughs did.

G. W. Thomas

Chapter I:
The Stasis Loop

Her footsteps crossed the cracked stone dais, leaving no impression in the fluorescent blue moss that covered the time-weathered stone like a cushion. Long, pale hair fell about her shoulders in a twisted profusion, amethyst glistening from sloe eyes smeared with some dark makeup. The bare flesh that peered from beneath her torn, reflective cuirass was tinted green, and her lips—the lower being fuller than the upper—bore a purple hue.

A scabbard slapped against her bare thigh, the narrow hilt of a rapier-like blade protruding. On her back she wore some sort of firearm unlike anything Garvey had ever seen, built with a wide bore and massive vents. The strange woman looked toward the stranded astronaut, and her lips parted. Just as Garvey Dire thought that she would speak, her lithe form began to shimmer, and she faded into nothingness like the apparition that she was.

Each time that she appeared it was the same. She sprang into existence near the shattered pillars at the top of the dais, and crossed from the collapsed passage to the bottom of the dais where Garvey sat nursing a broken right leg that had been shattered when his probe, the Mars Climate Orbiter crash landed on Mars' arid surface. Once he had even reached out to touch the woman, but his hands passed through her as though she were made of mist.

Officially, NASA designated Garvey's ship, the Orbiter, as an unmanned space probe, but elements within the space program were far more ambitious. They equipped the craft with landing capabilities, and enough supplies and equipment for one man to survive indefinitely on the hostile surface of Mars. Following the claustrophobic nightmare of the 286-day trip from Earth, Garvey began the descent onto Mars' surface and one of the landing thrusters gave out.

The only things Garvey managed to salvage from the Orbiter were the space suit he was wearing, a few days worth of food, and a small atmospheric generator, which was feebly pumping out oxygen next to him.

The air supply in his suit had long since been exhausted, and he rested his right elbow on the fishbowl helmet, grimacing as he once again felt blood flowing from his compound fracture, and pooling in the bottom of the space suit that he still wore.

It was only a matter of time now. After the crash he managed to crawl from the flaming wreckage and into the shelter of a rock fall, where he jammed himself between two boulders to protect himself from the gritty winds that swept across Mars' rugged surface. As he struggled his way deeper, the ground gave way beneath him, painfully depositing him among the rubble of this alien-constructed chamber buried beneath the surface of the planet.

She came every hour, her step and stride never changing. Garvey knew each movement and glance by memory; it never altered. Though the lure of adventure had ever been greater for him than the lure of human companionship, as his life wound down to its last minutes, and his breathing grew labored as the atmospheric generator faltered, Garvey found himself wishing that this woman was more than just a wraith, more than some phantasmal vestige of a decayed and lost civilization that Mars once possessed.

While he sat bleeding, waiting to draw his last breath, he tried to push aside the agony of his broken leg and in the dim light shed from a globe hanging on the cracked and heaving ceiling, his eyes searched for the mechanism that might be projecting this three-dimensional illusion. Finally, he perceived a trio of mechanical devices that pushed from the moss growing on the dais.

He checked the chronometer on his suit and saw that it was another ten minutes before his exotic visitor would once again appear. Curiosity got the better of him, and he decided that, even dying, he could not sit idly by while the great mysteries of Mars remained still unexplored. Clenching his teeth, he dragged himself up the broad steps of the dais, and began brushing the rubble away from the metallic knob protruding from the moss. Garvey ripped away a great clot of the bluish bryophyte and uncovered a metallic box that had once been hidden beneath the stone pavings of the steps. The lid was jammed tight, but Garvey withdrew a multi-tool from one of the pockets on his suit, and managed to pry it away with his screwdriver extension. Inside the box rested a dazzling array of capacitors and circuits constructed from no metals or materials, which he had ever seen. Thick cables penetrated the box from beneath, and Garvey guessed that these might be providing the power source for the projectors. Maybe a more brilliant man might have been able to adapt this alien source of energy to feed the dying atmospheric generator, but Garvey had no idea where to begin.

Once again the alien woman appeared at the top of the dais, her booted feet carrying her weightlessly across the moss. Garvey's atmospheric generator chugged to a halt, and black spots appeared before his eyes, marring his vision of the ephemeral beauty that walked toward him in her predestined, and unending circuit. It was only moments before he lost consciousness, but still Garvey's curiosity drove him to experiment. He lowered the metal tip of his screwdriver into the box until it touched the nearest capacitor.

Blue fire arced from the box, leaping up the screwdriver and climbing Garvey's right arm. For a brief moment a blue aurora played across the marooned astronaut's body, then the misdirected energy picked him up and hurled him through the air, directly into the image of the palehaired woman that crossed the dais.

This time, however, he did not pass through her. Their bodies met, flesh against flesh. She cried out and they went down in a tangled, rolling heap, blue fire playing about them, soaring in great jagged arcs. The scent of ozone hung thick in the air as energy crackled, leaping from mechanism to mechanism. A blinding flash filled the chamber, and then blackness descended like a great sheet.

Chapter II:
Lana Shar

Cape Canaveral, Florida 1998

Bradley Thomas leaned forward, resting his forearms on the polished mahogany surface of his desk. His tie was loosened, and the sleeves of his white shirt rolled up, revealing an anchor tattoo he'd foolishly gotten one drunken night when he still flew fighters for the Navy. An unlit cigar was clamped firmly between his teeth.

"Garvey, you're one of the luckiest son of a guns that I've ever known. You'll be the first man to set foot on Mars. You don't know how much I envy you."

Garvey Dire wore a pale blue polo shirt and a pair of black slacks. His dark eyes shifted to his long time friend behind the desk, as he took a seat in a heavy wooden chair. "I don't mind telling you, Brad, but the hardest part of this whole thing is going to be keeping it a secret. They gave this job to me because I'm known for being tight-lipped with a secret, but going to Mars and not being able to tell anybody about what I saw? That's a little much."

Bradley's eyes moved to the closed door of his office. "Just don't let any of the brass hear you say that. They'll take away your flight privileges, and give Arnold Stetcher the flight to Mars. He's been shooting you daggers ever since you got the call."

Garvey reached across Bradley's desk and stole an apple that was holding down a pile of paperwork. "I also don't mind saying that Arnold's the biggest jerk that I've ever met."

Bradley let a deep chuckle roll from his chest. "That's putting it nicely. I have a few other choice words that I'd use to describe him."

Garvey took a bite of the apple and carefully chewed it, his eyes far away. When he'd finally swallowed the masticated pulp he spoke. "I know that I'm supposed to be a good astronaut and blindly obey orders, but can you tell me why NASA isn't going public about a manned flight to Mars?"

Bradley scratched at the cleft in his chin. "Why don't you lock the door, then we'll have a little chat."

Mars, 47,000 B.C.

When Garvey Dire awoke he felt like his guts had been tied in knots. An odd sense of vertigo assailed him as he pushed his eyes open and found the green-skinned woman leaning over him, her pale hair brushing his cheek as she examined him with great curiosity.

The astronaut could feel the pulse of her breath, and the warmth in her hand as she touched his stubbled cheek with her fingertips. Whatever she was, she was no longer an illusion. Her amethyst eyes narrowed as she realized that Garvey was coming out of unconsciousness. Alien words tumbled from her purple-tinged lips, harsh but melodic. Garvey shook his head, unable to comprehend the language that she was speaking.

She took two fingers and pressed them lightly against Garvey's forehead, and the torrent of words that fell from her mouth began to take shape in his mind, and he was surprised to find out that he understood.

"You are not a torrack," she said. "Yet you appear to be a man."

"So I've been told," grimaced Garvey. His respite from the pain of his shattered leg had been brief, now it throbbed fiercely. The atmosphere, however, provided his lungs the sustenance that they had been denied before he disrupted the circuit of the device that had been projecting the image of this alien beauty.

"You understand me now," she said. It was more of a statement of fact than a question.

"I don't know how, but I do," answered Garvey. Bewildered, he turned his head and saw that the room which had previously lain in ruins, now stood as it must have thousands of years before he ever found the forgotten chamber. The polished walls of hewn stone stood straight, and the marbled pillars atop the dais were untouched by the ravages of time, supporting a domed ceiling carved with strange symbols. The steps that had formerly heaved and twisted stood perfectly straight, but the metal knobs, that had projected the image of the woman leaning over him, smoked and crackled with unleashed energy.

"It is a telepathic ability of my race to be able to communicate with others who speak differently than we. This is something I would expect most to know, but you are unlike any race that I have ever seen."

"What happened?" asked Garvey. "One minute we were in a ruined building buried beneath the sands of Mars, and the next the building is repaired and looks as though it must have thousands of years ago."

"Longer," corrected the woman. "I have been caught in a trap—a stasis loop—for unending eons, doomed to repeat my steps over, and over again. That is, until you interrupted the circuit and freed me from the Warlord Shaxia's snare. When you freed me, the temporal vortex pulled us back to the moment after I blundered into the Warlord's trap."

Garvey bit back the pain. "So, you're trying to tell me that we traveled eons back in time since I found you in the stasis loop?"

The woman didn't appear to hear Garvey's question but saw his grimace of pain. "You are wounded. Where are you hurt?"

"It's my right leg," answered the astronaut. Even as he spoke his vision swam before him, and he knew that the loss of blood was taking its toll.

She glanced at his space suit. "This is strange apparel that you wear. Is it some sort of armor?"

Without waiting for a reply, she drew out a knife from a sheath on her left thigh, and she began to slice away the layers of the space suit, until she was able to remove the right leg of it. Crimson poured from the boot, spattering on the stone, and Garvey steeled himself against the sight of his wound. The bone protruded from the flesh in a gory gash, and Garvey wondered if even a surgeon could fully repair the damage that had been done.

"'Tis a grim injury, indeed, stranger. How did you come by it?"

He hesitated to tell the tale, thinking that she would scoff at the truth–but what could he possibly say that might seem more outrageous than the events he had experienced in these last few moments?"

"My name is Garvey Dire, I come from the third planet in this solar system. A planet we call Earth. My vessel crash-landed and I was injured."

She shook her head. "I know of this Earth. The scientists of my tribe have studied it, and it is far too close to the sun to sustain life. Its oceans boil in the daylight, the vapor sinking back to the seas when darkness falls."

Garvey considered this for a moment. "You forget that I come from your future. The sun's rays have cooled, and the seas no longer boil. Billions of people inhabit the planet."

"My name is Lana Shar of the Muvari people. Since you saved my life, I'll not question your assertions, but I must admit that they sound like a tale the story teller of our people might invent."

As she spoke she put her hands on Garvey's wounded leg and exerted pressure, pushing the bones back into place. The astronaut stiffened, and cried out. "What are you doing?"

"Don't move," ordered Lana Shar. "We may be able to fix this."

Garvey grimaced. "You've got to be kidding me."

The alien girl reached into a pouch at her belt and withdrew a small handheld unit that projected with two diagonal stubs. She turned a knob.

"I kid you not. This is technology stolen from the Warlord Shaxia; technology withheld from the tribes that inhabit the surface of Mars."

She depressed a button on the curving metallic casing of the device and a yellow ray emitted from the double prongs at the top, bathing Garvey's leg in the sickly illumination. Intense pain shot through his nerves, and sweat burst from every pore, but the light transfixed him, and he was unable to pull away from its glow.

Even as he watched, bone begin to knit within the gaping gash, then flesh began grow over the top, until even the skin had closed over the wound. Lana turned off the alien machine, and the pain ceased—leaving only a dull throbbing where a broken bone had jutted only moments before.

"That's amazing," murmured Garvey, unable to fathom the technology that had regenerated his mangled body in a matter of minutes.

"It's some of the technology hoarded by the Warlord Shaxia," replied Lana. She licked her purple lips, and glanced nervously about the chamber. "But I fear that we've tarried too long. Some of the Warlord's torrack guards will surely notice that the stasis loop has been broken and will be down to investigate."

"You mean that we're in the Warlord's Shaxia's castle right now?"

Lana waved her hand dismissively. "Hardly. Shaxia has hidden depots where she sometimes conceals technology such as this device that healed your leg. This is one of them—I located it on the far edge of the Rift."

Garvey had no concept of what the Rift was. "The Warlord is a woman?"

"Yes," replied Lana as the glanced back toward the pillars through which she had crossed repeatedly for thousands of years. "Does that seem strange to you?"

Garvey shook his head as he gingerly hoisted himself to his feet.

"No more than anything else that I've experienced today." He was surprised to find that his leg supported him, but much of his customary strength was gone. He felt weak and frail, and was surprised to find that he could stand at all. It suddenly dawned on him that the reason he could still stand in such an enfeebled state was that Mars' gravitational pull was so much less than that of Earth's. He remembered vividly that Mars' gravity was 37.7% of that of Earth.

Lana's purple eyes opened wide when she saw Garvey stand under his own power. "I'm surprised that you can stand at all. Most men are so weakened after undergoing the healing process, that they can only walk with the aid of another."

"I feel as weak as a baby," admitted Garvey who regretted the words as soon as they left his mouth. Despite her strangely slender build and alien colorations, Lana Shar was a beautiful creature, and he found a secret desire to impress her lurking within his mind. Perhaps admitting to feeling weak would lessen him in her eyes.

Lana Shar eyed his broad shoulders critically. "You have a very powerful physique," she said. "Though you are far shorter than most men of my tribe."

Indeed, Lana was nearly as tall as Garvey's six-foot frame, and as she stepped closer her purple eyes peered directly into the astronaut's. Garvey noticed that Lana wore an inscribed gold hoop that pierced the upper cartilage of her left ear.

From somewhere beyond the pillars, in the dimness that shrouded the passage beyond, the sound of footsteps slapping against stone echoed to their ears.

"Come," said Lana. She brushed past him and began running down a long corridor, which was lit only by intermittent globes of light that peered from the stone ceiling. Garvey's knee buckled beneath him on the first step that he took, but Lana was too far ahead of him to notice. The astronaut regained his balance and took a first step, which propelled him about seven feet down the declining floor of the hallway. In a few moments he caught up to Lana, and adjusted his pace so that he did not outstrip her. They ran side by side for about a hundred yards and suddenly they burst forth from the corridor onto a ledge of bluish stone that jutted from a massive cliff face.

For a moment Garvey teetered on the edge of the precipice, staring down into a massive rift that tore through the crust of Mars' surface and dropped nearly a mile toward the core of the red planet. The lower depths of the rift were concealed in a thick fog that roiled up from the jagged teeth of rock below, and Garvey could feel the moisture beading on his bare leg.

Lana put out a hand and steadied Garvey. "I should have warned you we were reaching a dead end."

Garvey whirled and stared up the cliff face behind him, only to find that it rose at least a hundred yards above them. Given some time, an adept cliff climber might be able to pick his way up the face, but Garvey had an idea that time was at a premium.

"These torracks?" asked Garvey, "Do they carry weapons similar to the one on your back?" He nodded toward the thick black cylinder, with heavy vents that flared out from either side.

Lana Shar nodded grimly. "They can strike a woman from a distance, cutting her in half. However, they aren't terribly accurate, and the energy cells last only for a short time."

"Are they accurate enough to pick us off the cliff if we start to climb?"

Before Lana could answer a high-pitched scream resonated from the depths of the corridor from which they had just emerged. The strange sound was accompanied by a blue bolt of energy that burst from the hall. It nicked Garvey's space suit on his left arm and burned a hole through the suit. He grimaced as molten plastic and metal dripped on his bare skin.

"The torracks!" hissed Lana as she pushed Garvey to one side. "We must make haste."

"Agreed," said Garvey as he flattened himself the cliff wall next to the opening of the corridor. "But unless you can fly, I think we might be done for."

Chapter III:
Wings in the Mist

Cape Canaveral, Florida 1998

Garvey locked the door of Bradley Thomas' office while Bradley shut the blinds of the window, blocking out the brilliant sunlight, so that only a few dusty rays filtered through into the darkened room.

"You understand," said Bradley, "that even I'm not supposed to know this."

"Understood," answered Garvey, his eyes turning as hard and black as charcoal.

"It's all about mineral rights. When the rock samples that the Mars Lander retrieved for us were analyzed they showed rich deposits of gold, silver, and copper—not to mention derivative selenium. It's your job to establish an outpost and show NASA, and whatever commercial investors it brings together, that a mining colony on Mars is a viable option."

Garvey shrugged. "So they're sending me on the longest treasure hunt in Earth's history, why all the secrecy? So what if the general public knows?"

"Like it or not, it's also a national security issue. China has been stealing our top-secret technology left and right, and due to millions of dollars of Chinese money that somehow ended up in his campaign coffers, our former president let it slide. China's space program is on par with our own, and they are as capable as we are if they decide to put together a manned mission to Mars."

"Are they?"

"Our intelligence sources say that they are planning one in 2,002. It's imperative that we have a man there first."

Garvey still didn't look convinced. "Let me play devil's advocate for a minute. Let's say that NASA has an information leak, and China knows that Mars is loaded with precious metals. Mars is about half the size of Earth; that still makes for an awfully big planet. Isn't their enough precious metals to go around?"

"That brings us to the second, and most important value of Mars," said Bradley.

"I'm listening," said Garvey. He took another bite of Bradley's apple.

"Strategic. China has already put nuclear devices into orbit around Earth. These nuclear satellites can be dropped from the sky on any number of U.S. cities. Our scientists are working as fast as they can to get the Strategic Defense Initiative up and running so that we might have a shot at blowing these falling satellites from the sky before they hit their targets, but let's face it, we're decades away from having a complete Star Wars defense system in place. In the meantime, the only defense we've got is to jam China's signal before it gets to the satellites."

"Now I get it," said Garvey. "If China establishes a base on Mars before we do, they can transmit signals to their satellites from outer space—and there's nothing we can do jam the transmission."

Bradley threw up his hands. "Not unless we're there first. Unfortunately, NASA's funding is extremely limited, and in order to get the cash necessary to pull off such a huge undertaking we need to involve venture capitalists."

"And that brings us back to mineral rights," said Garvey.

Bradley nodded. "You're going to live on Mars for an entire year before we send a group of relief astronauts. You're going to get lonely."

A grin spread across Garvey's face. "You're jealous, aren't you?"

Bradley grinned back. "Dang right I'm jealous! But I've got a wife and three kids to think about. You—you're just an old hermit anyway. You've managed to avoid marriage more times than I can count."

"I keep telling you," replied Garvey as he tossed his apple core across the room. It thunked against the rim of the metal garbage can and bounced in. "It's the lure of adventure. If I get serious with a woman, or if I get married and start a family then I wouldn't be able to take neat little trips to Mars, and spend a year isolated from all humanity."

"Just don't wait too long. I don't want you to die shriveled, alone and bitter."

"I'll just die shriveled and alone," laughed Garvey. "I think Arnold Stechter is the bitter one."

Mars, 47,000 B.C.

As a second blast of superheated plasma burst from the dark corridor Lana Shar twisted to the right side of the door and leaned back.

Her hands groped in a narrow crevice that split the stone cliff and she pulled loose an apparatus that reminded Garvey of old film clips that he'd seen—movie footage showing old scientists and their failed attempts to fly using a variety of non-functional contraptions.

It looked like a backpack with wings attached. The wings were constructed with a hollow wooden tubing similar to Earth's bamboo, and stretched across this framework was a milky brown membrane, which Garvey could not identify. Lana shoved the backpack across the opening of the corridor and Garvey snatched it over to his side of the ledge as another blast of energy screamed by and dissipated in the mists that rose from the awesome gash in Mars' surface.

"Put that on," ordered Lana.

Garvey looked at the questionable device, a worried expression creeping onto his face, but Lana was already shrugging another such device onto her shapely shoulders. Perhaps Lana was some sort of Martian lunatic about to plummet to her death, or perhaps such a device would work in the lower gravity that bound Mars' surface. Garvey could not say, but he could hear footsteps pounding against stone as their pursuers came nearer, and he could smell the scent of their energy weapons, still lingering in the air—similar to odor of smoldering plastic.

The displaced astronaut followed Lana Shar's example and pulled on the wings. "Why did you bring two sets of wings?" he asked.

Lana halted for a moment, her slender frame poised on the edge of the precipice, her membranous wings spread wide. "I did not come alone. Another warrior of my tribe was killed here."

Without speaking any further she leaped into the steaming void, miraculously gliding on the torrents of wind that buoyed her up. Garvey sent a prayer soaring to the sky as he sprinted across the ledge and leaped out into nothingness. As he leapt, five torrack warriors burst from the mouth of the corridor. Each stood nearly seven feet tall, their slender physiques rippling with lean muscle. They wore leather harnesses that crossed their bare chests, and each brandished a sword or a strange energy rifle like the one that Lana Shar carried. Expressions of rage passed across their green-tinted visages, their purple lips scowling as they lowered their rifles and fired at Garvey.

The rifles screamed, and a downdraft sucked Garvey into the rift. He plummeted, bright lances of energy criss-crossing his path and searing his wings. Drops of moisture beat at his face as he plunged into the thick mist, obscuring him from the view of the torracks that were attempting to cut him from the air. Garvey twisted and flailed, desperately attempting to beat the air with his wings, but he only fell. The fog sizzled and popped as blue energy seared through the air around him, but the weak Martian gravity had Garvey in its grip now, and unmercifully pulled him toward the jagged teeth of the rifts rocky bottom.

The wind beat at Garvey's face as he finally untangled his wings and spread them wide, attempting to slow his rapid descent, if but a little.

The cracked and heaving floor of the rift rushed up to meet him, towering stalagmites that glistened with shards of volcanic glass, beckoning him to his death. His wingtips brushed the sharp tip of a protruding stone spire, and then his wings finally caught the wind, and he swooped through a forest of stalagmites, dipping his wings to the left and right as he wove through the deadly maze. A dozen feet below Garvey, the cracked stone earth whipped below him—his momentum hurtling him forward at over a hundred miles an hour.

Garvey began to pump his arms, desperately beating the wings in order to gain some height. He knew that if he were to impact with any one of these stalagmites, or even hit the earth that his fragile body would be pulped beyond recognition. He didn't have enough skill with his wings to slow his speed and make a landing, and even if he did the last thing that he wanted was to become lost on the floor of this massive canyon.

To Garvey's amazement, his wings began to lift him, and he slowly began to rise, finally elevating himself above the loftiest of the crack-spidered spires. His wings carried him through plumes of hot steam that rose from glowing fissures in the bottom of the canyon floor, the heat stinging his skin and burning his lungs.

He fought his way through the thick white billows, rising ever higher, where the heat of the steam diminished so that it was merely uncomfortable, and not dangerous to linger within its obscuring fogs.

Garvey's heart beat wildly. Slowly his breathing evened as he recovered from the adrenaline-inducing free fall that had nearly cost him his life. He lifted his eyes and searched for Lana Shar's slender form, but his vision failed to pierce the hazy air.

The canyon walls were pocked and cracked, and Garvey could make out ledges and even the mouths of dark caverns that pierced the red rock wall. If he tired, he figured that he could take temporary refuge on one of these ledges now that his speed had slowed considerably. He slowly spiraled upward, seeking to break through the layer of mist that clouded his vision, and hindered his search for Lana Shar.

Finally his wings pushed aside the veil of mist and he rose above the billows. The astronaut's eyes searched the wide, and uneven rift, and did not see any familiar sights. The alien landscape jutted and heaved before him, bathed in the golden glow of the sun as it filtered through Mars's thin atmosphere. The scene was utterly incredible, and breathtaking—and Garvey suddenly realized how very alone he was.

He was a man displaced in time and space. His only friend, Bradley Thomas, was thirty-four million miles, and 39,000 years away.

What could bridge that awesome gap? How had he bridged that awesome gap, and for what purpose? Did God have some plan for him, or was it some cruel cosmic joke that had snatched him back in time?

A grim smile touched his lips. Surely, this was the ultimate adventure. Perhaps he had failed in NASA's mission to establish an utpost before China could gain a foothold on the planet's surface, but he had discovered life and civilization on Mars that none of Earth's scientists had ever dared imagine. Yes, they examined bits of meteor debris, and loudly proclaimed the existence of organisms on Mars—but surely they had never imagined such as he had already discovered.

A faint glint caught the corner of Garvey's eyes, and he sent his body rushing forward with a thrust of his arms. The movement of wings through the clouds held his attention, and he flapped his own wings hard, trying not to lose sight of what he was sure was Lana Shar. The sunlight glinted again from her metallic cuirass and Garvey shouted out to her.

Lana heard the cry as it bounded from the walls of the rift, and she bent her wings and circled back toward Garvey, meeting him in the ethereal tendrils of mist.

"I thought that perhaps you had plummeted to your death," she said, her face betraying no concern at the grim thought.

"It took me a little too long to figure out how to make these things work," answered Garvey. He gave his wings a push, and awkwardly glided into a circle around Lana.

She laughed at his crude efforts. "You still lack some finesse, but it is fortunate that you learned their function in time to save yourself. You will be quite a prize, and the elders of my tribe might not forgive me if I had lost you."

Garvey raised his eyebrows. A prize? Perhaps this beautiful Martian was taking a liking to him. "Why would the elders not forgive you?"

"A man is a rare thing." A smile touched her purple lips. "Almost as rare as a visitor from Earth."

Garvey furrowed his brow. "What of the torracks who attacked us? Aren't they men?"

Lana Shar's almond-shaped eyes widened ever so slightly, and the corners of her mouth curled up. "They are not men or women. They are neutered beings that are created solely to serve as warriors for the Warlord Shaxia. So even if they weren't sworn enemies, our tribe would have no use for them."

Garvey wasn't entirely sure what Lana was referring to, but his being male seemed to put him in good stead somehow. He had more questions, but Lana seemed anxious to be moving on.

"Nightfall will be coming soon, and it is best that we are not out in the open when darkness falls." She turned, and bent her wings toward the North, her slender arms moving them with a grace and agility that Garvey could never hope to attain.

He followed clumsily, the power in his broad shoulders and arms somewhat compensating for his lack of grace and skill with sheer speed and force. Lana expertly rode the winds, while he stayed aloft only with a determined effort. They cut through the mists, never leaving the rift, which broadened out before them, dark shadows crawling up the cliff faces as the sun fell over the horizon.

The outlines of Mars two moons, Phobos and Deimos, became visible in the sky. Since Phobos made three revolutions around Mars per day, it orbited faster than the planet rotates, so it rose in the West and descended in the East—opposite of its burlier and slower brother, Deimos.

Deimos' face was pitted and pocked with craters, and Phobos showed a series of parallel scars across its face.

Slackening her pace, Lana Shar had fallen back alongside of him, observing him while he gazed up at the scars that slashed across Phobos.

"Those are the cities of the Karpathesians; they raid the planet, taking slaves and concubines. Even the Warlord Shaxia fears them."

Garvey looked doubtfully into the shadowing skies. "They have craft that will take them from Phobos to Mars?"

"They have great ships coated in glittering metal that reflects the plasma blasts created by the Warlord Shaxia's rifles." Lana bobbed her head in the direction of the rifle that she wore on her back.

"Is that why you wear that metallic cuirass?" asked Garvey.

"Yes," replied the winged warrior. "They are effective against only a glancing hit. A direct hit, or a sustained blast will melt right through the thin metal foil and burn out your innards."

"You have a way with words," replied Garvey. "Are the Karpathesians the reason why you fear to be caught out after dark?"

Lana Shar returned an icy glance with her purple eyes. "It is not fear, it is wisdom—and no, it is not the Karpathesians of which I am wary.

There are plenty of other creatures native to Mars of which we need be more concerned."

The sun's fiery light was fading into oblivion as an extensive series of battlements built onto the cliff side came into view. A plethora of caves dotted the sheer stone face, and a network of stone and wooden ramps, built with spiked rails, connected the cave openings. A large wooden deck projected from the stone ledge of the largest of these caverns, and Lana gently alighted on its surface. Garvey came down harder, tumbling forward and snapping the tubing of his right wing. He was utterly exhausted from the flight, his arms and chest were burning, but with a groan he managed to push himself back to his feet.

As he stood upright, a dozen spear tips were thrust toward him, hovering inches away from his slashed and melted NASA environmental suit. A score of slender, green-skinned women crowded around him, their purple-hued lips pushed back in snarls, and their violet eyes burning with malice.

Chapter IV:
The Caves of Ledgrim

Cape Canaveral, Florida December 11, 1998

Garvey Dire settled himself into the tight confines of the Mars Climate Orbiter long before NASA allowed reporters onto the grounds. NASA's press releases stated that the Orbiter was an unmanned craft to monitor weather conditions on Mars. To all appearances, the orbiter was designed to do exactly that. It was a small, squat construction placed beneath the nose cone atop a Boeing Delta II 7425 four stage rocket.

Each of the four solid rockets that surrounded the base of the rocket held 26,000 pounds of hydroxyl-terminated polybutadiene propellant, or as the rocket scientists liked to call it—HTPB. It added up to about 100,000 pounds of thrusting power.

That was just for starters, Garvey knew that he was also sitting on top of three stages of rocket fuel—nearly a quarter million pounds of juice. If something went wrong, there would be more than enough heat to incinerate him in a blink of the eye—but Garvey barely gave this a thought. He knew the risks, and he put them at the back of his mind.

He could hear the countdown in his headset. Five minutes and he was on his way—the first man to set foot on Mars. If only he could survive the year long journey there without going insane.

Bradley Thomas spoke in Garvey's ear from a small private control room within the vast halls of the Cape Canaveral complex. Perhaps twenty people knew that the Climate Orbiter was actually a manned mission—and they wanted to keep that knowledge to as few as people as possible.

"All systems are go," said the speaker in his ear. "We'll continue to monitor the systems, but it looks like you're going to be on your way to Mars in a few minutes."

Garvey looked around at his cramped quarters. "Tell Stechter that I'd love to have him along, but there's not enough room for his ego…let alone his big head."

"He's one of the best we've got," said Bradley, "but he's not taking this well at all. He already got into a scrap with one of the math wizards, gave him a black eye."

Garvey raised an eyebrow. "You've got to be kidding me? What was the scrap about?"

"Nothing, really. Stechter's just in a foul mood. He'd give his left arm to be in your place."

"I don't blame him, really." Garvey watched the countdown scroll down to four minutes on his cockpit screen. "There's no place I'd rather be right now than in this cockpit."

"Well, Stechter won't even get to see the launch. He's been banned from the site for today. No doubt, he'll be back in the good graces of the brass in a week or two. They've got him in mind for your relief mission next year."

"Funny," mused Garvey. "I won't have even reached Mars by the time they send him out to retrieve me. Still, after two years of solitude I'll probably be glad to see even his ugly face."

They lapsed into a tense silence as the countdown continued.

Already, the cockpit of the Mars Climate Orbiter seemed unbearably hot. Sweat rolled down Garvey's forehead. The astronaut quietly said a prayer, all the while the automated countdown continued. Garvey had yet to finish his fervent prayer when the rocket began to vibrate, the shaking jarring his teeth and rattling his bones. The countdown was complete. The four solid fuel rocket boosters jutting from the circumference of the first stage ignited, and one hundred thousand pounds of thrust pushed Garvey deep into the padding of his seat.

With deliberate slowness the rocket rose from its pad, the great skeletal structure that supported its ponderous weight fell away—and for a moment Garvey wondered if the rocket might topple, too. But inexorably the rocket needled skyward, its first stage bathed in leaping, roiling flame that rebounded from the scorched concrete beneath.

The rocket lifted into the sky, smoke rolling across the launch field, and white hot flame bathing everything in an eerie iridescence. At thirty seconds the rocket reached Mach 1– 738 miles per hour. At forty-five seconds the rocket reached maximum dynamic pressure, the gravity forces pushing and tearing at the skin of Garvey's face, each breath coming slow and painfully, as though an elephant were sitting on his chest.

At one minute three seconds the solid fuel boosters quit burning, and without Garvey lifting a finger they jettisoned away, falling free and into the warm waters of the Atlantic. The first stage continued to burn—RP 1, a highly refined kerosene also known as Rocket Propellant 1, powered the RS–27A engine, which in turn burned the 212,000 pounds of liquid oxygen that the eight foot section of rocket carried.

Minutes passed, the rocket pushing through Earth's atmosphere, the G-forces pounding Garvey's body. The first stage shut off, its fuel exhausted, and six seconds later the empty shell was discarded, falling lazily back to earth. Two seconds later the second stage ignited, pushing the rocket into a low earth orbit. Garvey checked his altimeter and confirmed that the rocket had reached 13.4 miles above the surface of the planet. At this altitude the rocket came to rest, traveling at 2,423 miles per hour as the world spun beneath it, the payload fairing splitting and falling away to reveal the Mars Climate Orbiter and the third stage booster to which it was still attached.

Now it was time for Garvey to wait until he reached the proper coordinates, and then to ignite the third stage, which would propel him toward his final destination—Mars.

Mars, 47,000 B.C.

Garvey went down on one knee, his arms burning and exhausted from his long flight, and the membranous wings that were attached, brushed the dirty stone ledge that jutted from the cliff side dwellings of the Muvari people. The spear blades glinted at his throat, held there by a few of the dozen warrior women that surrounded him, their spears pressed against the thick plastic armor of the NASA space suit which he still wore.

Weaponless and exhausted, Garvey held no illusions about how he might fare against these newfound foes. He had thought that Lana Shar was his ally, but now, by the ferocity in the eyes of these women, Garvey wondered if he might not have been led into a trap. His adventures on Mars were about to come to an inglorious end.

The woman who held a spear tip beneath his exposed and stubbled chin jabbered out something in a language, with which Garvey had been an unfamiliar a day ago, but his brief telepathic link with Lana Shar left him with an understanding of this stranger's words.

"So you try to make a meal of my sister? See what my spear tastes like instead!"

The muscles rolled beneath the green-tinted skin of her bare shoulders as she drew back to gain some momentum for the thrust.

Because of the dozen spears that poked and prodded at every side of him, Garvey did not dare dodge the blow. Instead he tucked his chin down tightly to his chest so that his throat was not exposed, and raised his plastic-armored forearms in front of him in the small hopes that it might help deflect some of the damage of a thrust that was meant to kill him. His wings swept forward with him, inadvertently knocking away many of the spears that bristled around him, and propelling his body upward and forward so that his body fell upon the spear tip that was meant to pierce his throat.

Fortunately, the woman had not yet begun her forward thrust and the tip lodged in the thick chest piece of Garvey's space suit without penetrating through to his flesh. The warrior woman surrounding him lifted their spears, about to plunge them into the astronaut's back and sides, but then a cry rang out from Lana Shar's purple-tinged lips.

"Halt! He's a friend!"

The spear tips wavered, but before any of them could think better of sparing the life of the wayward astronaut and complete their preempted thrust Lana Shar lofted herself into the air with a push of her wings and came down beside Garvey. The warrior women backed away, some relaxing the grip on their spears while others still held them at the ready, but not so close to Garvey's body.

"This man is not of the Galbran. He freed me from the Warlord Shaxia's stasis trap."

The woman who had claimed to be Lana's sister wrenched her spear free from Garvey's suit and lowered the blade to the ground, but Garvey could still read suspicion in her purple eyes. Though most of the women that surrounded him were as tall as he, she was shorter by three inches. Her face was more angular than Lana's, set with high cheek bones, and dozens of pale braids splayed about her bare shoulders and over the tanned leather hide which fell to the middle of her thighs. She appraised Garvey with the same critical demeanor that Lana had. Garvey noticed that unlike many of the woman who had attacked him her ears were unadorned by any piercings.

"You are wider, more muscular than any man I have ever seen. I can see now that you are not one of the Galbrans, but from where do you hail? You certainly fly as clumsily as the Galbrans."

Garvey defended himself. "I've had little time to learn the wings. In my homeland we do not have any devices quite like them." He did not want to become branded a liar so early in his acquaintance with this tribe—which was obviously paranoid about visitors so he held back on a few of the details which he had shared with Lana. "I hail from a land called Florida quite some distance from here."

This did little to satisfy the woman who had attempted to kill him. "And what is the name of your tribe?"

"They call us Americans."

She narrowed her eyes, her long lashes coming together. "I've never heard of the Americans."

Lana interjected. "Excuse my sister. Very rarely do we come across a stranger that means us no harm. You'll have to forgive her suspicious nature."

"My name is Garvey Dire," introduced the astronaut.

"Mine is Ntashia Stridj. I am guard leader of the third patrol." She shot a glance at her sister. "What do you plan to do with him?"

"Of course, I'll need to take him before the Muvari elders, and seek their council, but he has nowhere to go. His people are far away, and perhaps he would seek refuge with us."

"He is not as the torracks?"

"Not so far as I know," answered Lana seriously. "But there will be time enough to establish his eligibility."

Now Garvey noticed that the attitude toward him had somewhat eased. The warrior women eyed him with curiosity and not malice, and Garvey was not sure if he was imagining some of their gazes to contain more than just curiosity. He quickly discarded this thought. On this planet his physique must be considered somewhat freakish by the slender Muvari.

If the Muvari men were as tall as the torracks who had attacked them as they escaped from Shaxia's hidden technology depot, then they were a full seven feet in height. Their builds had been frail by an Earthman's standard. Garvey figured that he must appear to be a dwarf to these women who were surely used to looking up to the men of their tribe.

"I'll order some warriors to escort you to the inner sanctum," said Ntashia.

"That won't be necessary," responded Lana. "He is weaponless and exhausted—unlikely to pose any threat to us in his condition—even if he were to harbor ill will against us."

In a motion that must have indicated deference, Ntashia crossed her left arm across her breasts, pressing her left palm against her right shoulder. Lana returned the gesture, though she touched lower on her right arm than had her sister.

Lana Shar turned to Garvey. "Come, let us meet the presiding elder. Perhaps he will be able to find a place for you here."

Garvey followed Lana's lead and stripped off his broken wings, which were collected by several unarmed female attendants with ears unadorned, and whose clothes were woven from a thin, red-dyed fiber which the astronaut did not recognize.

Lana led him toward a large cavern, and as they came closer Garvey realized that the area just inside its ragged mouth had been meticulously carved into an open archway. When they passed through, Garvey saw great hinges upon which were hung massive iron doors wrought with a Martian glyph. As they passed through Ntashia and her group of guards took hold of long rope lines attached to hooks on the inner door and began pulling the gigantic metal slabs closed, shutting out the dangerous Martian night. They slammed tight and rang like a gong, the last echo barely fading before thick timbers were laid into brackets behind the door to ensure that it was secure against marauders.

The last few glimmers of sunlight disappeared behind the lip of the rift, coloring the sky with bloody streaks. The shadows within the cavern deepened, but the blackness was broken by lanterns that hung from hooks pounded into the living rock walls. These were not lanterns such as Garvey knew from Earth. No flame flickered inside the glass housings, but instead a frosty luminescence emitted from hunks of rock captured within. This cold light revealed the vast central chamber that they had entered. The broad central floor of the cavern was a hive of activity, and reminded Garvey of depictions of medieval bazaars that he had seen.

Booths swathed in colorful cloth dotted the area, constructed with no rhyme or reason. Tall slender women with varying shades of purple in their skin hosted the temporary shops, and entertained equally slender women who picked among the baskets of strange vegetable matter, and purchased cuts of meat that were unrecognizable to Garvey.

Among the hundreds of impossibly thin women, Garvey saw only a few men. These were easily six-and-a-half feet in height, and some closer to seven feet. Like the women, they possessed a slender, though slightly more muscular, build that would only be possible in the light gravity of Mars.

"Where are the men of the tribe?" asked Garvey.

"There are only a few," replied Lana. "For some reason our women bear many girl children, but only a few males. It is for this reason that the women are the warriors of the tribe. If we sent our men to be killed in battle our tribe would be stripped of our ability to increase. We would become extinct."

Garvey carefully digested this fact. "How many women does the tribe have compared to men?"

"When the babies are born only one child in ten is male. War and some disease reduces our female numbers so there are six adult women for every adult man."

"What did you mean when you told Ntashia that my eligibility would be more fully established?"

"If you are healthy you will be expected to stay here in Ledgrim and become a member of the Muvari tribe."

Garvey's forehead creased between his brows. He didn't have anything against becoming a member of the Muvari Tribe, but he knew so little about them or Mars, for that matter, that he hardly felt capable of making an informed decision. Still, he didn't really have any other options open to him. The only other race he had come across had tried to kill him, and it sounded as though he could expect little more from the other inhabitants of Mars. He had been lucky to come across an ally as resourceful, and beautiful he added mentally, as Lana Shar.

His leg had been shattered in the crash of the Mars Climate Orbiter. Doubtless he would have bled to death by now if he hadn't have come across the hidden chamber and the alien woman caught in the stasis trap.

"I would be honored," replied Garvey.

"The Council of Elders will be pleased," said Lana. "They will send for the eligible women of the tribe, and you will be expected to pick your wives."

Garvey's jaw fell open. "Wives?" He looked around, wondering if there was some way to escape. Lana didn't seem to notice his shock. "You shouldn't have any trouble finding several women who please your Earthling sensibilities of beauty."

Suddenly Garvey's legs felt weak. He'd spent all of his thirty-five years fleeing from commitment, so that he could pursue his adventurous lifestyle without impediment. The responsibility of having just one wife seemed overwhelming to him, let alone multiple wives of an alien race. How was it that he was suddenly a candidate for enforced matrimonial bliss?

"What if a man is not ready to become married?" Garvey purposely couched his question in a way that suggested his query was purely suppositional.

Lana looked at him seriously. "Anyone of marriageable age, that refuses take upon themselves the responsibility of helping to ensure the continuation and longevity of the Muvari Tribe is of little use to us."

"So they wouldn't be accepted into the Muvari Tribe?"

"That is the least of it," said the warrior woman, her purple eyes somber. "Any one who refuses to his duty is subjected to the ritual of fire."

The ritual of fire didn't sound too promising to Garvey, but he didn't yet want to rule it out as a possibility. "And what does that entail?"

Lana Shar looked at him, disdain creeping into her amethyst eyes as though she were beginning to suspect that Garvey wasn't enthusiastic about the great honor that the council would likely bestow upon him. "It little matters what the ritual entails," she answered sharply. "It will suffice you to know that none have ever survived it."

Chapter Five:
Attack on Ledgrim

December 11, 1998, Earth's Orbit

At exactly thirty-nine minutes and fifty-three seconds into his flight, the rocket orbited into proper position. Cape Canaveral and the Atlantic Ocean were long gone, and now the brown mass of the Australian content thrust up from the glistering blue of the Pacific as Garvey hit the buttons for the auxiliary jets and slowly rotated the Mars Climate Orbiter into the proper position so that the final stage—stage three—could be ignited.

The craft was devoid of its outer casing now—long since jettisoned, and the seven–foot-tall by six-foot-wide craft was visible. Its eighteen-foot solar panels were unfurled, collecting the unfiltered rays of the blazing Sun, and storing away the energy for the long, cramped voyage ahead.

Bradley Thomas' voice came into Garvey's left ear. "You're on target. Let her fly!"

"Roger that," replied Garvey, but it came through parched lips and on dry tongue.

He pressed the ignition button and third stage pushed him back into his seat, a bright flare spreading from rear of the craft and into the cold sky. A minute and a half later the acceleration ended. From here on out he coasted to Mars. It was nearly a year's journey before he reached the red planet. He hoped he could fight the claustrophobia that already tickled at the edges of his mind.

Mars, 47,000 B.C.

THE lanterns hung in grape-like clusters from wood beams that crossed the arching dome of the elder's council chamber, shedding chill illumination on the assemblage below. Escorted by Lana Shar, her pale hair flowing behind her, the fine strands glowing with captured lantern light, they entered the chamber and crossed the patterned tiles of the floor until they stood at the sunken center of the long room, surrounded by a low wall and rail, behind which the elders of the Muvari Tribe sat at red-hued tables.

Though a few were white-haired and venerable most appeared young and strong, their purple eyes glowing with vitality. A mixture of men and women sat at the table, and all eyes were upon the strange outlander as Lana began to speak.

"Honorable elders of the council." She folded her left arm across her breasts, clasping her palm to her right shoulder. "I bring to you a man of a tribe so distant he has no hope of returning. I bring to you, also, a man who saved me from the Warlord Shaxia's stasis machine. He disabled the trap in which I was caught and escaped with me from the torracks using our wings of flight."

A wrinkled man with wispy white hair that fell down across his narrow shoulders, tightened his puckered violet lips and straightened himself in his high wooden seat. "And what of Rajeia?" he asked, his voice raspy and trembling.

Once again Lana clasped her hand to her shoulder and addressed the ancient man who spoke. "Bel Ratham, I am sorry to inform you that the torracks slew her as we stole the plasma rifle that is now on my back, and one of the healing devices which we find so valuable. She fought bravely and died with honor."

Bel Ratham bowed his hoary head, so that the others could not see his pain, and Garvey guessed that Rajeia had been his daughter or granddaughter.

Now from one of the side tables a handsome man with high brow, and dark flowing hair tinged with purple rose to his feet. The cartilage of his left ear was pierced with a golden ring, and he grew a mustache on his thick upper lip.

"Lana Shar," he asked as he laid his large but narrow hands upon the polished wood of the table behind which he stood. "You know the laws of Ledgrim and of the Muvari Tribe. No stranger can come to Ledgrim lest he undertake the responsibilities of a tribe member. If he refuses he shall be cast into the pit to endure the ritual of fire."

"Clivok Shar, this stranger had no where else to go, and I did not inform him of his obligation should he follow me back to Ledgrim."

"Nevertheless," answered Clivok. "He must now accept the responsibilities of a member or be initiated in fire."

Clivok Shar turned his blazing eyes toward the wayward astronaut and pointed a slender finger in his direction. "What is your name stranger?"

"Garvey Dire."

"Very well, Garvey Dire. Choose your fate and choose it well. Will you swear to serve and guard the Muvari Tribe, or will you refuse this honor and responsibility that we offer you?"

Garvey hesitated. Perhaps it really was an honor to receive this invitation to join the Muvari, but he'd been thrust back into the past of Mars for less than a day and he was being asked to commit his life to a tribe with whom he was scarcely acquainted, and take to wife Muvari women so that he might help propagate their race. He glanced at Lana Shar and wondered if she might be one of the marriageable women of the tribe—perhaps he was not being given such a raw deal after all.

"What say you?" bellowed Clivok.

Garvey opened his mouth to speak when a metallic boom rang through the caverns of the Muvari. Garvey knew that sound—it was the same that he'd heard when the great iron gates of the Muvari cliffside fortress had closed. Had they been opened again during the nighttime hours, and then closed?

That didn't seem likely to Garvey, and his suspicions were confirmed when the entire assemblage of twenty leaped to their feet, and reached for the sword blades at their sides.

On quick feet a lithe young girl with raven hair ran into the chamber. "The gate is under assault!" she cried. "The Galbrans attack!"

There was a swift rush for the doorway as all the Muvari sped to defend their city. Lana turned her violet eyes upon Garvey. "Now is the time to prove your worth to the Muvari. Use your strength to throw back the filthy cannibals that assail our gates, and you will be rewarded with your pick of our most beautiful women, and with a spacious home in the safety of Ledgrim."

Garvey didn't say so, but Ledgrim didn't seem so safe to him right now, and the attack on Ledgrim nearly seemed a welcome reprieve from his forced commitment. But if forced to marry he already had an idea of whom he would pick for a wife. "Give me a weapon."

Chaos swirled around them and Lana pushed through the press of humanity, leading Garvey to a weapon rack carved into the rock wall—one of dozens that Garvey had already seen as Lana had led him through the winding halls to the council chamber. Inside thirteen swords, and as many spears beckoned him.

Garvey was a pilot, an astronaut; he had little experience with weapons of such an archaic nature, but that wouldn't stop him from trying.

He grabbed four spears, and a three-foot blade with a broad tip that came down to a razor taper.

"I'll lead the way," said Lana.

Garvey shook his head. "You'd only slow me down."

A press of Muvari flesh barred his way at the arched entrance to the council chamber. Garvey got a running start and with his earthling muscles defying the weak Martian gravity he leaped into the air, hurdling the Muvari elders, and sailing over their heads, through the archway, and landing on the stone floor beyond.

He went down to one knee as he hit, but instantly regained his feet to bound down the long corridors, each stride taking him eight or more feet. The Muvari elders gasped, but Garvey was no longer there to see their astonishment.

The city smelled of fear, and everywhere he looked the Muvari poured forth from small side passages, armed, and ready to defend their pitiful piece of Martian soil. Garvey leaped past and over them, their eyes wide with uncertainty as they wondered who this strangely appareled man was—and how he could leap through the air as though he were flying.

Garvey entered the main hive of the city. Most of the booths had been removed for the night, and those that still stood were now abandoned. He sped through the maze of shops, leaping over empty booths with careless abandon. The door rang out again and again, and Garvey couldn't imagine what was striking with such force.

Inside the cavern wall, on the upper tiers, the female warriors stood at arrow slits carved into the living stone. They poured volley after volley of crossbow bolts into the night beyond. Screams of pain, and great roars of rage filtered through the rock—occasionally an enemy arrow found its way through an arrow slit and a Muvari woman would fall shrieking from her precarious perch. Some were dead before they hit the stone floor sixty feet below. Others died on impact.

A phalanx of warriors formed up inside of the gate, spears bristling and braced should the great doors give and allow the enemy inside.

Though he was running as fast as he could, Garvey had yet to reach the phalanx, and suddenly the doors shook, and the hinges groaned, bending and tearing away from the crumbling rock in which they were moored. The line of warrior women gave out a cry and turned to flee, but for many it was too late. The massive doors tottered and fell, tons of iron crushing a dozen women beneath their merciless weight—their lives snuffed out in an instant. The floors running violet with their blood.

The Galbrans gave out a horrible cheer and poured through the archway waving steel-tipped spears and blood-encrusted scimitars—an avalanche of Martian flesh. Unlike the Muvari they wore little clothing or armor, and it was equally men and women who surged forward in the howling horde. They wore loin clothes, and their bodies were painted and pierced, their hair hanging in knotted mats about their grotesque and twisted faces—faces that bore the crudely stitched scars of many battles before.

Their teeth were filed to a point, and some dropped their weapons and fell upon struggling or wounded Muvari, rending and tearing at their victims' flesh with only their teeth. Now Garvey understood why Ntashia Stridj had accused him of attempting to make a meal of Lana Shar. The Galbrans were cannibals, and they hunted for human flesh—and somehow she had made the less than flattering assumption that he was a Galbran.

But as horrifying as the onslaught of Galbrans was, they paled in comparison to what stood beyond. Rearing on two massive legs stood a thing twenty feet tall. The beast's upper arms ended in hooked claws that looked like massive scythes, and its razor-toothed snout opened wide and let out a fearsome roar, which chilled Garvey to the bone. Its beady eyes darted to and fro as if searching for something.

Galbrans rushed beneath its thick legs, wrinkled skin the color of brick dust, seemingly unconcerned about the vicious beast that had torn the heavy iron portals from the gates of Ledgrim. Ponderously the beast moved through the arched gateway and into the caverns beyond, each step crushing unwary Galbrans who happened to be in the creature's path.

The battle scene was horrifying beyond anything Garvey had ever imagined, yet he had never shirked from danger or adventure, and this was adventure on a grand scale. He might die, but he would die as a participant—not an onlooker in this momentous struggle. As he poised himself to leap into the fray a swarm of Galbrans wafted through the open gates, borne on membranous wings. They swooped down low, lashing out with bent short blades that cleaved and decapitated the earthbound Muvari warriors who were defending their home.

Garvey jumped over the rear rank of Muvari warriors, and in midair his path intercepted the flight of an airborne Galbran. The astronaut lashed out desperately at the surprised cannibal, chopping through his arm, so that one winged appendage spiraled free in a gory spurt of violet blood. With one wing missing the Galbran veered head first into the stone floor of the cavern, his skull cracking on impact.

His sword blow threw Garvey off-kilter and he spun in mid-air coming down in a jumble of his own spears. He quickly rolled into a kneeling position and thrust his sword blade out at a Galbran who rushed forward with an upraised cudgel as if to brain the fallen astronaut. Instead the Galbran impaled himself on the point of Garvey's violet-spattered sword blade.

Garvey wrenched the tip of the blade loose and sent the groaning, dying Galbran spinning back into the oncoming horde of his fellow cannibals. The astronaut jumped to his feet and followed the dying man into the enemy with earth-born speed that startled his opponents. Garvey wielded his blade with brutal imprecision. His lack of sword skill was balanced by his earthly musculature, and his blade hewed through flesh and bone, wreaking gory carnage wherever he struck.

Fortunately for Garvey, the Galbran were not swordsmen, or they might have easily turned aside his crude hacking and killed him—but they wielded their weapons with less finesse than even he, and he cut down their ranks as they swarmed around him. Those Muvari warriors who had not fallen to the initial onslaught of the Galbran retreated to their second line of defense, which was bolstered by the Muvari citizens flowing from the caverns that riddled the cliff side.

Garvey found himself alone in the swirling maelstrom of clashing weapons, gnashing canines, and twisting misshapen faces that temporarily emerged from the violet haze that he threw up about him with the blade of his sword—only to be thrust back again by its keen edge.

The Muvari pressed tightly around him, their numbers seemed unending, and Garvey began to despair that this might be the end for him. Then he saw a struggling figure in the midst of the Galbran cannibals. Only twenty feet away she fought savagely with her slender blade, her purple-tinged braids of pale hair flying wildly about her angular face as she cut and thrust. Garvey recognized her as Ntashia Stridj, Lana Shar's sister, who had stuck a spear in the chest of his NASA space suit.

Garvey was still wearing the cumbersome thing, but it hung in tatters around his frame, cut and bashed by spear, sword, and club. Probably it had saved his life a half–dozen times. He could see that Ntashia, like himself, was on the verge of being overwhelmed by the enemy.

Alone they would be subsumed by the tide of Galbrans, but just maybe if they fought together they could make a stand against the foe. the astronaut leaped into the air, over the heads of the Galbran and landed a few paces away from Ntashia, spearing one of her opponents through the back. Blood gushed and the Galbran screamed, violet pouring from his mouth as he wriggled like a worm on a hook. Garvey cast him aside and wielding his blade like a butcher, swept his sword across the throats of two Galbrans.

"So American, already you prove yourself an asset to the tribe. Too bad that we shall die so soon."

Bravado came to Garvey's lips as he cut down a Galbran who ventured within distance of his sword. "I'm not planning on dying any time soon. Stay close and mayhap we'll both live to see another Martian sunrise."

Ntashia took off the tip of a Galbran nose with the edge of her blade, and danced back to avoid the swing of a spiked club, her back pressing against Garvey's. "Bold words for a man who holds his sword like a cleaver. But I think that our doom is coming."

Garvey shot a look in the direction of Ntashia's gaze and heard the roar of the massive beast that had unhinged the doors of iron from the great archway of Ledgrim. It tramped into the cavern crushing Galbrans beneath its great splayed feet; feet stained with the purple blood of its masters.

"The hobranx cometh," said Ntashia.

The hobranx swung its great arms and its dark pincers whirred scythe-like through the air. It lowered its wrinkled, red behemoth head to within a dozen feet of the Ntashia and Garvey and let out a bellow, the foul stench of its breath carrying in a fetid wave that engulfed them.

"How long are we going to live now, American?" asked Ntashia.

Chapter Six:
The Mind Master

September 23, 1999

Garvey was restless when he fired the Orbiter's main engine five minutes before he reached Mars. The planet glowed beneath him, filling the small porthole screen with its pocked crimson surface. He longed to stretch his legs on alien soil. For nearly ten months he had been confined inside the walls of his miniscule spaceship, catching up on every book he'd ever wanted to read, exercising with his Bowflex, and listening to music.

Now his destination loomed below him, and he could scarcely stand his confines any longer. A voice relayed from the 112-foot diameter antenna at the Deep Space Network complex near Canberra, Australia crackled in the Orbiter's speakers. Garvey recognized the voice as belonging to his old friend Bradley Thomas.

"You're almost there, Garvey. How does it feel?"

"I can hardly wait," answered the astronaut as he stared at the surface of Mars– so large that seemed he could reach out his window and touch it. "The problem is that I've still got a couple weeks of aerobraking ahead of me while I orbit the planet."

"Well, hang in there. You've lasted this long without going insane. I'm sure that you can manage a few more days."

Garvey glanced over at his handheld reading pad that contained over five thousand books and four hundred hours of music stored on its solar powered hardrive. "I guess I'll start in on War and Peace while I'm waiting. Then if I have time I'll read the Old Testament again."

"You may even make it all the way through. How is your oxygen pump working?"

"It's working great," replied Garvey. "I'm running it completely off the power gathered from the solar array, and haven't had to dip into any reserve energy. As long as I can set up the solar panels shortly after I land they should keep me in breathing air until relief arrives."

"We shot Arnold Stechter into space a month ago. So he should be arriving to keep you company in less than a year."

"Only for a few weeks, though," grunted Garvey. "That hasn't changed has it? Then I get to go home and Stechter does a shift on Mars."

"That's the plan," confirmed Bradley. "We've got about fifteen seconds before we lose contact. See you on the other side."

"See you on the other side," echoed Garvey, and no sooner had he spoken when interference fizzed across the intercom speakers. The Mars Climate Orbiter slipped behind the red planet, a speck in the spectral glow of its thin atmosphere.

In order to get into the ellipitical orbit necessary for aerobraking, Garvey needed to fire the bipropellant engines for about sixteen minutes. Once he had moved into the proper orbit the Mars Climate Orbiter would cruise around Mars ocassionally passing through the upper reaches of its atmosphere—the resulting friction gradually slowing the speed of the orbit.

This method of aerobraking reduced the fuel needed by the Hydrazine thrusters when it came time for Garvey to lower himself through the atmosphere to the planet's surface.

Garvey reached up and carefully watched his coordinates. At exactly the right time he fired the bipropellant engines, a bright flame blossoming from his fragile craft, and pushing him toward his orbit. The spacecraft rapidly approached the orbital path, and five minutes into the burn Garvey realized that something was dreadfully wrong. The strength of the thrust was preprogrammed into the onboard computer—carefully prepared by the mathematicians of NASA—so that the propulsion would drop the spacecraft into perfect orbit, but the Mars Climate Orbiter was hurtling toward the surface of Mars at tremendous speed. Someone had severely miscalculated, and unless Garvey could cut off the thrusters he and his spacecraft were going to add one more hole to the crater–pocked surface of Mars.

Ledgrim Mars, 47,000 B.C.

As the hobranx fixed them with his baleful glare Garvey felt something roll beneath his feet. A quick glance showed him the same spears that he had dropped after leaping into the fray. With earthborne reflexes he scooped up the closest, pulling it from beneath the feet of an attacking Galbran, whom he sent stumbling into the legs of his fellow attackers.

Garvey's arm went back and as the brick red head of the hobranx lunged forward with jaws wide—revealing nasty double rows of foot long teeth—he threw the spear down the open gullet of the beast. The astronaut threw with such power that the spear went through the back of the creature's neck, emerging in a violet spray of blood.

The hobranx recoiled in pain, letting out a blood-laced roar. Its feet thrashing about, turning slow Galbrans to pulp beneath his enormous weight. Ntashia's purple-tinged lips fell open when she saw the power of Garvey's throw.

"No, not the Hobranx!" she cried, when she saw that Garvey might have the arm to make a longer throw. "Throw at the shaman; the Mind Master." She gestured with one long arm, adorned with golden circlets that pressed into her violet spattered flesh.

Garvey followed her finger and saw a gnarled and painted Galbran dressed in feathered skins of rainbow hues. He stood far from the fray, at the broken gates of Ledgrim, his eyes rolled back in a glassy stare that made him appear entirely oblivious to his surroundings.

"But he's no danger," protested Garvey.

"Trust me," spat Ntashia as her sword blade blocked the downward swing of an axe.

Garvey leaned back, his legs gathered beneath him—then he snapped the spear forward, sending it far over the horde of Galbrans. It sliced through the air and descended, spitting the defenseless Mind Master through the chest and sticking him to the wall. The Mind Master's gaze suddenly became lucid, and blood spilled from his mouth as he struggled like a pinned fly.

Then Garvey's vision of the Galbran shaman was obscured by the red bulk of the hobranx as it loomed over he and Ntashia. He dodged to the left and found himself beneath the belly of the beast as a massive foot came down crushing the flesh and bone of fallen foes. Ntashia had not been so fortunate, as she leapt away she slipped and fell, and the Hobranx dipped his head to snatch her up in his cruel jaws.

Garvey cried out and plunged his sword blade into the belly of the hobranx, the sharp point punching through the leathery hide and into the bowels of the beast. Perhaps it was little more than a pinprick to the gargantuan creature, but it was enough to momentarily distract, and the hobranx reared up, its thrashing tail indiscriminately sweeping away Galbran and Muvari.

The American Astronaut wrenched his sword free and waited for the worst to happen. Surely he would become the target of the beast's razor scythes or its devouring maw. Instead, the hobranx gave out a great cry as it wheeled in the air and fled through the great arches of Ledgrim. The hosts of the Muvari gave out a great roar of victory and more closely pressed the ranks of the invading Galbran.

Garvey fought to Ntashia's side, and diverted several sword blades that were meant for her. He reached down and caught her arm, bringing her to her feet once again.

"Why did it leave?"

"The hobranx are wild beasts, only a Mind Master—a Galbran shaman—can control such a creature. You slew the shaman and the Galbran lost control of the hobranx."

The Muvari were gaining the advantage now, and the Galbrans fell back, sweeping Ntashia and Garvey with them until they stood on the ledges outside the arches of Ledgrim, pressed from all sides by the enemy. Somewhere Lana opened up with her plasma rifle, and bolts of energy lanced through the twisted hordes, severing extremities and slicing Galbrans in half to the left and to the right.

Screaming invaders pushed toward the cliff, pressing Garvey and his companion-in-arms toward the edge, and the dark Rift that yawned beyond. Plasma bolts cut through the Galbran ranks, a half dozen of them slicing the air dangerously close to their tenuous position—and Garvey began to wonder if they would die by being pushed over the precipice or by a stray bolt from Lana's rifle. It was doubtful that she could see them amongst the press of Galbran flesh.

Garvey and Ntashia fought back to back, but their blades could not work fast enough and their arms grew heavy; their strokes became slow, and each time they lifted their swords they felt as though they were holding tree trunks in their grasp.

Many of the Galbrans who still wore their wings took flight, and they wafted into the darkness of the abyss. Others who had cast aside their cumbersome wings for the attack, snatched them up and desperately tried to fit them on while the fleeing horde squeezed them tighter. A few succeeded, but many more plunged to their deaths.

Finally, lungs heaving, Garvey and Ntashia teetered on the edge of the precipice, their limbs leaden and their bodies spattered with violet blood. The swing of a Galbran club tore Garvey's sword from his hand, and Ntashia's blade slipped from her benumbed fingers.

The Galbrans surged in retreat and Garvey and Ntashia were swept from their perilous foothold. As they plummeted into the pitch night, Garvey reached out to grab hold of Ntashia's wrist in a vain effort to save her. They tumbled head over heels into the void, clutching tightly to each other when suddenly some force tore Ntashia from his grasp, and he was alone—the dark winds whistling in his ears as he fell; his stomach in his throat as he wondered when he would strike the unseen bottom of the rift.

He did not wonder for long, for a hook snapped out from the harness of a Galbran above, tearing through the thick skin of the NASA space suit, and buoying him upward on flapping, tenebrous wings. When they passed from the deep shadows of the rift and into the rays of the double moons, Deimos and Phobos, the twisted and gnarled form of the Galbran that had captured him was illuminated in a wash of crimson light. A scarred and misshapen face glared hungrily down at him, drool glinting on the sharp incisors of his captor.

Even if Garvey had the energy to resist, which he no longer possessed, he wouldn't have struggled against the hook that held him. To struggle free meant resuming his plunge into the impenetrable darkness beneath. For the moment, this Galbran had saved his life—even if it was only with the intent of making a meal of him later.

In the light of the twin moons Garvey could see other winged forms, fleeting in the dark, some carrying the forms of captives, both dead and alive, by means of hooks attached to their harnesses. He vainly sought for the sight of Ntashia. He knew that she had been ripped from his grasp, and suspected that it had been by a Galbran—but hoped to reassure himself by finding her in the night-thickened gloom.

Fatigue and dizziness assailed him, and the astronaut's vision wavered before him. Instead of resisting the pull of unconsciousness he willingly let the twilight of sweet oblivion embrace him—letting the horrific reality slip away for just a few moments of forgetfulness.

When he emerged from the twilight realms he found himself in a dank chamber below the earth. The scent of death was strong in the air, and the groans of injured captives echoed hollowly against the slime-coated walls. A lurid flickering flame cast an unsteady shaft of light from a barred trap door above, and as Garvey staggered to his feet, strength once again flowing to his limbs, he stumbled over the corpses of slain Muvari. He quickly realized that he was not in a prison; he was in a larder. The only difference between him and the others, was that he would be fresher meat when it came time for the Galbrans to eat.

Chapter Seven:
Lair of the Galbran

September 23, 1999

The Mars Climate Orbiter shuddered, rocked by the atmosphere of Mars as it plunged recklessly toward the surface, the bipropellant rockets forcing the craft faster and faster toward inevitable doom. Even as Garvey reached his hand up to cut the rockets he could feel the temperature inside the small craft rise twenty degrees. He flipped the switch and the bipropellant thrusters went silent, but the damage was already done.

Without a doubt the NASA engineers had severely miscalculated the amount of thrust necessary to push the spacecraft into an oblong orbit that would allow him to coast through the edges of the planet's atmosphere, slowly decelerating the ship for two weeks before he made the final descent to the surface of Mars.

The hydrazine thrusters meant for the descent to the red planet contained just enough fuel to make a safe landing, but only from a carefully decreased orbit and from a much slower speed. Garvey could fire off the hydrazine right now, but he realized that it alone wouldn't be enough to slow his descent to less than four hundred miles per hour—and that would still guarantee a spectacular crash landing which would leave nothing but little bits of flaming debris.

Garvey could only think of one other possible option. It was unconventional, and Garvey knew that the Orbiter wasn't built for such a maneuver in atmosphere, but he had to give it a try. His altimeter quickly dropped from one hundred to seventy miles over the planet's surface as his fingers played over the control panel. The retro rockets at the ship's side, meant for adjusting the direction of the craft, still contained a bit of fuel. Garvey fired them full on, and the ship lurched sickeningly as it changed direction, twisting around in mid-air.

Now Garvey hit the bipropellant thrusters—a bright flare that burst suddenly from the reversed tail of the ship. The heat tiles of the craft glowed red from the friction of re-entry, and the ship rocked violently the solar wings, that were a vital power source to Garvey, shredding and ripping away as though they were constructed from tissue paper.

The astronaut's breath came shallowly as he watched his entry speed drop, a small hope flickering in his breast. Just when he thought he might be able to slow his descent enough to make a landing the bipropellant thrusters ran dry, and the ship resumed its unchecked plunge.

Garvey didn't know if he had enough fuel in the retro rockets to complete another 360-degree turn, so that he could maneuver his hydrazine thrusters into proper firing position. All he could do was try. His finger depressed the trigger and the retro-rockets briefly flared, dying as soon the ship began to spin. In desperation Garvey hit the button again and again, but it was futile; the fuel tanks for the retro rockets were dry as bone.

Still, the brief burst of the retros had started a spin, and slowly the ship began to rotate—even as it was buffeted by the atmosphere. The heat tiles moaned as they expanded, coloring a molten red. Garvey sat drenched in his own sweat, waiting for the hydrazine thrusters to swing into position.

Slowly the ship rotated, and the moment his only remaining thrusters were pointed toward Mars he lit them up. The hydrazine rockets flamed orange, and the metal of the Mars Climate Orbiter creaked as divergent forces threatened to rip it apart. But miraculously the spacecraft held together, the hydrazine thrusters mightily resisting gravity's pull.

Mars became an all-encompassing vision that blocked out everything else, its rocky surface flying up to meet the fragile ship. At a thousand feet the hydrazine rockets had slowed Garvey's descent to less than forty miles per hour. He had to meet a velocity of less than ten miles an hour to land the craft without breaking it to pieces, and by five hundred feet above Mars' barren surface Garvey brought the ship to thirty miles an hour.

At four hundred feet the hydrazine fuel dried up, and the Mars Climate Orbiter plummeted like a rock. There was nothing aerodynamic about the craft, it was built for traveling the reaches of space, and now there was naught to hold it in the air. The superheated tiles that had protected Garvey during the descent burst from the ship upon impact with the hard ground of Mars, their broken pieces scattering for a quarter mile. The Orbiter crumpled like a tin can beneath a booted foot, and it smoldered in a scorched crater of its own making—the only thing preventing it from exploding, the fact that all its fuel had been exhausted on the trip down.

The impact broke Garvey's leg, and an equipment bank tore loose, clipping his head as it flew by. The astronaut lay stunned in his seat, horrible pain shooting up his leg, and his vision swimming in a crimson haze before him. The self-contained atmosphere of the craft hissed as it leaked out in great filmy gouts, dissipating in Mars' thin air. Already Garvey could scent the alien odors of unexplored Mars as the red planet's environment replaced the stale air in the capsule. Carbon dioxide made up 95% of Mars's atmosphere, and oxygen less than a tenth of a percent. The carbon dioxide would be lethal shortly, and his long trip finished.

So this is how it all ends, thought Garvey—still groggy from the blow he had received to the head. A shame that he never actually got to set foot on the planet. A shame he wouldn't actually be the first. A shame he would suffocate here in his seat, trapped in the collapsed and ruined wreckage of the craft that had carried him 145 million miles, at 55,000 miles an hour, across the cold, black void of space—only to die before he could tread the alien sands of Mars beneath his feet.

Suddenly Garvey's mind cleared, and his thoughts turned to action. Perhaps he could fight his way clear of the wreck and salvage enough equipment to survive the intervening months until Arnold Stechter came to relieve him. Maybe there was some small chance. Garvey unstrapped himself from the seat in which he had been trapped for so many months.

He cried out in agony as he jarred his shattered leg, but gritted his teeth and pulled himself out of his chair. The ceiling of the ship was caved in, and he only had inches to spare as he slipped to the floor and crawled toward the niche next to the hatch where his NASA space suit still rested.

With some effort he managed to pull it free from the crumpled compartment, and slowly, painfully, he attired himself in the bulky suit. He glanced down at his right leg, and saw bone protruding from the open wound—a compound fracture. The blood loss might kill him if the lack of breathable air didn't do the job first. Most of the oxygen had escaped the ship now, and by the time that he snapped the fishbowl helmet of his suit into place Garvey's blood stream was filled with carbon dioxide that had seeped in from outside. He pressed a button on the chest of his suit, and an oxygen tank hissed as it released its precious cargo into the astronaut's helmet.

In a few minutes Garvey felt better, and he focused his attention on the task of escaping his metal coffin. He could only access a portion of the exit hatch, and it appeared to be jammed tightly shut, not yielding to any of his efforts to kick it open with his good left leg. His right leg was sticky with blood, and a constant source of pain. Finally Garvey gave up on trying to force the hatch open, and he remembered that a cutting torch was among the ship's equipment—if only he could find it.

He crawled across the floor that was wet with the acid of broken solar battery cells. Though the acid would be strong enough to cause a nasty burn on bare skin, it did little to the shiny shell of his space suit.

Wreckage hung a few inches over his head as he pulled himself forward on his belly. Eventually he located a small wall storage compartment that had broken open during the crash. He rummaged through the various tools that had spilled from the compartment and found the cutting torch among the confusion.

The cutting torch was NASA-designed to work in Martian atmosphere, providing both fuel and an oxygen mix to create a high-temperature flame, which would melt through steel as though it were icing on a cake. He didn't bother crawling back to the hatchway, and instead commenced cutting a hole right through the wall of the ship. Ten minutes later he had cut a gap large enough for him to crawl through, and with grim exertion he struggled through the freshly sliced space and pulled himself onto the rocky red soil of Mars.

With great effort he grabbed hold of the ship's crumpled side, and pulled himself to his feet. With a smile touching his lips behind the Plexiglass shield of his helmet he took one painful step. Tears of joy gathered in his eyes. He had done it! The first human being to take a step on Mars. Whatever happened now, he would go to his grave knowing that he had accomplished that which no other had.

He looked to the maroon skies, darkening in the distance. A sinister shape gathered there, swirling and gaining strength, only to billow forth as Garvey watched—a scathing sandstorm that swept forward obliterating all in the blackness of its shadow. The Martian winds howled, crying out for the sacrifice of its newest son, and Garvey stood in awe of the destruction that raced through the craggy terrain, dwarfing all with its awesome might.

47,000 B.C. In the lair of the Galbran

The trap door lay a full ten feet above the reach of Garvey's outstretched hand.

"It's too strong for us to break, American," said a familiar voice from the darkness at his right elbow.

Garvey whirled and without pausing to think he embraced the lithesome form that stood hidden in the shadow. "Ntashia! I thought that maybe they had killed you."

With a slight smile touching her violet-tinged lips, Ntashia slowly disengaged herself from Garvey's arms. "Quiet, American! We do not want to attract the attention of the Galbran."

"I'm glad to see a familiar face," he said. "Are any others of the Muvari alive?"

"Only two," answered Ntashia grimly. "The rest were dead before they arrived."

As if on cue, a slight Muvari woman emerged from the darkness. Her limbs were extraordinarily long and she towered over both Ntashia and Garvey, her violet-hued hair—entwined with oswagi feathers, spilling down her bare spine. She wore little else but a stained leather halter and skirt. Her feet were naked and bruised, sloshing in the violet blood that slowly congealed on the floor of the larder, and her left shoulder exhibited a nasty cut, which had not yet been attended. "My name is Omonyi Nash," she said. "I fell when the first wave of Galbran came through the door. When I regained consciousness I found myself here."

A man fully as tall as Omonyi, with a slightly stouter frame and a thick mustache that spread its wings into flowing sideburns appeared behind the woman. "I am Cray of the Lith family. "I was knocked unconscious and seized while I defended my wives."

"That was a foolish thing for a man to do," commented Ntashia harshly. "This American, here, is a stranger to our ways and does not yet understand the value of a man in perpetuating our people. You are no stranger to the Muvari, Cray, yet you stand in front of your warrior wives who have been trained to guard and protect you at the very cost of their lives."

"My second wife is with male child," protested Cray. "Surely her life and that of my coming son is worth more than mine."

"Perhaps," said Ntashia, "but that is not a decision for you to make."

"The last thing I want to do is get involved in tribal politics," interrupted Garvey, "but perhaps we should figure a way out of here before we're all eaten."

"We have time," said Ntashia. "We still live. They will eat the dead first, then slaughter us for food when the dead are consumed. We have weeks yet to live before they turn to us for nourishment."

"As calming as that is, I don't particularly want to stick around that long," replied the astronaut.

"We'll have to bide our time and hope for a chance to escape," said Omonyi.

Garvey shook his head. He didn't like the sound of such a passive plan. "That's strictly a second resort. We need to make something happen, not hope that it will."

Omonyi frowned. "When it comes to tactics of war, the women of the Muvari make the decisions. Only a decision from the council of elders supercedes our voices here." She pointed to Ntashia and then to herself.

"I'm not technically a member of the Muvari Tribe, yet," pointed out Garvey. "Besides, I have an idea."

His legs coiled beneath him and he sprang the intervening ten feet between him and the hatch door overhead, grabbing hold of the bars to support himself in mid-air. While Omonyi and Cray stifled a gasp of surprise at Garvey's amazing leap, he pulled himself up so that he could peer through the bars and into the room above.

The chamber above was a dank place as foul smelling as the larder below. Three Galbran huddled around a bare spot on the stone floor and tossed bones—shoveling a pile of loose bracelets and jewelry looted from Muvari victims around the ring as their fortunes changed. None of them noticed Garvey's fingers as they wrapped around the bars.

The astronaut made a quick survey of the room and found that it contained little else but a few piles of filthy rags that served as beds for the Galbran guards. He was about to drop back down into the larder below when Garvey started; a few inches from his face a cankered brass key protruded from the lock of the hatch. Apparently the guards, so certain that none of their prisoners could reach the lock, had left the key in the hole so it would not easily be misplaced.

Hanging by one hand, Garvey reached over and quietly plucked the key from its hole. Then with little more than a scuffing noise upon landing, he dropped back into the larder below.

"Have you been chewing blue-rings[1]?" whispered Ntashia, her voice fierce. "If we make trouble for them they won't wait to eat us last."

Garvey brandished the cankered key. "Do you think that this might be helpful in our escape?"

Ntashia's purple eyes widened, as did those of her two fellow tribesmen. "How did you—?"

"Now we'll wait," stated Garvey with his accustomed self-assuredness—something, which he'd lacked since crash landing on Mars. "Maybe the Galbrans will give us a better opportunity to use this."

Ntashia nodded her angular head, her green-tinted skin shining in the torchlight, and her pale braids falling over her face. "Before we found you, the Galbrans took up bodies on which to feast. They are being prepared and the feast will commence shortly. The Galbrans are prone to drunkenness."

Garvey caught Ntashia's drift and hoped that her prediction would prove accurate. Now it truly was time to wait. He looked at Omonyi's still bleeding wound. "Maybe we can at least bind that up. These aren't the most sanitary of conditions, though."

"I can rip a piece of my skirt loose," offered Ntashia. "Perhaps it will at least help to stop the blood from flowing." In a few minutes she finished binding Omonyi's wound, and the four of them huddled in the reeking darkness.

As Ntashia suggested, the Galbran guards above began feasting, and with their meat they drank prodigiously, their drunken songs, echoing into the larder like a chorus of injured wolves. The boisterous and harsh laughs continued for hours. Garvey could only understand a few words of their language, spoken in guttural tones inflected with spite and envy.

Finally their conversation became more infrequent, and their occasional dialogue slurred and slow. The heavy breathing of sleep finally overtook the guards, punctuated by the soft snores of at least one of the Galbrans.

Garvey had himself drifted in and out of sleep during the festivities. He awoke to Ntashia gently shaking his shoulder. "It's time, American. I think

---

1 Blue-rings are a hallucinogenic mushroom sometimes used by shamans of certain tribes to induce visions. The behavior of shamans under the influence of blue-rings is often erratic and foolish.

that they are all sleeping."

The astronaut gathered his wits about him then silently rose to his feet, crossing the corpse littered floor of the larder until he once again stood beneath the trap door that lay so far above. Ntashia stood a few feet away as he eyed his goal.

"Do you think you can make the jump again?" she asked. "No Muvari woman could make such a leap."

"And the men?" asked Garvey curiously.

"Of course not," scoffed Ntashia. "Are all the men of your tribe so able?"

"Some," admitted Garvey. "Are all the Muvari women as beautiful as you and your sister?"

"I have twelve sisters," said Ntashia, "of which one are you speaking?"

"The only one I know is Lana Shar."

"She and I are of the same mother, though my abnormal shortness detracts from whatever beauty I was born with."

Garvey glanced at the Muvari warrior, and only now noticed the ravishing beauty of her face that could scarcely be concealed in her disheveled condition, and the smoldering eyes that peered from behind a screen of falling braids. He had been so blinded by Lana Shar's beauty that he had not seen that the beauty of her sister was nothing short of stunning.

"I think that you underestimate yourself."

He crouched and sprang upward, just high enough so that his fingertips were able to wrap around the bars of the overhead hatch. Hanging by one hand, he took the key from between his clenched teeth and carefully slipped his right hand between the bars so that he could insert the cankered brass into the keyhole. The muscles of his left arm quivered as they supported his weight; slowly he turned the key. The lock did not turn smoothly, and finally it gave with a clang that seemed to resound in Garvey's overly-sensitive ears.

The snoring Galbran started and then rolled over. Garvey waited, breathless, until finally the guard resumed the rhythmic breath of his regular sleeping pattern. The astronaut let his body out to full length to stretch out his cramping arm. He glanced down and saw Ntashia, pale braids spilling over her bare shoulders, the slender and tall Omonyi, and the stubborn Cray waiting below with bated breath.

Now came the difficult part. Though the hatch was now unlocked Garvey needed to figure out how to lift it. The fact that he was hanging from the hatch was a considerable impediment to this next operation. The hatch was set in a small stone box, carved into the living stone of the larder's ceiling—this bit of workmanship had created a shaft about a foot thick. Garvey maneuvered so that his body was wedged into this narrow shaft. He let go of his handhold while lodged in this precarious position and pushed the hatch back. It fell open with a loud bang, and Garvey began to slip. Before his body plummeted to the larder floor he reached out and grabbed the edge of guardroom floor. Stone crumbled away, and Garvey's body dropped into a hanging position once again.

The bang of the hatch hitting the stone floor immediately woke at least two of the Galbran guards, and still besotted they reeled to their feet grabbing sword and club as their heads moved to the left and right, searching out the source of the noise that arrested their slumber.

Using the power in his shoulder and arms, and abetted by the weak Martian gravity, Garvey propelled himself from his hanging position, and up through the hatch so that he landed on his feet in the guardroom above.

Before the first Galbran could lift his club, Garvey took two long strides and thrust one hand into the guard's tangled beard. He yanked hard, his earth borne strength hurling the Galbran across the room and through the open hatch, to land awkwardly on his neck at the Ntashia's feet. Ntashia picked up the guard's fallen club, and silenced the screams of the Galbran with several well-placed blows to his misshapen skull.

Garvey turned in time to see the second Galbran advancing, waving the tip of his sword to and fro. The astronaut backed away, nearly tripping over the recumbent form of the still sleeping third guard. As quick as the eye, Garvey crouched and hoisted the half-naked Galbran, holding the unfortunate wretch in front of him as though he were a shield. Garvey took quick steps forward and impaled the rudely-awaking Galbran on the outstretched blade of the second guard.

The impaled Galbran let out a horrible shriek, blood flecking his gnashing teeth as Garvey let his weight crash to the floor, carrying the entangled sword blade with him. This left one unarmed Galbran opposing the misplaced Earthling, and Garvey wasted no time leaping across the writhing form of the dying guard. He let loose with a vicious punch that the Galbran was too late in ducking. Violet blood spattered as Garvey crushed the Galbran's nose and sent him reeling against the stone wall, unconscious.

Garvey grimaced and shook his stinging hand, wondering if he might have inadvertently broken some fingers. He carefully flexed, and determined that his bones were bruised, not broken. A coil of knotted rope lay in a pile upon the floor, already tied to a piton struck into the stone of the guardroom. With a kick Garvey sent the rope through the hatch, uncoiling as it went.

Ntashia came first. She looked up at Garvey who stood overhead. "Catch," she called.

She tossed her stolen club into the air, and the astronaut caught it as it sailed through the hatch. Nimble movements carried Ntashia up the rope, and a few moments later Cray and Omonyi joined them.

Garvey appropriated the sword from the still-writhing body of the impaled Galbran.

"Finish him off," said Ntashia.

Garvey hesitated. "I suppose it would be the merciful thing to do."

"Mercy has nothing to do with it," she answered. "He is our enemy. If he survives the wound he'll attack the Muvari again. These beasts understand nothing of mercy."

Lips and eyes tight, Garvey thrust the tip of the blade into the Galbran's heart, and the thrashing slowed and stopped. Among the fallen Galbran they managed to recover three knives, and Ntashia disseminated these among the group. "They're not much defense against a longer weapon," she apologized to Omonyi and Cray, "but they are better than nothing."

The slender-limbed Omonyi studied her knife intently. "This is a Muvari blade. No Galbran knife would hold an edge as well as this."

"They are scavengers," spat Cray. "They steal what we create, and eat our very flesh to survive."

Garvey's attention turned toward a long torch-lit passage, which wound upward, its walls rough-hewn or of a natural cave formation. Without saying a word he glided into the tenebrous corridor, followed by Ntashia and then Omonyi, who pushed Cray aside as she took the position from the protesting Muvari male.

"The males must be protected," hissed Omonyi to Cray. "What kind of warrior would I be if I let you take the lead?"

"Garvey leads us all," pointed out Cray.

"It is not honorable that Ntashia allows him to endanger himself thus, but I understand why she does."

"Why is that?" grumbled Cray.

"Isn't the reason obvious? He is as strong as the three of us put together."

Ntashia turned as they wound through the pocked and porous caverns, putting two slender fingers to her violet lips to signify silence. Cray and Omonyi ceased their whispered conversation and they continued on, only the scuffing of their feet against the stone making a sound. They passed by many side passages, but Garvey kept to the lit corridors, guessing that these might be more likely to take them toward an exit.

Garvey let a smile cross his lips as he saw a faint wind flicker the torches; perhaps he was on the right track. The passage took on a steeper grade and Garvey mounted a series of crude steps and climbed to the mouth of the corridor, where he halted suddenly.

Before him yawned a drop of sixty feet to the floor of a massive subterranean cavern which spread out before his vision. The stalactite-studded ceiling of the cavern arched up into impenetrable darkness, but below them a hundred fires burned low, casting a hazy pall in the air.

Scattered around the fires lay the huddled forms of sleeping Galbrans—thousands of them. Some lay beneath thick furry hides, and others lay where they had fallen, rough hewn bowls of grog still clutched in their twitching fingers as they slept the slumber of the drugged.

Garvey felt Ntashia's presence as she halted alongside of him and whispered in an awed voice. "No one has ever been inside the Galbran's stronghold and lived to tell about it. They are so much more numerous than the Muvari."

"There is no shortage of males here," commented Garvey.

"Degenerates. They have no family unit—living and breeding in their own chaotic filth, incestuous and inbred. They are no better than animals."

"Worse," said Garvey as he searched for an egress from the great cavern of carnality. Finally he thought that he detected a glimmer of dawn's light seeping through a small hole on the northwest side of the cavern.

Around it several silent forms lay slumped, great axes clutched across their malformed chests. He pointed out his discovery to Ntashia who nodded her head in agreement.

Several knotted ropes were tied to pitons in the rock, their frayed ends brushing against the cavern floor below. Garvey tested the first rope, giving it a pull. Satisfied that it would hold his weight he backed over the edge of the cliff, and jumped outward, letting a few feet of rope slide between his hands at a time so that he descended as if he were rappelling.

The friction heated his hands, but in the lighter gravity of Mars he was able to complete the descent bare-handed, something he would have been incapable of on Earth.

To Ntashia, Garvey's leaping descent appeared to be the action of a man gone insane. She quickly lowered herself down a second rope, and arrived at the cavern floor a little bit later, soon to be joined by Omonyi and Cray.

Scattered about the base of the cliff were a half-dozen Galbran—still deep in their besotted slumber, the scent of fermented fruit hanging about their bodies in a palpable alcoholic aura.

Omonyi's arched brows lowered, her eyes burning holes of hatred. She lifted a dagger and took two quick steps toward the nearest Galbran, ready to pull back his head and cut his throat from ear to ear. Before she could plunge her fingers into the drunkard's matted hair Ntashia caught her arm. She shook her head.

"But we can kill many of them," objected Omonyi, her whisper sharp like the dagger that she held.

"Yes," agreed Ntashia, "but we can do more good by returning to Ledgrim and reporting the location of the Galbran's refuge. We can seal the cavern off and entomb the entire tribe."

Omonyi was thirsty for revenge, and it was only with great restraint that she lowered her dagger. Cray crouched and retrieved a rusty and dulled sword blade from beneath the limp grasp of an unconscious Galbran. It wasn't a fine weapon by any means, but it would give him a longer reach than the dagger he currently held.

Slightly better armed, the quartet of escapees crept through the tangle of recumbent forms lit only by the glowing embers of the dying fires. They stole through the den of the enemy until they reached the gateway to the cavern. It wasn't nearly as impressive as the great metal doors that had stood at Ledgrim, but Garvey wondered if it might not be more effective.

It was a round tunnel about waist high. The only way to negotiate the passage was to lean over or crawl through on hands and knees. The guards to the gate still lay sleeping, their fingers touching the hafts of their chipped and rusted axes. Garvey remembered that the Vikings had built longhouses with similar entrances—so that if an enemy attempted to enter he was forced to lean over, and the Viking guard could easily behead the enemy as he set foot inside.

Garvey crouched down and looked through the passage that delved about thirty feet through solid stone. The morning glow of the sun cast a hazy effulgence down the tunnel, and Garvey figured that as long as there weren't wakeful guards standing at the outside of the tunnel that their escape would prove successful. No Galbran had noticed their flight. They wouldn't know that their prisoners were gone until they awoke hours later.

He was about to enter the tunnel when he heard a gurgling cry from one of the Galbran guards. Omonyi stood behind him; her long fingers entangled in the guard's hair, and her other hand holding a knife that dripped violet. The Galbran's throat was slit, and his eyes opened wide as the pain jerked him from his deep slumber—a blood-choked cry bubbling from his lips.

A second guard jerked from his slumber, bleary eyes snapping to the left and right. Omonyi leaped to this Galbran, and plunged her blade into his heart before he could gain his wits about him. The dying Galbran cried out, reaching up and wrenching at Omonyi's feather-entwined hair, pulling her to the ground, before his body began to spasm, and his limbs fell limp to his sides.

Ntashia moved quickly to Omonyi and untangled the corpse's still-warm fingers from her friend's hair. She reached down and jerked Omonyi back to her feet.

"You fool!" snapped Ntashia. "Do you think that the four of us can kill three thousand Galbrans?"

"But we are nearly escaped!" protested Omonyi.

"Just because the Galbran sleep during the day, does not mean they are afraid of the light."

The death cries of the guards had indeed aroused other Galbrans, and they rose quickly—snatching up their weapons and letting loose with bellowing cries that echoed in the vast chambers; cries that roused yet more of their fellow tribesmen.

The third guard leaped to his feet, his hand groping for his axe. Garvey and Cray quickly dispatched him with thrusts of their blades. Garvey lowered his dripping blade as the Galbran fell heavily to the floor and roughly grabbed Ntashia's firm arm. "Get into the tunnel, I'll hold them off."

"The tribe can't afford to sacrifice another man," objected Omonyi as she pushed Cray toward the tunnel. Cray hesitated but saw no point in arguing while a thousand Galbrans roused themselves from sleep and closed in for the attack, so he ducked into the tunnel and disappeared from sight.

Ntashia looked at Garvey, her eyes a burning deep purple. "This time she's right."

A crossbow string twanged and a bolt sang through the air, its tip emerging violet from between Omonyi's breasts. She staggered and fell to one knee. Ntashia went to her side, but Omonyi waved her on. "Go," she choked out. "I'm as good as dead now."

Chapter Eight:
Escape from the Galbran

The Surface of Mars: September 23, 1999

The storm swept toward Garvey, a massive wall of suffocating sand that threatened to engulf any and everything in its path. His first thought was to take refuge within the broken remains of the Mars Climate Orbiter, but he quickly discarded that idea. Already the winds were howling with such force that the Orbiter was rocking in its crater, threatening to lift and tumble along with the hurricane forces that buffeted it. Only by leaning into the wind was Garvey able to stand, and he knew that the worst was yet to come.

His broken leg lancing pain, he crawled back into the Orbiter and retrieved what little he could; rations, a first aid kit, a carbon dioxide converter to provide oxygen once the tanks in his suit ran out, and as an after thought he grabbed the electronic pad that held his books and music.

Each step was excruciating as he fled the Orbiter and trekked toward the rocky outcroppings that emerged from the sandy surface of the planet. The large converter unit was a burden and made every footfall a stabbing symphony of pain. The wind pulled at him, carrying him several feet to the south each time his feet left the ground. Only the lighter Martian gravity gave Garvey the extra impetus he needed to reach the relative safety of the rocks.

As the sands descended, scathing rock and rill, he found a deep crevice and pushed himself inside. Two hundred mile per hour winds kicked at the face of the planet, and above their howl Garvey heard the groan of protesting metal, and saw a metallic glint as the Orbiter left its crater and tumbled by, pushed by the relentless gusts.

The sands found even Garvey's hiding spot, scratching the glass of his helmet and scathing the plastic-coated containment suit. His leg hurt abominably, and Garvey was loath to move, but he worked up the willpower and wormed his way further into the darkness of the crevice. Finally, his back came up against something hard; rock, Garvey figured. The sound of the wind was muted here—and further muted by the fishbowl helmet that he wore, only the faint sound of rattling sand came to his ears this far down the crevice. The astronaut lifted his glow lamp, and his jaw fell open in shock.

The walls around him were carved with designs that nature, itself, never made. The rock was carved with strange beasts and symbols, which he had never seen before. Among them were human figures.

For a moment the awe of his discovery caused Garvey to forget the pain in his leg. The implications of these carvings were tremendous. Not only had there been life on Mars, but also there had been intelligent life. More than mere bacteria had existed upon the surface of the red planet!

Garvey moved to closer examine the carvings holding the glow light up to study the detail. The ground caved beneath him and he plunged into darkness.

Lair of the Galbran: 47,000 B.C.

Another crossbow bolt split the air, shattering against the stone wall of the cavern a few feet from Garvey's head. The astronaut knew that Omonyi's assessment of her mortality was probably right. Short of them stumbling across one of the Warlord Shaxia's amazing healing devices, or a hospital equipped with a surgeon and staff, Omonyi's life was nearly over.

Omonyi stumbled back to her feet and turned to face the Galbran that closed in—a wave of savage, twisted flesh. Garvey slipped inside the tunnel, followed closely by Ntashia. Before they emerged, they heard Omonyi's horrible cries echoing down the passage as the Galbran rent her limb from limb.

They found themselves on a broad ledge, the misty depths of the Rift far below them, and the lofty reaches of its jagged cliffs towering far over. Several narrow pathways branched out from the ledge along the cliff side, and these were the only escape routes, which Garvey could see. Neither one provided much cover from Galbran spears or crossbow bolts, and with the sounds of Galbran pursuit echoing up the tunnel Garvey didn't give much for their chances should they decide to take either route.

Garvey wished he could find some way to block the tunnel, but the cliff face was sheer with no loose boulders or rock that he could bring down upon the ledge—even if he had the means. "It looks like Omonyi has forced our hands."

Ntashia nodded in agreement, understanding perfectly what Garvey was getting at. "We're going to slay the Galbrans now. We have no choice in the matter, but to make our last stand here."

Cray stroked at his extravagant black mustache as he examined the pitted surface of his sword. "I wish my blade were keener, but if I'm going to die this is a good way to go."

"No," said Ntashia. "We have only two sword blades between us. Garvey and I will hold the entrance while you escape to Ledgrim. Be sure to mark this spot well, so that our people can return and take their vengeance."

Cray bit at his lip. "It seems cowardly for me to go with so much slaying to do."

"You know the creed of the Muvari as well as I do," replied Ntashia. "Men and children first."

"What of Garvey?"

"I'm not an official member of the tribe, yet." Garvey poised himself alongside the entrance with his sword blade raised.

Ntashia stretched out her hand to Cray. "Quick, give me your sword. My dagger will do little damage."

Cray tossed his sword to Ntashia and she snatched it out of the air, before tossing her dagger back to the Muvari male. He let the blade fall to the earth between his feet and retrieved it. "Fare you both well, may the One God be with you."

"And with you," answered Ntashia.

The matted head of a Galbran emerged from the tunnel and Garvey struck, his blade sheering through the warrior's neck, and sending the head bouncing across the ledge. He lifted his sword and waited for the next. "We'll take turns," he said. "That way we can rest between blows."

Ntashia nodded, and she expertly beheaded the next man through the hole. They came one after the other, pushed by the fear of their tribal chieftain to meet their doom. The ledge was slicked violet with blood, the heads of a hundred Galbrans littering the ground. Alternating blows, Ntashia and Garvey struck in rapid succession as the Galbrans pushed each other from behind, hoping that they could emerge before the next blow fell, or while a blade was still caught in the body of their fellows—but the two warriors struck quick and clean blows, disabling or killing their enemies before they could struggle clear of the tunnel.

The entry became clogged with bodies and gore, and finally the Galbrans ceased their futile efforts. In this respite, Garvey and Ntashia leaned against the cliff side, regaining their breath in the warm winds that blew from the Rift beneath.

"Do you think that they've finally given up?" asked Garvey between breaths.

Ntashia shook her head, her braids flowing around her face in an odd effect that could never be reproduced in Earth's gravity. "The Galbrans are quite persistent. They aren't going to allow us to camp out on their doorstep."

"Maybe we should make a run for it while they regroup," suggested Garvey, looking down the narrow ledges where Cray had long since disappeared from sight.

The Muvari warrior looked to the sky, displaying her flawless profile. "I think that it is too late for that."

Garvey followed Ntashia's gaze, his eyes searching the misty heights of the canyon and finding a flock of winged Galbran cleaving through the sky. "They must have a second entrance."

"Or perhaps more."

As the Galbran drew nearer Garvey counted their number at twenty, and even as he watched he could see more winged shapes emerging from a crevice in the cliff side far above them.

"It was a pleasure working with you," said Garvey. "We've survived far more than we had a right to."

"The pleasure was mine, American. It is a shame that you will not survive long enough to become an official part of the Muvari Tribe."

"Just as well, I suppose," said Garvey fatalistically. "I always did have a fear of commitment."

"To your tribe, or to your women?" asked the Muvari.

"A fear of marriage," admitted Garvey as he watched the Galbran grow larger.

"It is the duty of any true man. Why would you shirk such a grave responsibility?"

"It is not the same in my tribe. There are as many men as women, and my people number in the millions."

Ntashia frowned, her face showing disappointment with a touch of loathing slowly creeping into her expression. "But Lana said that you were not as the torracks? Are you not drawn to women?"

Garvey turned away from the impending Galbrans, raising an eyebrow as he looked into Ntashia's face. "Oh, I'm drawn to women—but like I said, my tribe is much different than yours. I was worried that being married might take me away from my life of adventure."

"Is this not enough adventure for you? And would you not desire a Muvari woman such as I standing at your side?"

"I know no Muvari women, except for your sister Lana," answered Garvey.

Ntashia's voice took on a bitter, rancorous tone. "Lana is not for you. Of that I am sure."

Garvey's brow furrowed. Somehow, even though they were staring into the face of death, he had managed to hurt Ntashia's feelings and she his. "And why is that? Is an outsider such as I not worthy of such beauty?"

Ntashia's eyes narrowed, her narrow brows pushing inward. "Best to look for some Muvari who'll return your love, blind American!"

As she finished speaking the Galbran were upon them, a horde of flapping, twisted death. These Galbran wore razor tips upon their wings, and as they dove in toward the two defending warriors they swept them forward to slice and sever Muvari flesh. Ntashia leapt forward, a ferocious scowl upon her face as she cut down the first. She ducked down beneath the spread of the razor wings as the dismembered Galbran hurled over her and slammed against the jagged cliff.

Garvey sheered off a wing tip and a hand of a Galbran as he veered by, and then the astronaut leaped to meet a second. Garvey's tremendous strength, and the fifty mile per hour speed of the diving Galbran met, and the astronaut's sword quivered as it cleaved from shoulder to pelvis. The split wings veered off to the left and the right, and Garvey tumbled to the earth– coming to his feet just in time to fend off the attack of a third Galbran, who twisted away to avoid the gory blade.

"Stand up against the cliff!" he called to Ntashia.

She already realized that standing up against the jagged outcroppings of stone at the cliff side was her best tactic, and together they took refuge in the jutting granite growths that grew near the tunnel entrance. Like a swarm of angry crows the Galbran veered back and forth, diving and climbing, then diving again, but they could not come at their prey for fear of catching their wingtips on the extending granite that protected their intended meals.

"I wish I had one of those plasma rifles right about now," muttered Garvey.

"Or even my bow would do," agreed Ntashia who stood at his back.

Out of the corner of his eye, Garvey saw movement in the tunnel. Bodies were being pushed out of the way, and the path cleared. Before he could react, a gore-covered Galbran burst free with a jagged sword in his gnarled hand. The Galbran raised his arms in triumph, but with strength not seen on Mars Garvey burst across the intervening space and impaled the Galbran on the tip of his sword. The dying cannibal brought his sword down upon Garvey shoulder, tearing through the NASA space suit and cutting the skin.

Garvey shook the dead Galbran from his blade and turned to find a pair of Galbrans already emerged from the tunnel, and more pushing through. Besides these new threats, he had left his refuge and was now exposed to the razor-tipped wings of the flying Galbrans. He heard the whoosh of displaced air, and instinctively ducked.

A razor wing swept over his head and decapitated the nearest earthbound Galbran. Garvey thrust his sword up into the air, but the winged enemy was already past. A sword blade rang on the stone near his crouched body, and Garvey leaped back as a half dozen recently-emerged Galbrans pursued him, gnashing their sharp incisors, and frothing at the mouth.

He fell back to the stone outcropping and once again joined Ntashia. Here there was only enough space for two or three blades to come at them at a time, and so they fought grimly as an unceasing stream of the enemy came at them. Overhead the wind-lofted Galbrans send out shrieking cries to disparage and demoralize their enemy.

The two warriors fought for long minutes, throwing back the Galbrans time after time, by virtue of Ntashia's skill and Garvey's brute strength. Still, their arms began to tire, and it was inevitable that they would go down beneath the overwhelming numbers of their enemy. Neither of them dared hope for more than to take down as many Galbran as they might, before being slain.

When a stone plummeted from above, accidentally crushing an advancing Galbran Ntashia and Garvey realized that their time was running short. The winged Galbrans, realizing that they were not able to attack their enemy while they took refuge in the granite outcroppings, landed on ledges overhead, from which they dropped and hurled stones.

Rock rained down from above, breaking against the granite, and spraying them with debris or splitting at their feet as they narrowly missed. The earth-bound Galbran assailing Garvey and Ntashia backed off a few feet so that they wouldn't be struck by the missiles of their fellow tribe members.

Realizing that it was only a matter of moments before one of the missiles crushed them beneath its weight, Garvey gave out a cry and charged into the midst of the Galbran. He hewed to the left and right, his blade biting through flesh and bone wherever it struck.

Ntashia was about to sprint after him, but a series of stones pummeled the ground directly after Garvey, inspiring her to press her body up against the stone spire of their erstwhile refuge. She saw a Galbran swoop from the sky toward the astronaut's exposed back, razor tipped wings glistening.

"Behind you, Garvey!" she cried.

Garvey crouched low and twisted, thrusting his sword upward. This time he was not too late, and he caught the flying Galbran in the heart. He wrenched the violet blade from his spasming foeman and tore the wings away, before using the unfortunate Galbran as a flail to push back the press of enemies. Bleeding from a half dozen cuts, Garvey lifted the locked, and ragged wings and threw them so that they glided to the rocky outcropping where Ntashia still took refuge.

"Fly home," he cried.

A knotted club crumpled his NASA suit, and Garvey fell to his knees as pain paralyzed his left side—locking his muscles. The Galbran swarmed over him, pummeling him with cudgel and sword, and the American astronaut was subsumed beneath the weight of their flesh—hidden from the stunned Ntashia's wide purple eyes.

Chapter Nine:
Captive of the Sinthral

October 12, 2000, Mars

Arnold Stechter's feet crunched on the gravel that scattered beneath his long steps as he left his four-wheeled dune buggy. In the sand-strewn Martian valley below he saw a glint of sunlight reflected by a shiny metallic object—something man made.

Stechter's pinched and pale face shone through the faceplate of his oxygen suit. Beset by illness and lethargy, the long trip to the surface of Mars had not been kind to the once cocky astronaut. Still, his earthly muscles, weakened though they might be, responded marvelously under the lighter gravitational pull of the red planet, and he bounded down the sandy slopes—taking twenty feet in each stride.

At the bottom of the slope he paused and took a pull on a water tube inside the fishbowl helmet, and then he continued his walk. A few minutes later he stood by a sandy mound that protruded with odd angularity from the wind-rounded contours of the dunes around him.

Stechter put out a gloved hand and brushed away the sand, revealing the scorched metal surface that was hidden beneath. In ten minutes he had cleared away enough debris to see the blackened inscription on the side of the ruined spacecraft—*Mars Climate Orbiter.*

A speaker in his helmet crackled, relayed from his landing vehicle, which was in turn relayed from Cape Canaveral Florida by a space antenna in Canberra, Australia. It was the squeaky voice of Allen Rigby at NASA Control.

"Has your search turned up anything?"

"Negative," answered Stechter. "I've gone over the projected landing sites with a fine tooth comb. I can safely say that there is nothing within a hundred mile radius."

Rigby unwrapped a sandwich; Stechter heard the crackling of the wrapper on another planet. "What was that? I may be getting some interference."

"That's me about to bite into a Meat Lover's Submarine sandwich," answered Rigby. "Well, if your search hasn't turned anything up, I guess that means that the Orbiter either burned up or had a fuel leak and exploded while going into orbit."

"The metal detectors show absolutely nothing."

"I guess congratulations are in order, Arnold. You're the first man to ever set foot on Mars."

Stechter smiled thinly. "I guess I am."

Mars, 47,000 B.C.

As the slavering horde of Galbrans rushed in her direction Ntashia slipped on the torn wings, which Garvey had thrown to her. She took three steps out from her granite-bound refuge and flapped the wings, launching herself over the heads of the angry cannibals.

A dozen winged Galbrans excitedly swooped toward her, anxious to see that their prey did not escape. They had the advantage of altitude, but she knew that if she could get across the ledge and out over the Rift that their advantage would be somewhat less. She would considerably open up the space in which she could maneuver.

These thoughts only flashed through her mind; a mind that was focused only on Garvey Dire. She had seen the astronaut go down beneath a wave of Galbran, and now as she glided overhead she watched them rend and tear with their teeth at a downed form clad in the protective skin of a thick NASA space suit.

Ntashia did not have enough speed to effectively use the razors imbedded in the ridges of the wings she wore, and she knew that swooping down to slash at Garvey's tormentors would result only in a crash, and her death. Still, she could not bring herself to abandon the man by whose side she had fought. It was anathema for the women warriors of the Muvari tribe to abandon a male to the enemy, but Ntashia felt additional emotions stirring within her for the stranger.

Though she had only known him for a short time she was duly impressed by his bravery, and if not for him she would not be even wearing the wings that she now used—instead she would be at the mercy of the enemy. A few of the Galbrans standing on the ledge overhead let loose with their missiles, missing Ntashia, but crushing and injuring several of their compatriots below.

Garvey's limbs were pinned, and sharp teeth worried at his suit and flesh. He writhed futilely, hoping that he could somehow break free, but the weight of the mob was too much for even his tremendous strength to overcome. Just as he thought that he was finished, a series of rocks fell from above, crushing bone and mangling flesh. Garvey, himself, might have been struck but for the tangled mass of Galbrans that pressed in on him, and several of these let out great shrieks and ceased their efforts to devour the astronaut alive.

This brief and partial respite gave Garvey the opening that he needed, and mustering his earthly strength he hurled Galbrans from his limbs. Struggling to his feet, he cast attackers aside as if they were chaff before the wind. For one brief moment he stood, clear. It was plain that his reprieve would be only temporary, that in seconds he would once again be mired in the overwhelming numbers of his foe.

He leaped high into the air, above the frothing mob, and when he came down upon the back of a Galbran he leaped again, propelling himself over the edge of the cliff. The warm winds of the Rift leaped up to embrace him, kissing his torn and bloody skin. He spread his arms wide as he fell, the misty cloud banks that lay along the canyon floor seemed to rush up to meet him.

The wind whistled in his ears, but above this he heard the sound of rustling—growing louder by the moment. He twisted his head around so that his sight was no longer fixed on his fate, and saw that Ntashia approached—her vibrating wings tucked at her side as she dove, rocketing towards him, her braids flailing behind.

Perhaps his fate wasn't fixed. Perhaps there was still a chance—but Ntashia dove completely past him, and into the edges of the curling mists beneath. For a moment Garvey lost sight of her in the foggy tendrils, and then he saw her rising from her dive—coming up rapidly beneath his falling form. With expert movements of her wings she brought her angelic form up beneath him so that he fell upon her back. The muscles worked beneath her skin, and Garvey frantically thrust his hands beneath the straps of her wing harness, and maneuvered his body so that it did not hinder the movement of her wings.

For a moment they pitched and rolled as Ntashia struggled to gain control of her flight. Garvey spread his body out, letting his legs and torso float free in the air, finally allowing the Muvari warrior the unhindered movement of her wings.

"Am I glad to see you," said Garvey.

At first Ntashia did not respond, working hard to keep them aloft. They plunged through the foggy white billows, their vision obscured.

Garvey looked out at the membranous brown wings, and noticed that tears were forming in the elastic material from which they were made—rips that grew as the winds beat against the wings.

"I won't be able to stay in the air for much longer," she gasped.

"Can we safely land?"

"That remains to be seen."

The wings slowed their descent, but they fell, emerging quickly from the thick layer of white that lay over the rift. A panorama of jagged stalactites and steaming vents spread out before them, and Ntashia tipped her wings, moving them ponderously, due to the extra weight that she bore, through the maze of stone pinnacles. As they came within twenty feet of the floor of the rocky chasm, Garvey let go of Ntashia's wing harness and slipped from her back—tumbling over the hard ground until he finally came to a halt.

The membrane in the right wing ruptured at the very moment Ntashia spread her wings to catch the air and lift her before she landed. She hit awkwardly and fell, snapping her left wing in two just above her outstretched arm. Stumbling to her feet she struggled free of the ruined wings and tossed them aside.

Bruised and bleeding, Garvey hoisted himself into a standing position and slowly wound his way through the stone mounds that dotted the ground between massive pinnacles of stone. His NASA space suit hung in ragged shreds, hardly a protection any more; the legs were torn and broken, and his shoe had broken off so that on one foot he walked bare.

As he made his way toward Ntashia he began unlocking sections of it and letting them fall to the earth—until finally he stood in torn tank top, a pair of Lycra boxers, and bare feet. His muscular frame was purpled, and smeared with his own blood.

"You don't look so well," said Ntashia. "My sister would never accept a marriage proposal with you looking like that."

"Doesn't bravery count for something?"

"It certainly does, but it wouldn't be enough to win Lana." Garvey sighed. He'd had enough talk of marriage. With no other options but to marry into the Muvari Tribe or to become an outcast on an alien planet, he had thought that Lana would be an excellent choice. Her beauty, like Ntashia's, was tremendous, and for some reason Garvey hadn't been able to help being intrigued by the exotic qualities of the first woman he had contacted.

Given a choice, however, he preferred to take the time to get to know his future wife or wives, for that matter—and he had to admit that the more time that he spent with Ntashia that the less the image of Lana dominated his mind. Though Lana had certainly taken Garvey under her wing, so to speak, she possessed a certain reserved, chilly quality, which he had presumed was natural to all of the Muvari women. However, as he got to know Ntashia he could see that was not the case; Ntashia was fiery in nature, a bit mercurial perhaps, but unreserved in her emotions.

"I never said that Lana would be the Muvari I chose to marry."

"Yet you said that she was the only Muvari woman that you knew, which wasn't true," she said hotly.

"No," said Garvey carefully, realizing now that any verbal misstep might further raise Ntashia's ire. "Now, I also know you."

"And you were also acquainted with Omonyi."

Garvey nodded grimly, his mind spinning for a way to defuse the situation. He briefly considered that at this moment he would rather be upon the cliff side battling the Galbran. "But she was merely an acquaintance. As you have, your sister saved my life—I must confess that I feel indebted to both of you, and with that I feel that I now know you both."

"So I have gained esteem in your eyes. I am now on par with Lana?" she asked shrewdly.

"I can't help but feel that perhaps I know you better, and by the time our journey is complete I may know you better than my best friend in America—someone I knew since childhood."

"What is her name?"

"His name is Bradley Thomas."

To Garvey's relief, this seemed to satisfy Ntashia, and with a toss of her braided head she changed the subject. "Your wounds need to be dressed. Perhaps we can find a spring and bathe them. Why does your body leak red?"

"It is my blood. I've spilled much Martian blood, and it all seems to be violet—but mine runs red."

"You are a strange man," she said.

"I suppose that I am," agreed the wayward astronaut. He leaned against a pile of stone and one of them clattered down the heap as it came dislodged.

"Best not to disturb those," advised Ntashia. She stooped and carefully replaced the stone.

A puzzled expression crossed Garvey's face. "Why is that?"

"These aren't natural formations. These are cairns built by the Sinthral to mark when one of their own has fallen."

"Are they buried here?"

She nodded. "For the most part. This is their holy ground that we have stumbled upon—and they don't take kindly to intruders."

"I'm not in any condition to be looking for trouble, maybe we'd better get out of here." These Sinthral were the fifth tribe that Garvey had heard of since being swept through the stasis loop. The first, of course, were the Muvari, and shortly after meeting Lana he had a rather rude introduction to the long-limbed and neutered giants of the torrack race—beings created and somehow reproduced solely to serve the Warlord Shaxia.

On his flight to Ledgrim Lana had pointed out the perpendicular scars across the face of Phobos and told of the cities of the Karpathesians who raided the planet's surface for slaves and concubines. His first meeting with the Galbran reinforced any suspicions that he might have had about the ferocity and dangers of the beings that inhabited Mars—could he expect anything less from the Sinthral?

"Are the Sinthral cannibals, too?"

Ntashia arched her fine eyebrows. "Worse…much worse."

Garvey shifted his gaze while he asked himself what could be worse than the Galbran. While his eyes were averted Ntashia leaped upon him, dragging him to the ground behind the cairn by which he stood. He was about to protest when he heard shrill cries rebound against the stone pinnacles that shadowed the thousands of cairns below. Winged Galbran flitted among the misty reaches of the far-spiring stalagmites, their cold eyes searching the rocky wastes for their escaped prey.

Ntashia and Garvey pressed themselves up against the warm stone of the cairn in order to hide from the enemy above. Finally the Galbran moved on, and the two escapees left their hiding spot to trek through the scattered cairns. The stone mounds seemed endless, but finally they emerged from the gravesite, gaining higher ground as they climbed a series of rocky plateaus that mounted against the west side of the Rift.

"Where are we going?" asked the astronaut, who was forced to be satisfied with the path that Ntashia was blazing.

"To the top of the Rift. It is far too dangerous to wander the canyon floor. If we can make the top of the Rift we may be able to find the Muvari outpost. They will give us the wings that we need to return to Ledgrim."

"You know the way to the top?"

"I have flown over the Sinthral holy ground many times, and I know that there are ways to the top—but I have never traveled them on foot."

"So, you're hoping that if we keep to higher ground we'll eventually be able to find a way to the top?"

Ntashia eyed Garvey suspiciously. "That is my plan. Do you have some difficulties with it?"

Garvey showed his palms as he shook his head. "It sounds like a reasonably good plan to me. I just wanted to know what our chances were, and I think I have a pretty good idea now."

"Our chances are minimal," said Ntashia bluntly.

"That's exactly what I was thinking."

They traveled for some hours, along the way Ntashia collected several broad-leaved plants that grew from between cracked rock, and they chewed on the reddish tubers, which grew in plentiful patches among gravel-strewn beds of earth. To Garvey the tubers had a grassy flavor with a hint of spicy radish. Though the taste put him off at first, he quickly became used to it and devoured many to help keep his strength up.

They always watched the skies for fear that the Galbran might come diving from those mist-bound reaches to whisk them back to their larder. On more than one occasion they hid themselves as a Galbran flier circled overhead. Garvey's legs felt like lead—the exhaustion of his earlier battle, and his wounds taking its toll. Ntashia fared no better than the earthling, and when their journeys brought them to a ledge dotted with steaming hot springs, and carved with a shallow cave entrance they resolved to make camp.

Tendrils of mist slipped from the mouth of the cave, and Garvey found a hot spring within the grotto—just at the back of its twenty-foot long corridor. Here they could relax away from the prying eyes of the Galbran, and though the mouth of the cave was rather wide, the two of them, side by side, might be able to hold it against an enemy if they were warned far enough in advance.

Ntashia stripped off her blood-stained clothing and slipped into the steaming waters of the rocky pool wearing nothing but her underclothing—a loincloth and a band of cloth that bound her breasts. She submerged herself to her shoulders, and for a moment Garvey stood stunned, still digesting the brief eyeful of alien anatomy to which he had been exposed.

Though of a more slender structure than the body of an earthling human, with impossibly narrow waist and long muscular limbs, the rest of the body was identical to that of an earth-born female.

Ntashia seemed blissfully unaware of the response that she might provoke in Garvey. She splashed at the bubbling water as she scrubbed the blood away from her arms. "Aren't you coming in? Your wounds need to be washed so that they do not become infected."

"Perhaps I'd best wait until you're finished," answered Garvey.

"You'll need help dressing your wounds," she objected as she motioned to the broad-leafed plants, which she had earlier collected. "The juice of the fennivrae is potent against infection. Before we discovered its uses, many of our people lost limbs due to infected wounds as small as a scratch."

When Garvey saw Ntashia's lack of self-consciousness he decided that he wouldn't make an issue of it and slipped into the effervescing waters and let the heat ease his aching muscles. He leaned back with a groan and closed his eyes, the sulfur-scented steam rising up around him. Only now did he realize how completely exhausted he was from their ordeal, and sleep quickly encroached on him.

He dreamed that he was in the Mars Climate Orbiter again, and that someone was with him, putting a hand on his shoulder. His eyes snapped open, and he found himself still sitting in the hot spring with Ntashia only a few feet away, steam rising about her high-cheeked face, gently shaking him.

"Don't fall asleep yet," she ordered. "We've got to fix up your wounds."

Garvey agreed groggily, but when she began to splash water upon his cuts, the initial sting quickly woke him. Once his wounds were cleansed, Ntashia made Garvey sit up out of the pool's waters while she squeezed the leaves of the fennivrae plant, letting the juices seep into his cuts.

This created a stinging sensation, followed by a numbing feeling in the wound, which made the pain of the cuts easy to bear. "That should do it," she said finally.

"Thank you." Garvey felt sleep closing in once more.

"Just lay down here by the spring," said Ntashia, seeing his fatigue. "I'm going to wash up my clothes before I sleep."

Garvey meant to ask if they should set up a watch and take turns standing guard but slumber was upon him before the thought could reach his lips. The warmth of the rising steam kept them comfortable during the chill of the night, and Garvey awoke as the late morning sun filtered through the foggy skies overhead and weakly illuminated the cave.

He sat up and looked around, but Ntashia was nowhere to be seen. Her leather skirt, tunic, and boots lay hanging on a boulder, still damp from the scrubbing that they had received the previous night—but Ntashia wasn't within the cave. Even her sword had been left behind, and Garvey found it unlikely that she would wander far unarmed.

He took up her weapon and called out to her, but his voice echoed hollowly against the cave. He quickly rose and passed to the mouth of the grotto where he looked out over the step-like ledges that descended toward the bottom of the Rift. Garvey could see no sign of his traveling companion and a sudden pang of fear grew in his breast. This was not fear for himself, but fear for Ntashia. Could something have crept upon them while they slept, and dragged her away while he lay only a few feet away?

It didn't seem possible to Garvey that he wouldn't have been awoken by her cries for help—and why would a creature attack her and leave him unmolested?

Still, the only other solution that Garvey could think of was that Ntashia had abandoned him—but after all that they had been through together this option didn't seem too likely to Garvey, either. He was about to begin retracing their steps toward the floor of the Rift to see if he might find any sign of the Muvari warrior when he noticed dark bristles pasted to a nearby boulder by the dampness of the mist. A little further he found a strand of blonde hair. He held it up to the suffused sunlight above and he could see the faintest hint of violet melanin.

Without a doubt the strand of hair belonged to Ntashia, but he couldn't determine what the bristles were from. He wound his way to the north, down an uneven jumble of stone that served as a stairway cutting down through a narrow, rock-flanked defile and he found strange prints upon the stone. They were not of human origin, nor did they possess the aspect of any other mammal of which Garvey could think. Of course, his knowledge was limited to earthly life. Nothing could have ever prepared him for meeting the hobranx that had been under the mind-control of the Galbran when they had attacked Ledgrim—and surely there were millions more mysteries of life on Mars, which he had yet to see.

Still, Garvey was sure that these prints came from something living—something, which had only recently passed that way or the prints would have dried by now. With a surge of hope passing through him, Garvey took up the pursuit—naked but for a pair of ragged boxers, a tank top, and the sword in his hand. Occasionally his steps took him wincing across sharp beds of rock, but for the most part the path smoothed out into broad ledges that carried Garvey beneath the overhanging cliff of the Rift.

Mist hung in the air as he followed the trail of odd perpendicular marks that seemed to fall with no rhyme or reason—with no pattern that Garvey could discern. Soon his path left the open air and into the wide and jagged maw of a cavern. The mouth hung thick with purple moss that fell in long bilious masses, nearly concealing the entrance. Garvey brushed this curtain of foliage aside as he entered, and found that the moss grew thickly within—the strange nature of the vegetation casting a violet luminescence that lit his way.

In this purple pallor he passed from cavern to cavern, in search of whatever thing had carried Ntashia away. The wet perpendicular tracks ceased, and Garvey searched blindly—hoping that if he followed the series of caves and tunnels for long enough that he might stumble across his prey.

Chapter Ten:
Escape From the Sinthral

February 12, 2001, The Surface of Mars

Arnold Stechter checked his solar panels, and carefully removed the wind swept debris that had gathered on their polished surfaces. Once he had assured himself that everything was in good working order he took bounding steps that carried him quickly through the low gravity atmosphere of Mars and to the small geodesic structure, which he had been living in for the past five months of his life.

He paused at the airlock and glanced once more to the reddening sky. He wondered if he would ever get used to staring at a vista so different than that of Earth's. He was about to open the airtight door hatch, when a flash in the atmosphere caught his attention.

It hadn't been a large flash, like the lightning storms that frequently swept across Mars, but a small crackle of light as though a meteor had plunged through the thin envelope of unbreathable gasses that clung to the planet. Or was it something else?

As he studied the sky, he saw another flash of light and then another. These, Arnold knew, were not caused by the friction of the atmosphere against a foreign object—but they were flashes of ignited rocket fuel. A craft was landing on Mars, and Arnold knew that it wasn't from the United States. A relief vessel wasn't due for another nine months.

Allan Rigby's voice suddenly crackled weakly in Stechter's fishbowl helmet. "Arnold! Are you there, Arnold?"

"Receiving," answered Stechter.

There was a long delay as the message was transmitted at the speed of light, from Stechter's helmet, to the small transmission tower that protruded in an ungainly fashion from the side of the geodesic dome, and through the cold void of space to Canberra Australia, and then to Cape Canaveral Florida.

"We've just intercepted transmissions from a Chinese craft that claims to be making a Mars landing only seven miles from your position. It took us a few minutes to break the encryption, but our triangulation of the transmission's source leads us to believe that it might not be a hoax."

Stechter watched the craft descend through the red-ribboned atmosphere, its stabilization supports already extended for the landing on the rocky soil of Mars. "It's no hoax. Do they know that I'm here?"

"We haven't officially announced your presence on Mars. We were waiting for the relief geology team to arrive and establish a firm presence before we told the world."

The astronaut gnawed on his thin lower lip. "That doesn't answer my question. Do they know that I'm here?"

After a long pause the voice of Allan Rigby squeaked through the helmet speaker. "We don't know for sure, but we suspect that they do. It seems more than a coincidence that they would land within ten miles of your base camp."

Arnold Stechter wasn't a man who was easily frightened. He had bridged the cold voids between Earth and Mars without fear once trembling his hand—but now he felt his heart race. He knew well the reason China was here. They wanted to claim Mars as their own—and to install a transmission base for controlling orbital nukes over Earth. They wouldn't let one American astronaut stand in their way, especially an astronaut that most Americans didn't yet realize existed. They could make him disappear and the United States had no recourse—because he didn't officially exist yet.

Stechter had longed for one thing since he became an astronaut: to have his name go down in history as the first man to set foot on Mars. He had lied and cheated Garvey Dire of the honor, so that he might have the distinction. In utter horror, Arnold Stechter realized that he would never bask in the adulation and glory of being the first. It would be stolen from him, just as he had stolen it from the astronaut who had come before him.

Mars 47,000 B.C.

The violet light of the phosphorescent moss gave Garvey's face a strange pallor as he crept through the caverns, sword tightly gripped in his freshly scabbed fingers. The fennivrae had worked quickly on his minor wounds, even closing a few of the scratches—but he was far from being healed; his body still a profusion of bruises and aches. Breathing shallow and quiet, his bare feet padding against the warm stone was the only sound that came to his ears.

This silence was shattered by a scream echoing through the chambers—and that chilling sound stabbed to his heart, because he was sure that it was the voice of Ntashia. He threw aside all caution and burst through the ragged, lichen grown entrance only to come to a sliding halt in the moss as a horrific sight reared up before him.

The thing stood on six spider-like legs, with a bulbous black body like that of an arachnid, which grew with profuse black bristles. Emerging from the front of the beast was a humanoid torso of slate gray skin, incredibly lean and narrow of shoulders with a slate gray head, impossibly long arms, and holding a ten-foot spear with a metallic point the shape of a spade. Though the face was humanoid, the eyes were small and slitted, and the nose, long, narrow, and sharply protruding; its ears were twice as large as a human's and ridged with multiple points.

A strange spatter of multi-syllabic words emitted from the gray lips of the beast. Garvey could not understand a bit of it, but the way the creature pulled back his spear, as if preparing to thrust it into the astronaut, spoke eloquently. Moving on sheer instinct, Garvey let his earthly muscles carry him forward and beneath the hideous body of the strange beast before the tip of the spear could ever fall. The six furry legs of the creature moved nimbly, one of them brushing Garvey, as the creature scuttled back into the room.

A sudden rush of images burst across Garvey as though the floodgates had been opened in his mind. The dark and sinister shape of the Sinthral, for now he knew that was what he was facing, moved across murky landscapes preying upon the unwary—hypnotizing them with bizarre mental powers and taking them captive.

The rush of images passed and Garvey found that he was down on one knee, the Sinthral hovering over him with a malicious smile slowly spreading across its slate face. A sibilant voice echoed in his head. "Submit creature."

It was a command, and Garvey felt strangely compelled to obey, but even as his body began to submit to the order something snapped inside the astronaut's head—and he was freed from the insidious mental bonds by which the Sinthral had attempted to ensnare him.

He lashed out with his sword and hacked a chitinous black leg away from the beast, which let out a great cry of pain as it tried to back away from the source of its woes. Garvey shoved his sword upward and into the bulging black belly of the Sinthral, ripping open the sack and letting loose a viscous stream of entrails. Now the keening cries of the creature rebounded from the walls, and Garvey hacked his way from a screen of wriggling legs and came free of the beast's body.

He backed his way across the cavern as the Sinthral writhed in its death throes, and noticed a second Sinthral—much like the first, slowly crossing the heaving floor toward him. This creature was bald and bare of torso like her companion, but she was obviously female, her dark, thickly lashed eyes barely comprehending of Garvey, but her narrow nose flared as she tracked him by scent.

She spoke through gray lips tinged with purple, and this time Garvey could understand the words. Apparently the Sinthral's attempt at subduing his psyche had also imbued him with an understanding of the language of these hideous abominations.

"What are you, creature? How do you resist the subjugation of your mind?" Her voice was sibilant, and even as she spoke Garvey could feel her words worming their way into his brain, trying to take control.

He was not taken so easily this time, and found that by focusing on the grim task at hand he could shut out the controlling influence of the Sinthral. "You are not like the woman that we took. Your scent is different; we did not recognize your scent in the cavern of the hotsprings. We thought you nothing more than a beast—your scent is similar to a rat's—but you are so much more dangerous—and large enough to make a meal for my offspring."

A glimmer of understanding seeped into Garvey's mind. These beasts were nearly blind, depending on their sense of smell to guide them more so than their sight. Because he was from Earth, the Sinthral had not recognized his scent, and thought that he smelled similar to the Martian equivalent of a rat. Not a flattering comparison, thought Garvey, but it had worked in his favor this time. The reason that Ntashia had not cried out and woken him from his slumber was because the Sinthral had put her under the influence of their mental control, silencing any attempt at an outburst as they carried her away. Probably it was also his alien mentality that now saved him from being subdued by the Sinthral.

"Where is this woman that you took?" demanded Garvey.

"Have I so beguiled you that you do not see her, creature? She is right behind me. You will soon join her."

Once again Garvey felt the words impacting his mind, sinuous things that tried to crawl into his subconscious and take over. He scattered the words from his brain as though they were chaff before a wind, and cast his eyes beyond the Sinthral, finding that Ntashia hung wide-eyed from a thick rope that was cast over one of the heavy beams that passed overhead.

She still lived, but beside her hung a row of festering bodies—mostly Galbran—that had long been dead. Strange growths and pustules grew on these bodies, and with horror Garvey suddenly realized why the Sinthral kidnapped its victims. The bodies were used as hosts—incubation pods, for their offspring.

"Are you alright?" Garvey called to his Muvari companion.

She nodded weakly to him, but her voice wouldn't come. Already she had been paralyzed by the poisonous sting of the Sinthral, and her vocal cords were numbed—unable to function. Likewise, her arms dangled unfeeling at her side, and her legs uselessly. Despite her best efforts she could produce no movement in them.

The Sinthral made no movement toward Garvey, apparently satisfied for the moment to keep him pinned in the corner of the cavern. There was no path that he could take that would pass out of reach of the Sinthral's long legs.

"You have killed Gorgoth, my mate," she continued. "Why would you do such a cruel thing? Don't you feel horrible for the pain that you have inflicted upon me?"

Waves of guilt and sympathy bombarded Garvey's mind, drawing unwanted, unbeckoned tears to his eyes. He fought back these artificially induced feelings, quickly realizing why the Sinthral seemed satisfied to keep him in the corner. She was buying time, hoping that if she attacked Garvey mentally for long enough that he would succumb, and that she wouldn't have to face him physically.

Though Garvey had managed to fight off the first few mental bombardments, he noticed that the Sinthral female's attacks were growing subtler, more devious—and more effective. He felt like throwing himself on the ground and giving into the surging tides of guilt and despair that gnawed at his soul. The astronaut had no doubt that if he allowed the Sinthral to continue her mental assault that it wouldn't be long before she found a pathway into his mind and that he succumbed to her manipulations.

"Give me the woman, and I'll let you live," shouted Garvey. He felt a sudden burst of anger emanating from the Sinthral.

"Do you think that I, Shavrena of the Sinthral, would be so craven as to allow the slayer of my mate to go free? Make no mistake, creature, you will surely die. While you lay numbed by my poison, but still aware of all that goes on around you, I will lay my eggs in your body—and my new mate will fertilize them. When my offspring are born, they will feed on the flesh of your body—your muscles and organs will succor them in their hunger."

Despite himself, Garvey grimaced at the thought of the horrible fate that might be awaiting he and Ntashia. It was too grim an end to ponder.

"My flesh is poison to your kind," boasted Garvey, "and my blade is death!"

Shavrena was more than ready for any frontal attack that he might make, so Garvey decided to use his earthly strength in a manner that might surprise the Sinthral female. His legs coiled beneath him and he sprang high into the air, catching hold of an overhead beam that was studded with hooks and knotted with frayed and broken rope that marked the spot where the corpse of many unfortunate victims had once hung.

This surprised Shavrena, but did not put the astronaut out of her reach. She scuttled forward and jabbed her spear toward the hanging Earthling, but Garvey did not stay still for long. He pulled himself up on top of the beam before the shivering spear sank deep into the wood. Long black, armored legs reached up to snatch him from his perch, but Garvey hewed viciously whenever one came within reach, slicing the probing tips away from two of the appendages.

Shavrena hissed angrily. "Come down from there, meat!"

When Garvey didn't comply, Shavrena suddenly reconsidered her tactics and strode across the floor to the opposite side of the chamber where Ntashia hung. She reached up with a massive pincer and placed the mandible about the Muvari Warrior's body. "Give up, or I'll pinch this woman in two."

Garvey leaped fifteen feet from the beam he was standing to the next. Dust rose from beneath his feet as he landed. "If I surrender she is already as good as dead. You'd only be doing a merciful service if you killed her now."

"A merciful service!" shrieked Shavrena. "I'll be doing all of Mars a merciful service when I rid it of you!"

Before the Sinthral finished speaking Garvey launched himself from the rafter. He prayed that he could reach Shavrena before those pincers closed about Ntashia's exquisite body. As he descended from his leap he aimed a horrific blow at Shavrena's dark wrist—just below the pincer. Though double the size of a large earthling's wrist, Garvey's sword hacked through the thick chitinous layer and completely severed the pincers from her body.

Shavrena let out a horrible, piercing cry as her dismembered pincers toppled to the floor without so much as scratching Ntashia's exposed body. As Garvey hit the rocky cave bottom Shavrena reared up and thrust her right pincer at him. Garvey was on one knee when he saw the massive claw bearing down upon him. He had no time to bring his sword into play, so he tucked forward, rolling away as the pincers snapped a hair's breadth behind him.

He came up out of his roll and spun, his blade whirring through the air. It was a reflexive action—designed to counter an attack that he suspected Shavrena would make, less than to counter an attack he saw coming. In this case, it worked in his favor. He split Shavrena's pincer down the joint, so that the pincers that stood on either side of Garvey's body were rendered useless. Shavrena was unable to move them.

The female Sinthral staggered back, all the while emitting an ear-rending scream that threatened to burst Garvey's eardrums. He thought that perhaps he should pursue and finish the monster, but he took a step forward and his knee buckled beneath him. Instead of chasing, he watched the Sinthral flee through the luminous corridors, her long chitinous legs carrying her with a speed that perhaps only Garvey might have been able to match. With such grievous injuries Garvey doubted if Shavrena would be back. She still had two hands on her humanoid body, with which she could wield a spear, and with which she might be equally dangerous, but she had been dealt a nasty loss.

His legs finally recovered from the after-effects of his adrenaline rush and regained their strength. Garvey mounted the rafter where Shavrena had hung her captive. He took hold of the thick rope by which Ntashia was bound and pulled her paralyzed form up to the rafter where he severed her bonds, then gathered her half-naked body in his arms. Her purple eyes glittered thankfully back at him, and her lips opened as if to speak—but no sound was uttered. The paralysis had utterly overtaken her body, and her head and limbs fell limply.

"I'm going to take you back to the cave," he told her. In truth, he had little idea of what he was going to do after that. Having no prior knowledge of the Sinthral and their poison, he didn't know whether the paralysis would prove permanent, even fatal, or if the effects of the poison would soon wear off.

Holding Ntashia tightly Garvey leaped down from the rafter, his spring-steel thews absorbing the impact of the landing. He quickly retraced his steps through the caves, and back across the rocky ledges to the hot springs where they had camped the night before. Ntashia's sword and leather tunic and skirt still lay on a nearby boulder—as did the still-moist fennivrae plant with which Ntashia had dressed Garvey's wounds.

As the astronaut resolved to lay Ntashia next to the hot spring he suddenly heard her voice echoing in his brain. "Garvey," she cried. "Can you hear me?"

Startled he looked down at the stunning features of her visage, but her violet-tinged lips had not moved. The voice came into his mind again.

"You can hear me, can't you?" With her voice came the sweet solace of intimacy passing over him like a wave—both gratifying and soul-touching at the same time.

"Yes, I can hear you," answered Garvey slowly and out loud.

"Through the mindspeak the Muvari can communicate mentally," she spoke. "You being an American I wasn't sure if you were capable of hearing me. It took me the entire journey to break through to you."

"That explains how I was able to learn your language," said Garvey.

"Lana touched me and the words flooded over me like a tidal wave. I felt as though I had always known the language—as though I had always known Lana."

"It is no wonder that you cannot get Lana out of your mind or heart," said Ntashia wistfully. "Because of its intimacy the mindspeak is a form of communication which the Muvari reserve for marriage, or only for certain worship rituals. Lana risked her wedding vows by imbuing you with the knowledge of our language and of her."

These words came as a sudden shock to Garvey. "Wedding vows?"

"Foolish American," responded Ntashia—but her voice was sympathetic, unlike her reproof of him before, "you do not know the ways of the Muvari."

"That, I will freely admit."

"My ears are unadorned, symbolizing that I am eligible for marriage. Lana wears a ring in her ear—indicating the bonds of marriage, and the sacred trust that she has undertaken."

Garvey eased his aching arms by setting Ntashia down, but still he kept near, his hand locked with her numbed fingers so that their link would not be broken. "But why would Lana risk her vows for me…a stranger? And why do you speak to me now with the mindtouch?"

Garvey found that he not only heard her words in his head, but he felt her emotion at the same time. It nearly overwhelmed his body and soul because he felt her secret love for him, it pounded him as the ocean surf assails a rocky shore—it was an emotion that had been entirely absent during his communion with Lana. "I know not why Lana spoke to you thus—perhaps it was because you had saved her life, and it was important to communicate with you quickly if you were to escape the torracks."

"And why do you speak with me?"

"Because my life is in your hands, and because…" her communication faltered for a moment. "Because I love you. Can't you feel it?" she pleaded.

Garvey gasped as he felt the intensity of her emotions amplified by the mindtouch and ringing in his brain. "I can," he answered.

"Do you think you can set aside your infatuation with Lana and return my love?"

"It wasn't like this with Lana."

"So, you can not return my love?" she said sadly.

"There was no love, no desire in her mind—only expediency. With you my very soul burns with the power of your emotions."

Some part of Garvey wanted to give himself completely to this alien girl who had opened up the floodgates of her thoughts to him—but old habits died hard. For years he had built a wall of reserve, never completely giving his heart to any woman lest they should somehow restrict his selfish freedoms. "Perhaps," he answered. "Perhaps I can return your love."

"Then I will let that hope burn within me," she answered, "until the day that your lips can agree with what your heart has already decided."

Garvey knew then that Ntashia was reading his feelings as certainly as he was hers—and he felt ashamed that he could not bring himself to tear down that wall of reserve. "What of the Sinthral poison? Will you recover?"

"I will die…unless you mash the fennivrae and dilute it with some water. I can still swallow, and you must force me to drink the solution. The fennivrae will serve as an antidote to the poison."

Immediately Garvey unclasped his hand and ground the fennivrae leaves between two rocks. In the worn hollow of a flat rock he mixed the pulp with some hot water from the spring and drained this between Ntashia's lips. With much effort she gulped down the concoction and then she faded into unconsciousness—the ever-watchful American astronaut by her side.

Chapter Eleven:
Return of the Sinthral

October 23, 2000, The Surface of Mars

Arnold Stechter gazed blankly at the sensor screen, his exhausted eyes no longer comprehending the blurry shapes that swam before it and his ears not comprehending the warning alarm that repeated its distress call every three seconds. Fearing that a Chinese attack was imminent, he'd been awake for the last sixty-three hours—watching the sensors, looking out the Plexiglass windows of his geodesic oxygen dome for any sign of movement in the red sands.

Finally his adrenaline kicked in, pushing away the sleep-deprivation-induced hallucinations involving a woman he once dated back on Earth. He shook his head violently as though to clear away the mental cobwebs and sprang to his feet. The sensors showed three intruders had passed the perimeter alarms, which were set one hundred yards away from the dome.

Arnold Stechter looked out the window—Phobos and Deimos shed their amber light on the undulating waves of sand—but enough shadows existed in those rolling dunes to hide thirty or forty men. He reached for the intercom; maybe he wouldn't survive the night, but at least NASA mission control would know what happened to him. He put the intercom against his lips and pressed the transmission button, but a streak of flame crossed from a dune seventy yards out from the astronaut's base camp.

Before the first word could drop from his lips his transmission tower exploded into fragments of metal. As quickly as the explosion blossomed the flame withered and died, snuffed by the nitrogen heavy atmosphere. Stechter's jaw fell, and mumbled, shocked words dropped out. "They're using rocket-powered grenades."

The Chinese astronauts had set up their base camp some ten miles from that of NASA camp, and Stechter had been living in fear ever since. Now that fear had become realized. The Chinese weren't going to play friendly; they intended to establish the sole beachhead on Mars at any cost.

If the United States were allowed to have a base on Mars they might easily set up a radio base to jam any and all Chinese transmissions to nuclear platform satellites orbiting the Earth. That would put China and the U.S. on a level playing field again. China obviously wasn't interested in a level playing field.

Already they had cut off Arnold Stechter's only lifeline, and now he was at their mercy. He had watched them disembark from the Chinese lander, and knew that there were three astronauts. His sensors showed that all three of them had crossed his perimeter.

NASA hadn't seen fit to provide Arnold Stechter with any weapons. Every ounce within his spacecraft had been accounted for, and including a firearm and ammunition would have cost an extra four or five pounds. Besides, Mars was a dead planet—what possible need could he have for a weapon? Now, Stechter would gladly have given up half of his equipment for even a .22 pistol.

One stride sent Stechter floating twenty feet to the opposite side of his geodesic dome. A variety of tools and equipment lay against the wall, and he picked up a short spade with a light, but sturdy, aluminum head. On the west side of the dome the airlock door gleamed dully in the light from the overhead glow lamps. Stechter positioned himself beside the door with upraised shovel, waiting to strike the first man that came through that door.

He realized that one well-placed rocket powered grenade could blow his entire home to pieces and kill him in the process, but he reasoned that the enemy already would have done so if they didn't have other plans.

Resources were in short supply on Mars, and probably they wanted to avail themselves of whatever NASA equipment and rations they could take from him. A grenade would destroy everything.

For long minutes Stechter waited. Despite the moderate temperature within the dome his face and body were drenched in sweat, and his arm quickly tired from holding his impromptu weapon. Were they ever going to come?

A high-pitched whine unlike the sound of any of his equipment came to his ears, and Stechter cast about looking for the source of the noise. Finally he spotted it, a carbide-tipped drill bit poking through the double walls of his dome. The sneaky little swine were going to choke him out!

He heard the hiss of escaping oxygen as the drill bit pulled free and he abandoned his position beside the door, leaping across the chamber to his NASA space suit. Working as quickly as humanly possible, and with hands that had practiced this drill many times he donned his suit. By the time that he pulled his fishbowl helmet into place he was gasping for breath in the nitrogen thick air.

The helmet catches clamped into position, sealing his helmet and he turned on the oxygen tanks even as he sank, gasping, to the ground—gulping like a fish out of water. Sweet oxygen filled his helmet and his thankful lungs took in the life-giving molecules.

The door to the air lock slid open sucking all the remaining oxygen out into the barren Mars landscape, and a space-suited man about five and a half feet tall stepped through the doorway, sand eddying around his booted feet, and a Chinese made .228 caliber rifle in his hands. The name Chang was stenciled on his helmet, and Arnold Stechter could see narrow brown eyes through the Chinese astronaut's faceplate, and a long narrow mustache that grew down to the intruder's chin. White teeth flashed in a triumphant grin.

Stechter reached his gloved hand forward, his fingers closing upon the aluminum handle of his spade. Before Stechter could stand, Chang lowered his rifle and fired three rounds. Though the Chinese rifle that he bore was by no means high-powered and the rounds were of a low caliber they were ideal for the thin Martian atmosphere. They quickly picked up velocity and punched through Stechter's space suit, oxygen atmosphere bursting out in milky white trails.

47,000 B.C. Mars, the Rift Hot Springs

For three days Ntashia writhed in fevered dreams, Garvey stayed by her side leaving only to search out more of the fennivrae plant to create more of the healing drink, and to gather more of the tubers, which they had eaten on their journey across the Rift bottom. When Ntashia regained enough strength and movement in her jaw Garvey fed her these tubers.

By the fourth day Ntashia was able to sit up on her own, and take a few shaky steps across the cavern. During her convalescence her skin had taken on an unhealthy pallor, brought about by the poison of the Sinthral, but now some of her natural colorations were returning—a healthy green tinted her flesh, and the underlying purple hue came to her scarlet lips.

Garvey's anxiety over Ntashia's health was replaced with the anxiety that the escaped Shavrena would gather other Sinthrals to attack their cozy refuge. Everywhere he went he wore his sword belt around his waist. His shoes were little more than rags tied onto his feet and in the fifth day of her convalescence Ntashia resolved to make him some moccasins.

Using Garvey's feet as templates she traced around them with a sharp rock on her leather tunic. Recycling the sinew thread of her tunic she was able to stitch Garvey a pair of moccasins with a shard of bone as a needle.

She proudly presented this gift to Garvey on the seventh day. He was impressed at her handiwork, gratefully accepting the moccasins. "My feet thank you. I feel badly that you sacrificed your tunic for me."

She waved off the sacrifice as though it were nothing. "The Rift is warm enough that I need not worry about being cold. Your feet would turn to bloody shreds if you didn't have something decent to wear on them."

Of all his earthly possessions the only thing that remained to Garvey was the solar powered Clip Pad that stored thousands of books and hundreds of compact discs worth of music. As Ntashia rebuilt her strength they listened to music, and Garvey often read to her, translating passages from the Bible, Homer, and Shakespeare.

Ntashia was as amazed by the Clip Pad as Garvey had been by Ntashia's ability to construct a pair of moccasins with such rudimentary tools. "It's like one of the Warlord Shaxia's devices," she said one day when Garvey taught her how to use the pad. "It sounds as though there is a whole orchestra inside—and how does it hold all those parchments?"

"It's a bit of a mystery to me, too," admitted Garvey with a shrug. "My tribe has hundreds of devices that do amazing things. After a while you start to take them for granted."

"How could you possibly take something so wonderful for granted?"

Garvey smiled faintly. "I certainly don't take them for granted anymore. Beside my NASA helmet, that's the only connection that I have with my home. It's the only record of my people's culture that I have left."

"The Iliad is surely a story worth keeping, and your religion parallels our own in many ways, but that Shakespeare fellow speaks in gibberish."

She made a face to illustrate her point. "It certainly can seem that way," agreed Garvey. "He uses the idioms and phrases of his own time."

"Speaking of time, tomorrow I shall feel well enough to travel again," she announced.

"Good, one more night of sleep in our little hideaway then."

Ntashia chewed at the inside of her lip. "Why do you not return to your own people? Are you somehow exiled?"

"Not intentionally," answered the astronaut. He dipped his finger in the sand and idly drew images on the rock. "You've shared at least one secret with me, perhaps it is time that I share my secret with you."

"Does anybody else know this secret?"

"Only your sister."

"Oh," her face fell.

"But she only knows what, and I haven't told her why," he added quickly.

"Then share your secret with me," she said, "and let me be the only one to know the what and the why."

"Then I will share it with you, and only you," said Garvey. "But you must promise not ridicule me when I tell this to you."

"I would never ridicule you…except for maybe to laugh at the way you wield a sword."

"Crude…but effective is it not?"

"Very effective against unskilled swordsman, but I fear that you will not be so fortunate against a more skilled foe."

"Swordsmanship is not a common skill where I come from."

"Then I will teach you," Ntashia said with a smile. "But first you must tell me your secret."

Garvey acquiesced and they stayed awake deep into the night, talking by the firelight, as he related how and why he came to the planet Mars. Ntashia didn't laugh, but she was an unending fountain of questions as they conversed in the smoke-mingled mist of the cavern—occasionally slipping into the bubbling waters to soothe their battered and wounded bodies. Finally sleep overcame them both.

The morning sun drove away the shadows on the east side of the Rift, filtering through the heavy cloud cover that bathed the floor of the canyon in a perpetual twilight. Garvey awoke first, and he slipped out of the cavern to gather tubers from a patch he had been raiding down the trail about a quarter of a mile. As he uprooted the plants, he gazed down the rocky trail and through the cleft that dropped down onto a series of broad stone steps.

Dark shapes climbed those steps—long chitinous legs moving rapidly as six armed Sinthrals crept through the twilight. Leading them was Shavrena, her face holding the trace of a smile as she anticipated the revenge that she would wreak upon the ones who had killed her mate and shorn her of her pincers.

Garvey's eyes bulged when he saw that the buds of new pincers were growing where he had lopped off the old. He hadn't wounded Shavrena as badly as he thought. The six Sinthral traveled quickly and quietly. Male and female they came, their sinews pulsing through their thin gray skin as their bulbous spider bodies carried their humanoid torsos surely across the jagged and jumbled rocks.

The American astronaut knew that he was scarcely a match for one Sinthral let alone a half dozen. He needed to wake Ntashia and flee with her before the Sinthral came upon their lair. He scooped up the tubers that he had harvested and threw them into his NASA helmet, then he sprinted for the cavern where Ntashia still slept. It took him less than a minute to cover the uphill quarter mile, and he leaped over bubbling hotsprings, bursting through the screen of mist to find Ntashia wrapping her sword belt around her leather-skirted waist.

She smiled as she saw him enter, but when she saw the expression on his face her demeanor quickly turned. "What is the matter?"

"The Sinthral," panted Garvey. "They are back."

"They? How many of them are there?"

"Six."

"Then we should flee. We don't have a chance against that many of them—and I might once again fall prey to their hypnotic powers."

They owned little in the way of possessions to gather, so in the matter of moments they emerged from the cavern, which for a week's time had been their home. Ntashia led the way through a maze of jagged boulders, and up a narrow defile, which emerged onto an equally narrow path that ascended the cliff face.

"We must stay ahead of them," she said.

"How would they even know in which direction to search for us?"

"In addition to their other abilities, the Sinthral have an uncanny sense of smell. They'll be able to follow our trail by scent alone."

"This ledge isn't wide enough for them to follow us, though."

"They are able to climb sheer cliff faces if they so desire," answered Ntashia. "Climbing this path is child's play to them."

As they mounted the cliff side, pebbles slipping from beneath their feet and bouncing to the floor of the rift hundreds of feet below, Garvey tried to recall a way that scent could be defeated. He knew that by crossing a river the scent would be washed away, and that it might take some time for a bloodhound to pick up the trail on the other side—but there were no rivers here, and no hope of escaping the relentless hunters that pursued them.

Garvey looked back over his shoulder, and saw the first of the Sinthral emerging from the defile. As they came onto the ledge they walked with three legs on the path and three legs on the wall of the cliff, their slate gray torsos at an angle. Their legs seemed to stick to any surface they desired, and their pace did not slacken.

Ntashia and Garvey, on the other hand were forced to slow as they picked their way up the treacherous trail. One misstep could mean plunging to their deaths, and they could not afford to speed along the path as did the Sinthral. Garvey paused. "There is no way that we are going to be able to outdistance them. We're going to have to stand and fight."

He picked up a loose rock, of which there were plenty beneath his moccasin shod feet, and hurled it a hundred yards at the nearest Sinthral.

Because of the lesser gravity on Mars, his rock picked up amazing speed, but Garvey's aim went awry, and the rock splintered against the cliff a half dozen yards away from his target.

"Fool human!" called the lead Sinthral, his grating voice echoing up the canyon wall. "You'll have to do much better than that if you want to live out the hour."

"Can you throw any better than that?" asked Ntashia.

"Not much better," admitted Garvey, "but I might get lucky."

"You might," said Ntashia with a smile, "but I've got a better way of doing this." She made a circle with her thumb and forefinger to help indicate to

Garvey what she wanted. "You find me as many stones as you can about this size—the rounder the better."

Garvey crouched and tossed one up to her.

"This is good," she said as she unwound a piece of leather that she had wrapped around her waist. "But find them just a little bit smaller if you can."

The strip of leather was one that she had cut from her tunic and into a four-foot length. She doubled this over, and Garvey noticed that the leather was cut wider at the center, forming a small pocket for the stone that she placed there.

"I'm much better with a crossbow," she said as she whipped the leather and rock in an arc, "but I'm not half bad with a sling either."

She let go of one end of the strap and the rock sped free, it struck the bulbous black body of the first Sinthral, and he let out an unearthly shriek. Still, he came on, redoubling his speed, rage spreading across his parchment-skin face, his pointed ears lying back against the sides of his bald skull.

Garvey handed up another rock into Ntashia's slim hand.

"Pray that my aim is true," she said.

The American astronaut whispered a quick prayer while the sling revolved. Every moment the Sinthral grew closer—until he could make out the bristly black hair that covered the spiderous body. It would be only moments before the beast was upon them.

Ntashia let the rock fly and it spun through the air striking the bridge of the Sinthral's nose and pushing in through the broken cranium. Violet blood spattered, and with a choking cry the Sinthral lurched backward, toppling from the path and plummeting into the misty tendrils reaching up from the hot springs far below.

Garvey pressed another stone into Ntashia's palm.

"If they get any closer than that," she breathed, "I'll fall victim to their hypnotic powers. I could feel that one prying into mind even as I let go of the stone."

"I'm able to resist them," said Garvey. "I won't let them get you again."

Now the Sinthral came on in a concerted wave, their cries of rage chilling the hearts of the Muvari-born warrioress and the American astronaut. They came together, so that Ntashia had no hope of striking them all down.

Her next stone struck the upraised leg of a Sinthral, and Garvey could hear the crack of chitin from where he stood. But the Sinthral still had five legs, and the loss of one didn't seem to hinder her much. She came on with back arched, and spear upraised, her torso glistening from the gathered mist, and a savage sneer upon her hideous face.

The astronaut flipped one last rock to Ntashia, and as she inserted it in the pocket of her sling, Garvey stood and hurled a fist-sized stone into the black tear-drop body of the Sinthral. The rock rebounded from the pliable flesh, pulverizing organs beneath. The Sinthral staggered, her remaining five legs buckling beneath her. Her momentum carried her forward to fall at Garvey's feet, but her violet eyes swirled as she fixed Ntashia in her lethal gaze.

Ntashia gave out a cry as the female Sinthral probed into her mind, demanding her surrender. With one last surge of willpower before the hypnotic gaze of the Sinthral bent her to its will, she let her last stone fly from the sling. It struck the beast on the skull, and her torso fell limp, sagging from the hideous black body from which it sprouted.

Even as she fell, the third Sinthral climbed over the top of her still warm corpse, his lean gray torso showed every muscular striation, and his skin was marked with a number of pale scars. His right pincer snapped at Garvey even as his humanoid arms thrust a spear down at the human, who was puny in comparison to the towering Sinthral.

This Sinthral had used this very same tactic against numerous humanoids and experienced quite a bit of success with the maneuver. It was difficult for a human to avoid both a spear from above and a pincer from below. Fortunately for Garvey, he possessed something that none of this Sinthral's former foes possessed—earthly muscles. His steel-spring thews carried him over the clacking pincers and into the air. He knocked away the point of the spear that the Sinthral thrust down upon him. His leap carried him nearly as high as the Sinthral's torso, but he fell short—and as he fell he shoved his sword into the swollen black belly of the man-spider.

Viscous puss poured out as the blade ripped a wide gash. Garvey found himself pummeled by a half dozen chitinous legs as the Sinthral bellowed out a roar of pain. These pushed him away and sent him tumbling across the rocky ledge—even as the scream pummeled his ears. Garvey dropped his sword blade and it tumbled over the cliff as he desperately scrabbled for a handhold on the path. His body slid over the edge, the rough rock scraping his belly and chest. Loose pebbles scattered from beneath his grasping fingers as he slipped, a storm of flailing Sinthral legs whipping around him. Finally his left hand found purchase on a small coniferous plant that had taken root among a crevice. This protruding plant arrested his fall so that he hung by one hand—the jagged shards of rock at the canyon floor beckoning hungrily.

At any moment, Garvey was in danger of being struck by the death throes of the Sinthral he had slain, but Ntashia bravely waded in with her sword blade—violet blood spattering, and cracked chitin spraying as she cut into the legs that lashed wildly about. Finally, she reached the edge of the cliff and she leaned down, proffering Garvey a hand.

Garvey reached up his right arm and gratefully took it. Shavrena and the other remaining Sinthral had considered fleeing when they saw that three of their number had been slain, but emboldened by Garvey's precarious position, and by the fact that the only standing foe was one that she had once subdued with her hypnotic arts, she crawled sideways onto the cliff wall—walking above her slain counterparts as easily as if she were traversing a flat surface.

Because of the dying Sinthral's still-thrashing body Ntashia was unaware of Shavrena's more subtle approach from above. Treading softly and surely, Shavrena came quietly closer. Bereft of the pincers, which were her natural weapon, she readied her barbed spear, impatiently waiting until she was within striking distance.

Ntashia helped to pull Garvey upward when a loosened pebble bouncing past her caused her to look above. Shavrena's gray lips opened wide, and she laughed maniacally as she thrust her spear down toward Ntashia's exposed back.

Chapter Twelve:
Caladrex

December 29, 2001, Orbit above Mars

The anchor tattoo on Bradley Thomas' muscular forearm writhed as he thrust his hand in between the air scrubber and the coolant tanks. Finally his thinning fingers found what he was searching for, and when he pulled his arm loose he held the escaped gold oval between his thumb and forefinger. He smiled with relief, and sighed. "My wife would kill me if I lost my wedding ring."

A few feet away, fellow NASA astronaut Hank Giffen rubbed absently at his sparsely covered dome while he surveyed a repair manual on his Clip Pad. "Imagine surviving the trip all the way to Mars and back only to be killed by your wife the moment that you get home."

Between pulls on a container of Tang juice drink Brendan Melhoff laughed heartily through twelve months worth of beard. "Just before my divorce my wife took my wedding ring right off my finger while I was sleeping."

"What did she do with it?" asked Giffen.

"I think she pawned it for drinking money," said Melhoff after he finished the last of his juice. "My advice to you is never marry an alcoholic red head, because your life…"

"Will become complete hell," chorused Bradley Thomas and Hank Giffen, speaking Melhoff's oft repeated refrain before he could even finish the sentence.

Bradley put his wedding band back on his ring finger, but he had lost much muscle mass during the year of weightlessness, and the golden band hovered loosely now. Because NASA sent three astronauts to look after the first two missing missions, there wasn't enough room to include any sort of exercise equipment in the craft. Exercising using your body weight wasn't an option in zero gravity, and all that left them was a series of NASA-prescribed isometric exercises, which they were supposed to perform every day.

These exercises pitted one's own muscles against each other, and provided for some increased blood flow to the worked muscles—but they were static and all-in-all rather inadequate. As a result, all three of them had lost a large amount of muscle-mass.

Bradley had been the most muscular of the three when they blasted off from Cape Canaveral, and though he had lost forty pounds in the intervening months, while the others had lost only twenty apiece, he was still a good thirty pounds heavier than the other two astronauts.

The rigors of weightlessness were a fact a space travel; reduced muscle mass, bone density loss, and the necessity to keep everything properly contained. Even a minor water spill could turn into disaster if the floating globules got into the computer processor. The one advantage that Bradley could think of was that within a week of taking off his spine had decompressed and now he was a couple of inches taller. Of course, this decompression was accompanied by severe lower back pain until one's body became accustomed to the increased height.

It bothered Bradley how out of shape he had become. Though he had his share of scientific background, the others were the scientists of the mission. He was along to provide the muscle—and this time NASA had supplied them with weaponry. Intelligence sources pegged the number of Chinese astronauts based on Mars at six. The last Chinese rocket to Mars had consisted of a payload of high tech missile guidance technology stolen during the Clinton presidency.

The United States government had hoped to establish the sole outpost on Mars, but its first two efforts had failed. It was Thomas, Melhoff, and Giffen's job to find out why they had failed, and to set up a base camp of operation that was capable of jamming Chinese transmissions.

Their commission was to defend this base of operation at all costs—and that meant taking the life of any Chinese astronaut who attempted to interfere with their mission.

They nominated Thomas, with his extensive military background, for the job. He found it hard to say no, and finally, with great reluctance he bid goodbye to his wife and children who he wouldn't see again for two-and-a-half years.

Hank Giffen somersaulted over to an access panel and unhinged it. He reached into the wiring and made a few adjustments until the control panel flickered to life. "We've got our rocket controls again!" he announced.

"What was the problem?" asked Melhoff, whose hairy face reminded Bradley of a baby bear cub he had seen once at the zoo with his kids.

"The vibrations of our take off worked the power cable loose. It was just floating there by its lonesome."

"It's a relief that's working again," said Bradley. "I'm anxious to get my feet on some solid ground again."

"Yeah," said Melhoff. "Floating up here in this coffin with you guys for a year has been a living hell."

"Don't get smart with me," joked Bradley, "or the first thing I'm going to do when we get out of this tin can is give you a good beating!"

Melfhoff unhooked his Clip Pad from his belt. His fingers maneuvered over the key pad that currently showed on its surface, and he brought up two rows of photographs that showed the six Chinese astronauts thought to be currently living on Mars's surface. He handed the pad to Bradley—whose face sobered when he studied the hard visages.

"Save your energies for those guys," said Melfhoff.

"They look more like wanted criminals than astronauts," commented Giffen as he looked over Bradley Thomas' shoulder.

Bradley pointed to a Xio Cheng—a thin-lipped Chinese man with a mustache that dropped over to the edge of his razor chin. "This one's the leader. He's a former Red Army Captain that took part in the Tiannamen Square Massacre. After that he joined the Chinese flight program and quickly rose up through the ranks."

"Who are the others?"

"Anshi Ping, Chih-Hao Fung, Dong-Soo Hwon, Kien Kuong, and Yew Lun. All have been in the Chinese space program for some time…longer than Xio Cheng, in fact."

"It must piss them off to no end that Xio Cheng got put in charge," suggested Melfhoff.

Bradley electronically flipped through their dossiers. "All have exemplary records, some as scientists, at least one as a fighter pilot like me, but none are as aggressive as Xio Cheng. He's a proven killer."

"What of the others? Do you think they would kill?"

"I don't know," mused Bradley, "but something happened to both Garvey and Arnold, and I'm willing to bet that it was foul play."

Mars, 47,000 B.C., The Rift

Garvey saw the wicked tip of Shavrena's barbed spear thrusting down toward Ntashia's back and he yanked her arm, pulling her over the cliff ledge where he precariously hung. She let out a cry as she tumbled over the edge, bits of loose gravel spinning from beneath her feet, and Shavrena's spear shattering into three pieces as the point struck only stone.

Ntashia fell directly upon Garvey, and the already strained coniferous plant to which the astronaut desperately held gave up its struggle—its roots slipping from the narrow crevice in which it was ensconced. Limbs entangled, they careened down the cliff face—until suddenly they stopped– impacting against a projecting ledge some thirty feet below the path from which they had fallen.

"We're alive!" blurted Ntashia in shock.

"Not for long," said Garvey as he rose on bruised and scraped limbs. "Shavrena's not going to let us go so easily."

The female Sinthral witnessed their narrow escape, and now she crawled right over the ledge toward them, her feet sticking to the steep cliff face as she strode toward them on stilt-like legs of black. Her hairy spider body bristled, and her sleek projecting torso undulated as she withdrew a second spear from a sheath she wore on her back.

Unexpectedly she stopped just out of striking range, her cruel eyes studying them with disdain. Garvey found his sword blade on the ledge and snatched it up, waving it in Shavrena's direction.

"Well, what are you waiting for you hideous mound of flesh? I killed your mate and I'll kill you, too!"

Ntashia frantically searched the ledge for suitable rocks to fit her sling, but was having difficulty finding anything the right size. Shavrena looked on calmly…as though she were waiting for something.

Garvey let a curse slip from between his lips. Shavrena wasn't the last of the Sinthrals he realized. There had been six; of those six they had been fortunate enough to kill three. Shavrena was sitting in front of them serving as a distraction. The other two were nowhere to be seen.

The astronaut hazarded a glance down below the ledge and found the two missing Sinthrals creeping silently up the cliff side, their sleek gray torsos a sharp contrast to the hairy bulks, which bore them. Their great black pincers snapped eagerly as they realized that Garvey had divined their position, and they surged forward. One of them launched a spear, but it struck against the lip of the ledge and wobbled away into the depths of the Rift.

Garvey determined to sell his life dearly. He held little hope of being able to best three Sinthral as they attacked from above and below.

Turning his head to look above he saw Shavrena edging closer.

"Garvey!" cried Ntashia.

He looked and saw Ntashia pressing her slim form into a crevice in the cliff.

"There's a cave back here!" she shouted. Suddenly she disappeared into the darkness of the crack, her purple-tinted braids the last thing that he saw of her.

Garvey abandoned his idea of fighting to the death and leaped toward the crack, reaching it in one bound. Shavrena let out a piercing cry of rage as she realized that her prey was escaping her. She leaped down from her perch, the ledge trembling as her incredible bulk alit. Fine stress lines appeared beneath Garvey's feet where the ledge met the face of the cliff. They grew by the second, widening into a crack.

Shavrena hurled her spear, but her balance was precarious, and instead of taking Garvey in the skull it imbedded itself in the rock near his head. Even with her last spear gone and her pincers severed, Shavrena was not helpless. Garvey realized that she could easily reach out with any one of her six legs, pick him up, and hurl him over the cliff.

He squeezed himself into the narrow gap into which Ntashia had disappeared, but found that his human frame was not so ably suited for fitting through such a small space. He exhaled, pushing the air out of his lungs in the hopes of narrowing his broad chest just enough to slip through.

Shavrena probed into the crevice with one of her legs and caught hold of Garvey's waist, a sticky secretion from the chitin at the needled base holding fast to him. The astronaut, wedged halfway into the crack, was caught tightly.

He lashed out with his sword arm, but because of his awkward position it took him three strikes to chop through the thick chitin and hack way the leg.

Again Shavrena screamed, but they were screams of rage more than they were of pain. Garvey shoved himself into the crevice, his legs driving him on, skin scraping and giving way as he tumbled through, Shavrena's hacked member still hanging from his waist. In her unthinking anger Shavrena thrust several of her appendages through the narrow, sun-lit gap, desperately trying to grab the escaping human.

Now Garvey had more room to work with, and he ably smote off at least two of the arms. Shavrena withdrew now, but he could hear her on the ledge outside cursing and frothing. The air inside the hidden cavern held a damp-scent, but Garvey's sun–accustomed eyes beheld only blurry darkness. He turned his eyes away from the light that filtered through the gap, and let his vision become adjusted to the darkness.

"Are you alright?" he heard Ntashia asked.

"Except for this spider leg hanging from my waist," said Garvey. "My eyes are still adjusting to the light."

With an admirable lack of squeamishness Ntashia took hold of the severed appendage and pulled, but succeeded only in stretching out Garvey's Jockeys. "It's attached to your loin cloth," she said. "I've still got some leather left, I can cut you a new one that you can support with your belt."

To Garvey this seemed a much better option than hauling around Shavrena's leg with him wherever he went. "That will be fine. We may have to wait awhile before our Sinthral friends get tired of waiting and leave us alone."

Standing at a safe distance, they glanced through the crevice and saw two Sinthral crawling up from below and onto the ledge to join Shavrena—who bombarded the Muvari warrior and her Earthly companion with an unceasing stream of invectives. As the three Sinthral settled onto the ledge, Garvey and Ntashia felt the rock shift beneath them, and the earth creaked as the ledge outside their narrow doorway cracked and gave way, sending the three Sinthral tumbling from their perch with screams of horror.

Garvey's mouth opened in disbelief at their good fortune. "Thank God for miracles. The only downside is that we may be trapped here, now."

Ntashia took his arm and turned him around, pointing to a rough-hewn passage that spiraled upward. "This cave may initially have been formed by the winds or waters, but it has been expanded by human hands. We want to travel upward, and it looks like the cave is going in our direction."

"It's certainly better than our other option," said Garvey who didn't relish the prospect of trying to scale the cliff side with bare hands. He was anxious to avoid the fate of the three Sinthral who had just fallen victim to their combined weights.

Leaving behind Shavrena's sticky appendage, and loins girded with newly fashioned leather, Garvey led the way into the dusky corridor, his moccasin-clad feet carrying him over the uneven floor. They ascended into utter blackness, and Garvey reached back and found the warmth of Ntashia's firm hand—not delicate and soft like many of the earth woman that Garvey had known, but still slender and feminine, though possessing a strength not common to the more soft and civilized females a world away—and even some of the males.

Finally Garvey had to halt, the soupy darkness assailing his senses. They had nothing to burn to create light, but the astronaut's hand brushed the Clip Pad at his sword belt. He pressed a button on the pad, and its face glowed luminously, faintly illuminating the cramped intersection in which they had halted.

They both had to bend so as not to strike their heads on the rough stone ceiling. Tunnels yawned darkly to the left and to the right.

"Which way do we go?" asked Garvey.

"We go up," said Ntashia with a faint smile. "Always up."

From their position in the intersection Garvey couldn't tell in which direction the tunnels proceeded so he wandered a little way into the right tunnel and saw that it leveled out and gradually began to descend. He crawled back to Ntashia. "Let's try the left corridor."

By the luminous face of the Clip Pad they made slow progress up the left corridor, which continued to rise steadily beneath their tentative footfalls. They continued on interminably, alternately crawling and walking through the tight confines of the passages that wormed their way through the guts of the cliff.

Eventually they both grew tired and they sat down to rest in a small grotto. These caverns possessed none of the luminous lichens or mosses that had illuminated the cave of the Sinthrals, and so they sat in absolute darkness except for when Garvey used the Clip Pad to shed light on Ntashia's beautiful features, but he was worried that the solar batteries, deprived of any exposure whatsoever to sunlight, would wear quickly, and thought that perhaps he should conserve power.

Ntashia scooted close to him, and Garvey could feel the warmth of her body against his side. Her clear voice reverberated in the enclosed chamber. "I'm beginning to wonder if we shouldn't have taken our chances and tried to climb the cliff back to the trail."

"Me, too," said Garvey. "For all we know this cave ends somewhere a hundred miles into the planet's core."

"But we are traveling upward. It would seem that we eventually should reach the surface."

"Soon, I hope," replied Garvey. "There's no tubers in here, and I'm getting a bit hungry."

"And thirsty," added Ntashia.

Garvey checked the clock function on his Clip Pad, and saw that they had been negotiating the twisting tunnel for nearly seven hours since their battle with Shavrena and her spiderous allies. In the green glow of the Clip Pad he couldn't help but notice how full and inviting were Ntashia's lips; her flaxen braids brushed against his bare shoulder.

"What are you checking?" she asked, looking more closely at the face of the pad.

Garvey fought back the urge to press his lips against hers, and pointed to the three flashing numbers. This keeps track of how much time has elapsed. I've changed the settings so that it matches the twenty-six hour days of Mars.

"How many hours are there in an Earth day, American?" asked the Muvari warrioress.

"Twenty four. The planet Earth revolves just a little faster than yours."

"Mars is your planet now," she said. "From what you've explained to me, you are not only marooned here, but you are displaced out of your time. Does your clock account for that?"

Garvey shook his head and smiled. "I think not. Nothing accounts for that." He paused as he thought over the words that his beautiful companion-in-arms had spoken. "You're right, though. I'm never getting back to Earth, and even if I could I probably wouldn't even recognize it. Mars is my home now."

"Is that such a bad thing?" prodded Ntashia.

Garvey shook his head. "Even if I could leave, there's more keeping me here than ever kept me on Earth."

They slept in the pitch-blackness, Ntashia's head upon Garvey's shoulder as they leaned up against the rocky wall. When a noise awoke him with a start, Garvey wasn't sure how long he had slept or what had woken him from his restless slumber. His eyes could not pierce the veil of darkness so he let his hearing reach out into the inky voids as Ntashia still slept, her body resting against his.

There in the bowels of the earth he listened, only the rhythmic sound of Ntashia's breathing coming to his ears. Perhaps the noise that had awoken him had been imagined, the conjuration of his sleeping mind. He about convinced himself that this was the case when he heard the sound again—and he knew that it could not be his imagination. It came reverberating through the earth, a deep cough followed by a muted rumbling that continued for at least three minutes before dying. To Garvey the noise sounded mechanical in origin, akin to a backup generator kicking on. But what could it possibly be?

For fifteen minutes Garvey waited in silence, hoping that the sound would reappear. He became painfully aware of his empty stomach and parched throat. His body was battered and bruised, and needed food and liquid to supply fuel for its recovery. Then the noise came rumbling through the caverns once again, and he gently shook Ntashia's shoulder.

"What is it?" she asked clearing away the braids that fell over her eyes.

"Listen," whispered Garvey.

Ntashia quieted and they heard the continued rumbling. The Muvari warrioress leaped to her feet, and reached out to grab hold of Garvey's hand. "Come," she said. "We must see if we can locate the source of the noise."

Garvey switched on his Clip Pad and the luminescent glow bathed the small chamber in a pale green light. "What is it?"

"It may be one of the Warlord Shaxia technology troves, or even one of the ancient's cities."

"The ancients lived beneath the ground?"

"They lived everywhere; beneath the earth, in the skies, and even under the seas. They feared nothing."

Ntashia took the Clip Pad from Garvey and held it aloft as she began to lead the way down a narrow passage. "They grew too confident and forgot that God had given them all they had. They became wicked—worshipping idols and bowing down to beasts. They became consumed in pleasure and forgot their responsibilities."

"They were destroyed?" asked Garvey, relying on familiar biblical pattern to guess what happened.

"At God's command, the very elements which they had harnessed reached up and destroyed them. Millions died; the ancients were wiped from the face of Mars. Only a few scattered peoples survived."

"But some of their cities remain undestroyed and undiscovered?"

"Most were destroyed," said Ntashia as they wound through the arteries of the mountain. "The Warlord Shaxia has made it her mission to recover as much of the ancients' technology as she can—her torracks salvaging what they can from the ruined cities and hiding up what they find in secret technology troves. It is by relying on the technology of the Ancients' that she has risen to rule most of the planet. Most tribes give her obeisance, making yearly tributes for which she spares their lives."

"Does Ledgrim pay this extortion?" asked Garvey.

Ntashia's face-hardened. "We do, though secretly we are trying to uncover the hidden troves of Shaxia. Only by gathering the technologies of the ancients can we ever hope to cast aside her shackles and rule ourselves."

They came to a break in the passageway. The largest of the tunnels curled off to the left, but to the right, about chest height, lay a volcanic tube that was just large enough for Garvey to crawl into should he desire. First Ntashia stepped into the left passage and listened, then she moved to the right and put her ear to the opening of the tube.

She pointed down the dark and narrow shaft. "The sound is coming from down there."

"I was afraid of that," said Garvey, who wasn't anxious to enter a space even more confined than that of the Mars Climate Orbiter. Still, without further complaint he slipped into the tunnel, taking the lead on hands and knees. Ntashia handed the electronic pad forward and Garvey clipped it to his belt, the green glow allowing him to see about five feet ahead at any given time.

The two explorers struggled forward, and to Garvey's relief he found that the tunnel grew gradually larger until, eventually, they were actually able to stand. The rock within the tube was much smoother than that of the tunnels, which they had previously traveled—the surface being almost as slick as glass in some places.

The machine-like throb grew louder in their ears as they continued, and they were encouraged they were on the right track when the sound once again ceased—leaving them in the eerie silence.

"What now?" asked Garvey.

"Keep following the tunnel," answered Ntashia. "There have been no passages to the left or the right, so we go forward."

Suddenly Garvey extinguished the Clip Pad.

"Did the power run out?" asked Ntashia who now basically understood the concept of how the solar-powered pad worked.

"No," answered Garvey, his deep voice echoing down the tube. "Look ahead. We have light."

Ntashia cast her eyes forward and saw a faint glow of spectral light seeping through the pitch darkness. Without another word they crept on ahead, their eyes stinging as they came into the illumination that poured from between cracked portals. The tube had grown to over ten feet in diameter, and set directly across the passage was a round set of double doors, the circle of the portals bisected from ceiling to floor so that each door comprised a half moon shape.

They were constructed of a metal that Garvey had never seen before, heavy brass-colored rivets pocking the surface. Laying in the river of light that streamed from between the slightly parted doors were a jumble of maroon-clad bodies—skin waxen and yellow, shrunken to fleshless faces, and withered, bony limbs outstretched—jaws clenched or wide open in the once agony of their death throes.

For a moment they halted, taking in the weird spectacle that had opened up before them. "Are these the Ancients?" asked Garvey.

"Yes," answered Ntashia, but then she paused. "Or at least I think so. They are dressed unlike any I've ever seen. By the sparseness of their clothing

I can see that they certainly are not torracks."

Ntashia tentatively knelt alongside the first of the sprawled bodies, a woman with long golden hair on her withered head, her body naked but for the maroon skirt and halter. In her fleshless fingers she grasped a petite gun, which the Muvari warrioress pried carefully from her still-clutching fingers.

A needle protruded from the rounded tip of the pistol, the slim lines of the ancient gun still gleaming, and the indecipherable words scrolled on its surface faintly glowing. Holding it in her hand Ntashia regarded it with awe and wonderment. "This is a city of the ancients that Shaxia has not yet been discovered—else these weapons would already have been looted from the bodies of the dead."

"What does the gun do?"

Ntashia shook her head. "I know not."

"Perhaps you should see if it still works."

Lowering the gun and aiming it down the tube whence they had come, Ntashia pulled back the slender trigger. A crackling of light appeared along the needle, hissing and spitting, but it died as quickly as it had appeared. Ntashia tried pulling the trigger again, with similar results.

Garvey shrugged. "As well as it may have been built we can't expect all this stuff to work after hundreds of years."

"Perhaps not," agreed Ntashia, but she was clearly disappointed that her first find hadn't been in full functioning order.

Garvey stepped over the decaying bodies and through the doors. He had been awed to find even functioning illumination and bodies beneath the surface of the planet, but the sight that greeted his widening eyes was nearly beyond his Earthling comprehension. A massive shaft nearly a quarter mile wide sank deep into the bowels of the planet. Heaving and buckled walkways crisscrossed over the shaft to a central core that descended into unlit depths. Everywhere he looked shriveled bodies were scattered, apparently struck dead in mid-flight. There were no marks of violence upon the bodies, yet they had died suddenly as though from fatal heart attacks—each and every one of them.

Upon closer examination Garvey saw that each of these maroon–clad figures were imbedded with a metallic chip on the back of their left hand, it mattered not of what rank or status the individual had belonged.

Whether the body dripped with necklaces of precious jewels and gold chains, or whether the raiment was coarse and the adornment poor, all possessed the chip, and one had died as abruptly as the other.

Ntashia came through the door bearing a couple of other weapons, which she had retrieved from the bodies of the ancients. Her purple eyes sparkled with excitement as she surveyed the tangle of broken bridges and the central column of glittering metal and crystal windows. "If we can just return to Ledgrim and tell the tribe about this city we may be able to recover enough technology to overthrow Shaxia."

Ntashia's excitement was infectious and Garvey found himself grinning widely. Ever since he was a young child the urge to explore had been strong—and when the back yard was fully explored, he climbed through a loose fence board and discovered the empty lot behind their house. When the old tires and discarded couches no longer held their same excitement, he penetrated further—into the forest that bordered their housing development. It was only a matter of course that he became an astronaut—what was more natural for him than a desire to explore the endless reaches of space?

And here, bound to a planet not of his birth, and thrust back into time he was discovering civilizations that he never suspected of existing. What could be more exciting than delving into the silent halls, and crossing the crumbling bridges of a forgotten time and an unknown culture?

"Did you find any weapons that work?" asked Garvey.

"I don't know yet," she said. She raised a pistol with a massive cylinder and pulled the trigger. A tremendous sound that reminded Garvey of a fighter jet breaking the sound barrier echoed through the city, and a distant bridge exploded into fiery metal fragments and spouting flame.

Ntashia set down the gun and shook her stinging fingers. "The thing tried to jump from my hand."

Garvey picked up the gun and examined it, noticing that it was constructed on the same principles of a revolver, except this gun possessed only four revolving chambers, each containing a shell the size of a child's fist. Only three remained now. "This will only work three more times."

"Why only three?" asked Ntashia.

Garvey briefly explained the concept of loading the gun to her, but glancing at some of the other weapons she bore he quickly realized that his limited knowledge wasn't going to stretch to those other firearms. They tested the other three weapons, but either due to their lack of understanding or the age of the guns none of them appeared to function.

The astronaut gave Ntashia back the one functioning pistol that she had found. "Let's see what else we can find in here."

Ntashia agreed and carefully they crept out onto the span of the nearest bridge, stepping over desiccated bodies.

"What possibly could have killed all these people?" asked Ntashia. "Not a one of them shows a visible wound."

"In my world we have weapons that can do such things," said Garvey. "They are radiation bombs that can kill everyone in a city, but leave the buildings standing and unharmed."

Ntashia's violet eyes widened. "Do you think that we are in any danger?"

"If it were a radiation bomb that did this, then possibly low levels of radiation still might exist here. But I really don't know for sure what caused these deaths."

"We must explore further," insisted Ntashia, "no matter the cost. Our discoveries could mean salvation for the Muvari."

Garvey nodded. If they were being exposed to radiation it was probably too late now. They would take their chances and explore the city further, and hope for the best.

The bridge shifted as they crossed, but they managed to make it safely into the overshadowing eaves of a wide terrace that jutted from the central column of the city. From here they could see the web of bridges that extended from the core and into the mountain bedrock where the shaft was suspended. The sheer immensity of the city was mind boggling to Garvey, and especially to Ntashia who hadn't ever witnessed any man-made structure on so grand a scale.

From the corpse-littered terrace they broached the broad metallic outer doors, their footsteps clanging hollowly as they entered chambers that had lain undisturbed for nigh on a century. The hallways were high and still brightly lit by overhead globes that cast long shadows behind them.

They wandered into rooms that glinted with inlaid gems, the long and narrow couches draped with decaying velvets that crumbled at their touch, down cushions that turned to dust at the slightest movement. Strange designs and lewd images scrolled across the walls in an unceasing montage of perversions. On a marble dais a golden beast, the likes of which Garvey had never seen, stood poised and ready to leap.

The creature reminded Garvey of depictions he had seen of a saber-tooth cat, but this cat's head held four eyes—two in the front and two on the sides for better peripheral vision. The beast possessed four legs but extending from each ridged shoulder behind its low-slung neck were a pair of suckered tentacles, which writhed out from the creature as if ready to snatch up its prey.

"What is that?" asked Garvey.

Ntashia mounted the dais and ran her finger along the golden back of the carven beast, drawing a line in the thick dust that had settled there.

"It is called a vackri. I've seen a dead one killed by hunters in our tribe. The vackri are extremely dangerous, and the Muvari hunt them only in large numbers. The one that I saw killed three of our hunters before he died."

"Hardly worth it then, was it?" Garvey muttered to himself, but Ntashia overheard his comment.

"The vackri possess an adrenal gland, which if processed correctly is said to grant eternal youth to those who consume it."

"And does it really work?"

The four Muvari hunters killed the vackri I saw some sixty years ago, and one still lives with our tribe. She appears to be no older than I."

"What happened to the other three?" asked Garvey skeptically.

"They were killed in battle. Eternal youth does not grant invulnerability."

"So what is with the vackri statue? Did the ancients worship those things?"

"That is what the legends say."

Garvey went to the wall and studied the gems that encrusted a glittering band around the chamber. "On my world these things would be worth a fortune. These were one of the reasons that my people sent me here—looking for precious minerals and stones."

Ntashia shrugged. "They are often used as decorations here, but are as common as rocks. The Valley Idor is littered with them. They lay loose on the ground reflecting the sunlight so brightly that to travel there with unprotected eyes is to risk blindness."

Garvey dropped his hand and decided to leave the diamonds imbedded in the wall. They were of little intrinsic value to him, and only worth collecting if others thought them of some value.

Ntashia stepped over a crimson-robed priest that lay sprawled across the dais steps, his hands outstretched to the golden idol of the vackri. She stooped and withdrew a split-bladed knife from his sash. Its pommel was graven with the four-eyed head of the vackri, but the blade was uncankered by the passing of time. She shoved the knife into her belt.

"I just wish that we could find some food and water," she said. "I'm beginning to feel faint."

"Me too," agreed Garvey, who had been feeling listless from lack of energy for some time. "I'm not going to last much longer if I don't get some nourishment."

They left the chamber of worship and continued down the gem–studded hallways, following the sparkling bands until they heard a rush of water. They moved excitedly past many open doorways, and past many dead until they emerged in an octagonal chamber at the center of the core.

Overhead, artificial sun glistened through a dome of glass, spreading its effulgent light on a great fountain of water that gushed sparkling into the air, to fall in churning white waves that collected in a pool enclosed by a great golden chalice.

Lips dried and cracked, the two wanderers fell upon their knees and recklessly began scooping the waters up to their mouths and sucking in draughts of the fresh, life-giving liquid. They drank to their fill, and washed away the dust of their travels, finally sinking down alongside the fountain to rest.

Unlike the other rooms, which they had passed through, this one was devoid of corpses. The walls were free of the lewd images, which had flickered through the temple room they had visited. Despite the illusion of sunlight from above, Garvey still couldn't help but feeling claustrophobic—even more so than when he and Ntashia were spelunking through the tunnels. Perhaps it was just his uneasiness, or a sense of foreboding, but he didn't feel comfortable here.

"Can you sense it?" asked Ntashia.

"Sense what?"

"The evil. This city is impregnated with it."

"I feel it," said Garvey. "But we haven't yet even scratched the surface of this city. There is a lot more to explore."

Ntashia nodded. "We need food, though. We can survive on water alone for a couple of days. Perhaps we should head back through the tunnels and try to climb the cliff."

"It might be the surest thing to do," agreed Garvey. "There may be some other way out of here, but we can't know for certain. Maybe we can look around and see if we can find something to help us climb the cliff."

"Like a rope and some spikes," interjected the Muvari.

"Exactly. Then we can fill our bellies with water again and make the trek back. We should have enough strength to backtrack all the way. Once we make the Rift we can look for more of those tubers." In truth, Garvey would have liked to have filled his belly with a nice solid steak—but he realized he didn't have that option. Right now he longed for even a fistful of those radishy tubers.

They rested for a few minutes more and then they rose. Eight archways led from the fountain chamber and Garvey pried loose a diamond about the size of a peach pit from the wall and with the point of the gem scratched an X over the portal through which they had entered the room.

They randomly picked one of the remaining seven and before entering marked a number one over the arch, so that if for some reason their trail led back to the fountain through another portal they might be able find their way back to the Rift.

They passed through an unceasing maze of chambers and halls, all magnificently decorated with a band of diamonds around the walls—and some varied with amethysts and rubies, all of which Ntashia assured him were common stones on Mars. Though much decayed, the opulence in which the ancients had lived was apparent. Their fixtures were ornamented with gold and silver, and everywhere Garvey looked gem stones sparkled riotously.

Their search took them deep into the core of the Ancients' city, and finally they emerged from dusty hallways into an amphitheater with seven rows of benches on one side and six on the other. Their leather shod feet cast up plumes of powder as they descended marble steps toward the dais that stood at the front of the room. The walls were swathed in red velvet curtains with golden cords falling from pulleys.

"I see our rope," exclaimed Garvey. He peeled off to the right and strode across the stone benches, stuffed cushions crumbling beneath his feet. Fortunately the cords had fared better, and despite being stiffened from the years the material from which they were made had survived the ravages of time with little detriment. The cord was looped and Garvey cut it, and began reeling it over the pulley so that it coiled at his feet.

Ntashia continued down the steps, and climbed the dais until she stood in front of a pedestal crafted from silver and gold, and encrusted with more diamonds—the largest of which she had yet seen in the city. Set into the top of the pedestal was a clear crystal lens. Incomprehensible runes circled the lens, as did some sort of dial with an ornate pointer.

She reached down and drew her finger across the crystal, drawing a line in the fine debris that had gathered there over the centuries. Suddenly a light flickered on inside the pedestal, and it shone from the crystal lens as a beacon, illuminating the arched metal rafters of the amphitheater like a spotlight. A deep rumble emitted from beneath the stage, vibrating through her feet and tingling her legs. Strange patterns of neon lit the surface of the dais around her—circles with lines that connected and intersected.

The sudden rumbling from the stage caused Garvey to let the rope slip from his hands. It continued to unreel from above, its loose end finally falling free of the pulley as the astronaut turned his attention to the dais where Ntashia stood. Her exquisite form stood radiant in the illumination that burst forth from the pedestal, and strange energies played across the floor around her, crackling and spitting as they ran along geometrically-shaped circuits.

"What happened?" cried Garvey as he coiled his legs beneath him to leap the intervening benches, but his voice could scarcely be heard above the growing hum that ebbed and flowed with the swirl of light that coruscated from the pedestal.

Then Garvey saw strange images projected from within the beacon; horrific beasts that lunged and snapped, bold Muvari warriors, Lana and the Council of Elders. All these slipped by, fleeting like distant memories summoned forth, and fading before they could be fully realized.

Both Garvey and Ntashia stood transfixed by this spectacle. Ntashia's very memories were being called up and visualized in this three dimensional montage. Jealousy lanced through his heart as he saw an image of Ntashia, her locks entangled in another man's hand, droplets of their sweat mingling as they coupled in fevered passion. Suddenly their reverie was interrupted by a booming voice, so loud that it drowned out even the hum that permeated the room.

"Who dares intrude on my sanctum?"

Garvey and Ntashia turned their heads to see a man floating into the room on a metallic disc that hovered six-inches above the dusty floor. His flowing white hair fell to his waist in great waves. With narrow waist and shoulders and standing nearly seven feet tall, he cut a strange but imposing figure. He wore nothing but a red sash about his loins, and his green-tinted skin was paper-thin so that every fiber of his lean musculature stood out. He wore incongruously large bracers on each thin wrist, and his over-sized opaline eyes gazed at them hypnotically.

The strange newcomer lifted his right fist and pointed it directly at Garvey. "Speak, or I will turn you to the dust from which you were made!"

Chapter Thirteen:
The Ghost of Caladrex

January 17, 2002– The Surface of Mars

The Mars Vindicator lowered itself through Mars' hazy atmosphere, the bright flare of its landing rockets coruscating against the sand that swirled in the heavy winds. The lander swayed to the left and the right, carried by the vagaries of the gusting air—so that it looked like a pendulum on a grandfather clock.

Bradley Thomas worked feverishly in the cockpit, an unlit cigar clamped between his teeth, watching the wind gauges and compensating as best as he could. They had known that the weather conditions on Mars weren't optimal, but balked at delaying their landing on Mars for yet another orbit around the planet.

A downdraft pushed the Vindicator too quickly toward the rocky surface of Mars, the altimeter showing a 510-foot altitude loss in the matter of seconds, and Bradley fired the rockets, slowing the descent once again. The flare of the rockets gleamed redly against the metal surface of the lander, and sand swirled in bilious clouds that blotted out sight of the planet below.

With no visual contact, Bradley worked strictly by instruments, flying blind, calling out orders to Melhoff and Giffen who were strapped into their seats behind and to the right of him. Bradley had landed on the surface of Mars a hundred times in the NASA flight simulator, but it was nothing like the real thing.

Brendan Melhoff's stubby fingers played with lightning quickness over the switches, his eyes fixed on the gauges. He spoke through his bristling beard. "Switching to auxiliary fuel tanks in five, four, three, two—now."

The Vindicator didn't even hiccup as the fuel lines switched, and Melhoff grinned savagely in Bradley's direction. "Don't screw this one up. If we crash land we're going to be dripping in complete hell."

Hank Giffen didn't even acknowledge the use of Melhoff's favorite saying, he had other worries, and suspected the sheer stress of the situation might cause what little hair he had left to fall out before they even hit the ground. The Vindicator began to wobble unevenly and Giffen checked the fuel flow, then the thrust output. "Rocket number four is at seventy percent. I suspect it's gummed up with sand."

"Got it," replied Bradley, who reduced the fuel output to the other three landing rockets to compensate. The Vindicator began a more rapid descent, but the quick adjustment saved the craft from going into an unrecoverable spin.

Bradley once again ramped up the fuel to the thrusters, the rattle of sand against the titanium hull of the lander sounded like a tin roof in a hailstorm. The wind pushed the Vindicator a hundred yards from their intended landing spot, and Bradley gave the thrusters one last shot, the flames rebounding from the sand-swirled surface of Mars, and bathing the titanium hull in a fiery aurora. The legs of the lander settled unevenly on the rocky surface beneath the shifting sands, and as soon as the three astronauts shut down the rocket systems they slumped in their seats, wiping the sweat from their brows, and wiping their hands on their jump suits.

Bradley let a soft chuckle slip from between his lips. "I haven't seen action like that since I was dodging flack over Baghdad."

"You flew in Desert Storm?" asked Giffen.

"Garvey Dire and I both did."

"You think we'll find Garvey?" asked Melhoff as he slowly straightened himself in his chair.

Bradley sighed. "I know the chances are less than slim, but I can't help but feel that he's still alive against all the odds."

Giffen shook his head, knowing that the odds were astronomically against the survival of Dire. He didn't expect to find Arnold Stechter alive either.

"I hope you're right," said Melhoff, "and I hope that we can find him."

Giffen consulted a gauge. "We're not going anywhere for a little while. The winds are gusting up to sixty miles an hour now. We never should have attempted landing. We're lucky to be alive."

"Luck had nothing to do with it," said Bradley as he removed the unlit cigar from between his lips and saw that the stem was bitten through. "I said at least five prayers on the way down."

Melhoff chuckled. "I said at least a dozen, so between the two of us…"

Giffen raised an eyebrow. His precise and ordered mind had difficulty accepting anything that he couldn't see and touch, and the idea of a greater power still took more faith than he could muster. "We beat the odds," he said. "God didn't have anything to do with it."

Melhoff and Bradley smiled at his skepticism.

"I used to be a whole hearted atheist," said Bradley, "then one night over Baghdad my entire perception shifted, and I cleaned up my godless ways."

Giffen shrugged. "Everybody has got to believe in something."

"And what do you believe in, Hank?" asked Melhoff.

"I believe in Science."

"Well, say a prayer to Science," said Bradley, "because if this wind doesn't let up we're going to be buried alive in a sand drift the size of Texas."

Three hours later the wind let up, and as dusky twilight fell upon the red planet three astronauts emerged from the half-buried Vindicator and slipped down the sand dunes to stand on rocky earth, sand eddying around their feet—still shifted by the cold breezes of the alien planet.

Like ghosts they moved through the howling winds, mere shadows among the gritty gusts that swept the surface of Mars. Bradley Thomas took the lead, carefully consulting his Clip Pad as it estimated the distance between their landing craft and the base camp that Stechter had established.

Their muscles, even weakened by their long weightless journey, carried them in long springing strides, but the wind picked them up and carried them sideways so they shortened their strides to baby steps as they traveled through the gusts of vision-obscuring sand.

Without discernable hesitation Bradley led them through the shifting haze, and finally a skeletal tower and sand-scratched dome emerged from the hazy murk of the dirty air. Even though the three astronauts knew what they were looking for, each paused, taken aback by the sight. It was as though they had discovered a vestige of some ancient civilization.

However, as quickly as their hopes rose that they might find Arnold Stechter alive and well, they were dashed. The first sign that things were dreadfully wrong was the melted and charred aluminum of the transmission tower. It stood at only half of its original thirty-foot height, the framework scorched and peeled back as though it were a banana peel.

Scattered on the earth, the glittering shrapnel of what had once been the receiver dish reflected the suffused sunlight. The dome had fared only slightly better. Many of its concave panels were missing entirely and some of the framework gone, but as Bradley stepped forward and ran his hand along the dome's remaining framework he could immediately see that this had been dismantled differently than the tower. The dome had been taken apart piece by piece for salvage, and not by some sudden, violent act.

"What in the flaming hell happened here?" asked Melhoff.

Giffen picked up a fist-sized shard of metal. "It would have taken some sort of explosive charge to do this to the tower, but I'm not sure what."

"Then let me clue you in," said Bradley. "The Chinese did it, and then they took apart Stechter's dome for salvage—piece by piece."

"Why didn't they salvage the tower?" asked Giffen.

"Think about it tactically," answered Bradley. "They didn't want NASA to know what was going on up here. The first thing they did was blow up the transmission tower and cut communications. After that they were free to do whatever they wanted."

Out of old habit Bradley pulled his Swiss SG551 assault rifle from his shoulder and brought it to the ready. It was a compact weapon equipped with scope and a unique triple magazine feed system beneath its ridged belly. He stepped over a portion of aluminum framework and into the interior of the dome.

Nothing was left. Every bit of equipment and food was gone, all that remained behind was the floor itself, sand collecting in the corners and rattling beneath his feet. There was no sign of Arnold Stechter. Except for the remains of the base camp it was as though he had never existed.

Melhoff joined Bradley inside the desolate remains of Stechter's former haven. "What now?"

"We set up camp and perimeter defenses, because if the Chinese did this to Stechter they aren't going to have any compunction about doing it to us."

Mars, 47,000 B.C.– The Lost City of Caladrex

For a moment Garvey stood transfixed by the site of the barely–garbed newcomer, white hair billowing behind him in some unfelt wind, and lean muscles rippling beneath his pale green skin. Dust still hung heavy in the air, thrown up by the rope that Garvey had pulled down only moments before.

Ashamed by the revelation that had flickered across the column of light, and then startled by the appearance of this strange man, Ntashia involuntarily staggered back two steps, the column of writhing light and images fading from being.

The seven-foot tall Martian shifted his fist and bright light lanced out from the thick bracer that he wore on his wrist. It struck the stage near Ntashia, the searing squelch of its impact echoing through the theater. The stage turned black where the beam struck, and scentless smoke curled lazily upward into Ntashia's nostrils.

"Did I not tell you to stand still?" bellowed the newcomer, anger suffusing his expression. "I have no tolerance for insubordination!"

"What is it, then, that you want from us?" asked Garvey, hoping to turn the Martian's attention away from Ntashia.

"I want to know why you have dared to enter the sacred City of Caladrex—realm of the immortals, worshippers of the Great and Omnipotent Vackri?"

"We did not know to whom the city belonged," answered the astronaut. "We were trapped in caverns beneath the earth and we came looking for water and tools."

"So, you expect to fool the ancient and wise Sved into thinking that you are not spies here to loot Caladrex of its treasures and secrets?"

"We did not even know that Caladrex existed," said Ntashia, encouraged by the fact that this guard over the city had not yet disintegrated her.

"And who is this wise Sved?" asked Garvey.

"Why, you fool, do you not know to whom you speak? I am the wise Sved, the guardian and watcher of Caladrex and its peoples—immortalized by the power of the Omnipotent Vackri."

"I apologize, Sved," replied Garvey. "I am ignorant of many things of this world. I hope that you will likewise forgive my ignorance when I ask what has happened to the immortal peoples of Caladrex."

"Sadly, they are all gone now," admitted Sved. "I am the last of a great culture. The others fell to the cowardly attacks of their enemies. Many of Caladrex's people had lived for hundreds of years by the grace of the great Vackri, but now they are gone."

Sved's face took on an expression of great remorse as he spoke, but apparently he realized that he was being sidetracked from his initial purpose of interrogating the two trespassers. His face flickered abruptly, his opaline eyes turning angry. "But the question is not where are the immortal people of Caladrex, but who are you infidel interlopers? Answer my question or I shall string your bowels from the great tree!"

Garvey sensed something odd about Sved. His body seemed to shimmer and shift as if it were being projected from a scratched celluloid print. He ignored Sved's demands. "How is it that all of your people are dead, and that you have survived for hundreds of years?"

"Simpleton! I have partaken of the sacred phylactery of Vackri. I am immortal!"

"So I understand were the people of Caladrex. Why is it that you lived and they did not?"

"I was able to lock myself in a vault before the Silent Death fell upon the city. I had warning that it was coming, but just long enough to save myself. My concubines were not so fortunate."

Garvey gesticulated wildly as he spoke, hoping that Ntashia would take advantage of his misdirection. "Just how old are you?"

"I am four hundred and twenty-three years old since my inception."

"Your inception or your conception?" asked Garvey.

"You blithering fool! What difference does it mean to you?"

"I'm simply trying to ascertain if you are a man… or if you are something else."

Ntashia slipped the ancient weapon from her belt as Garvey spoke, brought it around and pulled back the trigger. The massive barrel jumped, and the boom rang hollowly in the theater, the shell flying so that it pierced Sved's chest…and traveled through his insubstantial body, striking the wall of the hallway beyond.

The floor shook as chunks of metal exploded outward in a great roiling ball, shrapnel cutting, and spinning from the stone benches, and one shattering the mind-displaying column that stood in front of Ntashia. As it slid into two pieces, and crumbled on the stage, smoke still pouring from the barrel of her pistol, Ntashia looked in astonishment through the flame-rimmed doorway and found that Sved stood unharmed, as though nothing had occurred.

"There is nothing that you can do to harm me," he said.

"That's because you're an illusion," shouted Garvey, "nothing more than a three-dimensional hologram."

"Do not underestimate me because of my lack of physical substance. I have the power to burn you to the ground with a mere thought."

Garvey strode toward Sved who stood his ground amid the flaming wreckage of the exploded wall behind him. His white mane billowed outward as though a sea-breeze were rolling off the ocean.

"You can't hurt us," said the astronaut. "You have no physical substance, therefore you can do us no physical harm."

"That is not quite correct," answered Sved, his lips turning sardonically. "Do you not recall the power of the laser gauntlet that I wield?"

"Illusion," stated Garvey. "Just like you."

Ntashia put her foot down on the scorched area of stage that had been struck by Sved's laser. She frowned when she saw that it was now her foot that was scorched, and not just the stage. Pulling her foot away, she found that it was as intact as ever—unburned and whole. It was some sort of illusion.

"You have the whole theater wired with holographic projectors," said Garvey. "You can make it look like anything that you want. You could make a dozen of me appear and kill every one of them, but you can't kill the real me. You can't kill the real thing because you're nothing but a figment of someone's twisted imagination."

Rage twisted Sved's hollow face and he lowered his fist so that it pointed directly at Garvey. For a moment the astronaut wondered if he had been wrong. Then Sved's face softened, and he lowered his fist sadly. "I'm nothing but a ghost haunting the former glories of a once great city. I keep company with nothing but the rats. Even the vackri have long since left, having gorged themselves on the meat of the fallen until it became withered and tainted."

Ntashia left the crumbled column on the stage behind her as she walked up the aisle to Garvey and the thing that appeared to be man, but was nothing more than a projection. "Vackri, you say that there were vackri in the city?"

"Of course," said Sved with uncharacteristic meekness, "it was the vackri that gave the inhabitants of Caladrex their perpetual youth. Me, I'm just a computer construct, as you have discovered. I will never age. Until the day my operating program fails I will be as young as I am now."

"Weren't the vackri dangerous?"

"Of course, they were," answered the holographic image. "But they were caged and given human sacrifices regularly—mostly slaves, captured enemies, or those of a lower class, but occasionally a nobleman or woman would offend the Shad, or a lover would displease him and he would order him or her fed to the vackri."

Garvey frowned.

"Ah, those were the days," added Sved wistfully. "Well, spies or not—here you are. I must admit that it is nice to have some company after hundreds of years of tracking dust particles for my own amusement."

"Maybe you can be of some help," suggested Ntashia, suspicion of this strange being still tinting her voice. "We are looking for some climbing spikes, and a hammer so that we can climb the cliffs out of here—and if there are any functional weapons…"

"Say no more," answered the holograph. "I know of a stockpile of goods and weapons, which may as well serve the two of you. The residents of Caladrex certainly aren't using them."

Garvey raised an eyebrow and glanced at Ntashia who couldn't conceal the gleam in her eye. To discover a stockpile of the Ancients' technology would certainly be a boon to the Muvari.

"Then perhaps you'd be willing to give us directions?" suggested Garvey.

"I can do better than that," replied Sved raising his chin haughtily. "I can lead the way."

"So you are not confined to just this room?" asked Garvey, his basic scientific knowledge leading him to believe that three dimensional projectors would have to be active all around the city for Sved to lead them elsewhere.

"Not at all. I can function anywhere in Caladrex—except for certain areas that have suffered power loss."

"The ancients were truly an impressive people," said Ntashia. She had no concept of how Sved had appeared to them, but grasped the idea that he was nothing more than a ghost of a people long since passed.

The image of Sved flickered as he crossed into the hall through the still smoldering wreckage that Ntashia's purloined weapon had created. Then his image solidified once more. The floating disc upon which he had stood at their initial encounter was now gone and he strode ahead of them, his incorporeal footsteps leaving no trace in the dust.

"There is really no need for you to acquire any equipment for climbing," he said, his voice hollow and distant in the halls. "You will want to better arm yourselves, of course, since you both are ill-equipped for travel, but there are better ways of reaching the surface."

"How so?" asked Ntashia.

"The people of Caladrex used pneumatic tubes to travel great distances in a very short time. We have such tubes still functioning, which lead to the surface of Mars." The apparition gestured down a dark, unlit hallway. "One such tube is down that hall. You must pass through a dead zone to reach it, so I am unable to lead you there myself."

"Are they difficult to operate?" prodded Garvey, hoping to get as much information as possible.

"Hardly," scoffed Sved. "Press a panel indicating your destination and the rest is automated."

"We cannot read your language, though. How will we know which panel to press?"

Sved waved this off as though it were inconsequential. "Don't worry about such trivialities until after you have better equipped yourselves. Am I not here to guide you?"

"So the pneumatic tube isn't in a dead zone?"

"Oh no, If worse comes to worse I can meet you there."

With the peach pit diamond, Ntashia continued to mark the corridors as Sved led them through a bewildering maze of passages, past grand tournament halls, and through narrow galleries littered with shriveled cadavers.

"There is no need for that," said the apparition. "With me here to lead you, you have no worries of getting lost."

Ntashia didn't like depending upon a ghost to guide them, and she continued to scratch marks, but changed the subject to something that had been bothering her since her encounter with it. "What was that column upon the stage?"

"That was a holy device the priests of Vackri used to illustrate their thoughts to the worshippers. If you are trained in its use you can manipulate the images that are shown. If you are not trained it reaches into your mind and grabs random thoughts and memories, displaying them for all to see."

Garvey had questions about some of the images that he had seen appear in that column of swirling light, but he held his tongue, thinking that they were better discussed during a time when Sved didn't accompany him and Ntashia. "Are not the vackri beasts? Yet you refer to them as a singular entity."

"The Great and Omnipotent Vackri inhabits the space beyond ours, and the vackri that roam Mars are manifestations of him."

The astronaut had no time to ask any further questions because Sved halted in front of a single door that reached five times their height, and nearly as wide. The portal was scrolled with intricate designs and the strange language of the people of Caladrex. A ring of colored gems-studded its surface at about head height. "This is the vault. I don't have a physical presence, so I cannot open it myself, but I do know the sequence."

Ntashia brushed back her braids, her violet eyes as deep as the cosmos. "The sequence?"

"Those gems on the surface of the door," the ghost said with forced patience. "Each color must be pressed in the proper sequence or traps will be triggered."

The Muvari warrioress stepped forward passing right through Sved's transparent image, and emerging to stand in front of the door. "I'm ready. What is the sequence?"

"Purple, red, blue, red, red, purple, yellow, yellow," recited Sved in a near monotone.

Ntashia followed his directions, rapidly following the sequence. The gems sunk beneath her touch, then rose again as quickly as she took her finger away. When she finished a deep grinding noise emanated from the walls and the formidable door began to slide back until it revealed a cavernous chamber stuffed to the brim with crates.

Garvey and Ntashia slowly entered, surveying the piles of goods that towered over their heads and toward the vented ceiling eighty feet over their heads. Each crate was marked with a number of symbols, which probably marked the contents, but were useless to either one of them. Short of breaking each crate open they couldn't know what lay within.

"Perhaps we should start with some improved weaponry," suggested Sved.

Garvey shrugged. "Why not?"

Sved's flickering image led the way deeper into the room until the gaping door of the vault was blocked from sight by mountains of crates. He stopped in front of one particular hillock, which mounted twice as tall as Garvey. We have a number of weapon choices." He shot them a look of disdain, as they stood bewildered, with little idea of where to start.

"Perhaps I should make some suggestions."

"Please do," replied Garvey.

Sved pointed to a crate. "A redlens rapid-fire narrow focus plasmatic rifle might serve you both well. They are of moderate weight, are accurate at both short and long ranges, and can be fired rapidly or in single shots."

The crates seemed to be made of a durable, but extremely lightweight material of a synthetic nature. The lids were sealed down tight and Garvey spent a few minutes trying to figure out how to open it up. He was about to pull his sword and start hacking the lid off when Sved impatiently interrupted his endeavor.

"Simply grasp the lid by both sides and depress this slight discoloration on either side." He demonstrated, his grainy figure leaning over and pushing his insubstantial fingers into dark gray semi-circles. "The lid will automatically open up for you. These crates are hermetically sealed and built from a polymer as tough as steel, the same polymer from which we built our armor. You'd do little more than break your sword if you tried to open a crate with it."

Garvey frowned and resheathed his blade. It wasn't so much Sved's constant lecturing that got on his nerves, but the tone of voice that he used—as though he were talking to a moron. He kept his temper in check by reminding himself that they were dealing with only a computer, any mannerisms or tonalities had been programmed in so that Sved would behave in such a manner.

Ntashia leaned over the crate as Sved had demonstrated and escaping air hissed from the crate as she removed the lid. Stacked inside were a half dozen rifles of gleaming blue. Ntashia carefully hoisted one, examining its sleek lines in awe. "I've never seen one like this before."

"Of course not!" snapped Sved. "These rifles represent the pinnacle of Martian weapon-making. Only the people of Caladrex ever achieved such a weapon. You can line up ten men and shoot the first. The one shot from this weapon will penetrate the bodies of all ten. One shot will penetrate three inches of uranium-depleted steel."

Having served in the Navy, Garvey was not unfamiliar with weapons of many sorts, but he studied this alien creation with concern. "How many shots do I get before ammunition runs out?"

"This is not a primitive projectile weapon. It is an energy weapon deriving its power from a cartridge of compressed energy. Each cartridge will fire about a thousand shots, then the cartridge must be replaced."

"Where are these replacement cartridges?"

Sved motioned toward a crate stacked higher in the hill of weapons. Garvey climbed upward and carefully descended the mound with his prize. He opened the crate and saw that it was packed with a hundred replacement cartridges. Each cartridge was quite heavy, so he took just three. Ntashia weighed the cartridge in her hand and decided to take just one replacement.

"Once we get back to Ledgrim we'll tell the others and come back for the rest of these weapons."

Sved flickered, his face impassive. "Further back, we also have blades of a much finer quality than the ones that you two bear. I'm surprised that you are able to even cut butter with those crude implements."

They followed the apparition deeper into the chamber and cracked open the crates that Sved indicated, finding gleaming swords and daggers untouched and uncankered by the ravages of time.

"Don't touch the edges," warned Sved. "You're liable to lose a finger."

Ntashia hefted a curved blade, which she had picked out. "Good balance." She aimed a blade at a crate lid and split it halfway through.

"I thought you said those crates were constructed of the same polymer as the armor you made," said Garvey pointedly. "That sword went through the lid like it was nothing!"

"Precisely!" answered Sved after a short pause. "These sword blades are made to defeat our finest armor. However, you must understand that the polymer undergoes a special strengthening process when it is used in armor—giving it ten times the strength as the crates. As the crates stand, they would likely defeat your primitive blade—but not a Caladrex-forged weapon."

Both Garvey and Ntashia, suitably impressed by these blades, cast aside their old weapons and girded up these new ones, but both still stood in very scanty attire—Garvey having discarded his tattered NASA suit, and Ntashia having cut large portions of her leather tunic and skirt to fashion moccasins and a sling.

"Now you both need some armor. Apparently you both are begging for death, going to battle in attire more befitting a debauchery."

"We had little choice in the matter," replied Garvey acidly.

"You do now. Follow me." Sved led them to the very back of the chamber and showed them stacks of reflective armor stacked on pallets. "These are good against short bursts from plasma weapons, deflecting sword cuts, and projectile weapons of lower calibers."

After picking through the armor for some time, Garvey and Ntashia donned the meshed gear, which covered their waists and torsos. They found it to be of an extremely lightweight, and even the mesh hose that fit their legs did not feel burdensome. Long gauntlets that fitted their arms still allowed for the skin to breathe, while adding protection to their limbs.

Finally they stood in their gleaming armor, equipped with blade and rifle.

Sved grinned. "You both look as though you could conquer the planet. It's almost too bad that you'll be dying shortly."

Ntashia turned her head sharply to send a dagger gaze at Sved. "What are you talking about, ghost?"

A mocking smile illuminated the apparition's face. "Don't you hear it?"

Garvey felt it now, rumbling through his feet, and vibrating through his body. "The door is closing!"

His earthly muscles galvanized, springing into action. He leaped wildly through the air, his muscular thews propelling him from the very back of the chamber and toward the door at the front. In moments he came into sight of the door. Already it had closed three-quarters of the way. Using all of the strength at his disposal he hurled himself toward the door, but reached it only as it slammed tightly shut—the displaced air whooshing in his face as he came up against the closed portal.

Sved appeared beside him. "That was a valiant effort. I underestimated your speed. It was a good thing that I lured you to the very back of the chamber before triggering the door closed."

"Why are you doing this?"

Sved shrugged, his mouth twisting in a lop-sided grin. "I suppose that it is in my nature. I do have standing orders to dispense with intruders by any means at my disposal."

Ntashia reached the astronaut and the betraying apparition. "What do you think you're doing, ghost?" she spat at Sved.

"Control your anger, woman," admonished Sved. "You've only got five, six minutes to live. You might as well enjoy it instead of wasting it on fruitless anger."

"You've trapped us here," said Garvey, "but you've hardly condemned us to a premature death. There is enough food stockpiled in here to keep us alive for a thousand lifetimes."

"Ah, that is true," admitted Sved. "But there will be only enough air to last for another five minutes." As he finished speaking great fans whirred to life in the ceiling far overhead. "Those will suck all the oxygen out of this room in a very short time."

"Why kill us?" raged Garvey. "You're defending nothing but a city of dead!"

"Yes, but it's my city." Sved began to fade from existence. "I'll leave you two alone to enjoy the last few minutes of your life with a little privacy. The next time I see you both you'll be a couple of corpses to add to my already vast collection."

The sound of Sved's laughter faded away as he disappeared into the nothingness from which he had sprung. The great fans whirled overhead, pulling at their hair as they sucked the very atmosphere away.

"That's the last time that I trust a ghost," said Ntashia.

Chapter Fourteen:
The Death Trap

March 7, 2007, Near the U.S. Mars Base

On his belly, Bradley Thomas wormed his way up to the top of the ridge, cutting a furrow through the sand, until he lay there between two speckled boulders. A dirt colored tarp lay draped across his back, serving as a camouflage should any of the Chinese astronauts casually observe the outcropping of stone at the edge of the valley where they had constructed their base.

The Chinese had picked wisely when they chose their building site. The natural depression in the Martian terrain sheltered their base from the howling winds that tore across the planet. Bradley was surprised at the size of the complex they had built. It consisted of a central dome of nearly twenty feet in height, and from this hub four spokes emerged that connected to an equal number of smaller domes.

Bradley recognized the material used in the construction of the second of the smaller domes—it had been cannibalized from the U.S. base, the one from which Arnold Stechter had disappeared. Various mounds of dirt around the complex suggested that excavation had been accomplished—probably some beneath-ground chambers had been additionally installed.

From these mounds a great skeletal tower emerged, thrusting against the red sky. Bradley thought he saw small figures clinging to the tower. He put his binoculars to his eyes and brought the figures into focus. Fully enclosed in an environment suit, a Chinese astronaut was ensconced about forty feet in the air, testing some electronic circuits in a box bolted to the frame. Bradley lowered his binoculars for a moment and retrieved his Clip Pad from his waist.

With the click of a few buttons he was cycling through the dossiers of the various Chinese astronauts. In a moment a sallow face, over-wide at the cheekbones and tapering to a cleft chin, flickered onto screen; the face of the astronaut checking the circuits—Anshi Ping.

The flash of an oxyacetylene torch came into the periphery of Thomas' vision and he glanced up to see the second astronaut twenty feet higher than Ping, apparently welding a beam into place. Bradley focused in on the face and once the glare of the torch died down and the astronaut flipped up the protective visor on his helmet, he recognized Chih-Hao Fung. Fung was missing several teeth, and a number of scars marked his face, some obscured by the wispy growth of a beard.

Fung spoke angrily in his helmet, his lips moving rapidly. Bradley turned his attention to Anshi Ping to see if he would reply, but Ping was lost in his work, oblivious to whatever derision Fung was spewing.

Bradley felt the Swiss SG551 rifle shift on his back. He slowly reached for it, and sighted the scope in—putting the crosshairs in the center of Fung's fishbowl helmet. He figured he could take both Fung and Ping out of the picture before any of the other Chinese astronauts knew what was happening. He had proof enough that the Chinese had cannibalized the American base camp—that much was obvious even sitting on this far ridge.

Bradley's finger tightened on the trigger. He realized that he didn't have direct proof that the Chinese had been responsible for Stechter's disappearance, but the circumstantial case was nearly airtight. Two bullets and he could even the odds. He checked the wind—three knots from the south—and slightly adjusted his aim.

As he was about to put a bullet through Fung's helmet, and start the first war that Mars had seen for thousands of years a blaring crackle over his intercom interrupted him. Wincing, Bradley lowered his rifle and adjusted the volume downward.

"What is it, Giffen? This better be important."

"We've been doing a sonar scan of the surrounding landscape…"

"And?"

"And we found something you might want to take a look at."

"I'm not in the mood for riddles," snapped Bradley. "What have you got?"

"The mass and geometry are a perfect match. Stechter told us it never made it to Mars, but I don't see how he could have missed finding it."

A chill started to creep up Bradley's spine. "Find what?"

"The Mars Climate Orbiter," said Giffen. "It's sitting in a sand drift three miles west of us!"

Mars, 47,000 B.C., The Lost City of Caladrex

Already the oxygen in the atmosphere grew thin, great fans sucking away the life-giving air. Ntashia's violet eyes glowered from her angular face, and she licked at her purple-tinged lips as she pulled the redlens rifle from her shoulder and leveled it at the great door of the vault in which the illusory Sved had trapped them. She let her dark visor fall down over her eyes, to protect from the flash of the weapon.

"If this rifle can punch through three inches of steel, then it should be able to cut us a way out of this death trap," she snarled.

Garvey raised a hand to stop her, but she pulled the trigger, her pale braids flailing about her face as power surged from the rifle, her magnificent figure illumined red with each crimson pulse of energy that spat from the gun.

The American astronaut leaped at her from the side, tackling her and bringing her to the metal-plated floor as a sizzling bolt of plasma scorched the air where she had been standing a split second before. The plasma bolts whined and shrieked as they ricocheted around the room, finally ending their flight as they burst through crates, melting or flash-burning the contents inside.

"The entire interior of the vault is reflective," said Garvey who still lay atop of her recumbent form.

"I should have known better," admitted Ntashia. "I let my anger at Sved goad me into rash action."

Garvey stood and helped Ntashia to her feet, smoke writhing from a sundered crate behind him. "No harm done, but we still need to figure a way out of here. It's already getting hard for me to breathe."

Ntashia's braids floated above her head, the suction from the overhead fans pulling at her. She tipped her head back and stared at the gleaming fan blades that whirled raucously above. Loose items whirled through the air, vacuumed upward to be stopped by a mesh that covered the intake shafts of the fans.

"That mesh isn't reflective," she observed.

"But the fan blades are. I'm afraid any attempt to put them out of commission will bounce a plasma bolt back in our direction."

"What was that floating platform that Sved rode into the theater?"

At first Garvey didn't follow Ntashia's train of thought. "That was nothing but an illusion; probably so we didn't notice that his footsteps didn't disturb the dust."

"But perhaps it was based on a real thing—something that we might be able to find here in the storehouse?"

Now Garvey's mind jumped onto the same track as Ntashia's. He cast about searching for a metallic disc similar to the one Sved had ridden. He leaped from mound to mound, cases spilling out from beneath his feet, as he looked. He noticed his breath was becoming labored, as though he had been sprinting for some distance. The oxygen supply was running low.

Finally he saw a round disc tilted against a far wall, and running down a mountain of crates, which cascaded behind him, he came to it and picked it up. The disc was about six inches thick, and large enough for just one person to comfortably stand upon it. Without any plan or idea of how the disc might function, Garvey threw it upon the ground and stepped onto the circular platform.

As soon as both of his feet rested on the dull gray surface, small hatches opened up, and metallic coils snaked out, crawling over his moccasin-shod feet, and binding them tight to the platform. Garvey had no concept of how he was going to eventually free himself from these metal bands, but he had little time to worry about it now. Even standing still, without the exertion of climbing or jumping, his breath came in ragged gasps.

Ntashia came running around the corner, her hair standing up as the fans pulled at her. "You found it!"

Garvey nodded. "I just don't know how to get it to work."

Before he finished speaking, another hatch folded back and a segmented coil like the ones that had wrapped around his feet emerged, snaking higher until it reached the bottom of Garvey's rib cage. Atop this flexible feeler of metal rested a small box that reminded the astronaut of a joystick for a video console. A tilt button with a four-way arrow graced the top of the box, and a series of three buttons, marked with symbols he did not understand, protruded to the left.

Ntashia climbed onto the platform with him, but no metallic tendrils emerged to wrap her feet, so she embraced Garvey tightly, the mesh of their armor kissing as Garvey pressed the top button. The platform lurched, a light flashing on the control pad, and they rose into the air, defying gravity ever so slowly. Garvey let go of the button and the disc came to an abrupt stop, hovering four feet off the ground.

Garvey could hear Ntashia's heavy breathing, her head resting against his chest. He pressed the button again, so that the disc continued to rise, and he found that by manipulating the arrows he could guide the platform in any direction he desired. Within a minute he directed the disc so that it rested below one of the massive fans. Here the noise was tremendous in volume, air whooshing by them carrying small particles of refuse to be caught in the mesh. Their lightweight armor stood on their limbs, as though it were about to be sucked from their bodies, and their hair stood upright.

In the midst of this turmoil Garvey noticed a scar on Ntashia's left upper ear where it had once been pierced, but he had no time to contemplate the fact as he stabilized the disc, which wobbled unevenly in the winds of suction.

"Lean back!" shouted Ntashia, who with her left hand grabbed tightly hold of Garvey's mail shirt.

Both leaned back simultaneously, Ntashia fully extended as she drew her Caladrex–forged blade and swung at the mesh covering the intake shaft. Sparks flew as the blade sheared through the mesh, and in a half dozen strokes she cleared away the web of metal. Instead of falling to the floor, the great sheet of mesh whirled into the turbine above. For a moment the spinning blades groaned as they chopped the mesh into metal chaff, and then sucked it away, rattling and scathing through the maze of ventilation tunnels above.

Now there was nothing between them and the blades, the latter offering only a quick death should they be caught by those massive flashing propellers. Carefully counterbalanced, they pulled together until they once again stood upright and centered on the disc.

Ntashia clinging tightly to him once again, Garvey maneuvered the disc with his right hand while his left hand fumbled at his waist and unclipped a plasma power cell for his redlens rifle. According to Sved this cell held enough energy to provide 1,000 shots from the rifle. Garvey didn't know how stable the cell was. What would happen when it was struck at two hundred miles an hour by a sharp blade?

As Garvey maneuvered the disc past the shaft he tossed the heavy cell up into the intake shaft. The cell was too heavy to have ever been sucked up to the shaft from the floor, but Garvey and Ntashia were only a few feet below the fans, and he was providing the cell with some extra momentum. This added impetus sent the power cell careening into the scything blades, which shattered on impact, shearing open the battery.

Garvey and Ntashia heard the clatter of broken metal spitting from the shaft as they buzzed away as fast as Garvey's newfound skills would allow him to operate the disc. A fraction of a second later a noise like a sonic boom reverberated through the chamber. White-hot flame rolled from the shaft, billowing out in incinerating gouts that turned an entire hill of crates into fluttering ash.

The heat of the explosion scorched their faces and limbs. The hair on Garvey's arm shriveled and fell away, but strangely the new armor that they wore seemed to protect their bodies from the sudden surge of blistering temperature. A wave of air, pushed by the heat, rocked the disc, and they careened through the air, Ntashia's muscles straining to hold onto Garvey as they lurched wildly.

Desperately Garvey worked at the controller as the disc spun—beyond his meager skills to recover control. The wave of air pushed them rapidly toward the wall of the vault, and just when it looked as though they would be pulped against those formidable steel plates, the disc veered away and Garvey shakily lowered it to the floor.

He took his sweating hand away from the controls, and Ntashia sat gasping on a blackened crate. The air was extremely thin, and though she and Garvey had put one of the fans out of commission, five more continued to whirl—unharmed by the plasma explosion.

Garvey wiped his sweaty palm. "Come on, we've got to get out of here."

Once again, Ntashia stepped onto the disc, clinging to Garvey as he slowly guided them toward the melted and mangled shaft. Black spots swam before his eyes, and he fought to maintain consciousness, his lungs laboring to find oxygen in the burnt air. Clinging to the vestiges of his mental faculties he maneuvered the disc up the still hot shaft, past the stubs of dripping crossmembers that had once held the fan blade, and into a labyrinth of ventilation tunnels strewn with the wreckage of the shaft, and scorched by plasma.

Finally the air grew thicker with oxygen, and they stopped just so they could let their breathing calm, and let their racing hearts settle to a safe level. The ventilation shafts were large enough that they could hover through them with little danger of striking anything, but as they continued their exploration they found that some of the passages were barred by further fan systems.

Not wanting to risk another plasma explosion they explored alternate ventilation ducts until they found themselves hovering over a grate, which lay over a hallway littered with the decaying corpses of the citizens of Caladrex.

Garvey set the disc down, and Ntashia stepped off to examine the grate. "It's bolted into place," she said, "but I think that maybe you can bend the slats apart enough for us to drop through."

"I can certainly give it a try," said Garvey as he pressed the buttons on the suspensor disc, hoping to find some way to release himself from the metal coils that held him fast. "Assuming I can ever get free from this thing."

"You may have to fly everywhere you go from now on."

She meant it as a joke, but somehow it didn't soothe Garvey's mind. "I've tried everything, but it won't let me go."

"Sved wouldn't have any control over that, would he?"

"I don't think so. If he did, I doubt if he ever would have let us escape the vault in the first place."

This seemed to satisfy Ntashia who came over to examine the suspensor disc that had saved their lives. It was a bit scorched, but despite the fact that it wouldn't release Garvey it seemed to be none the worse for the wear for its misadventures. "These things are certainly a lot less effort than wings."

"Which is great," said Garvey, "except for the fact that I could figure out how to take off my wings."

Ntashia ran her long fingers across the surface of the disc, and then found a catch just beneath the lip. She pressed it, and the metal tendrils slipped free, coiling back into their recessed panels.

"How did you do that?" asked an astounded Garvey.

"It just takes a Muvari touch," said Ntashia cryptically.

After Garvey stepped free, she flipped it over and showed him the catch in the bottom side of the disc. "Press here."

Garvey left the suspensor disc where it lay, and crossed to the grating, peering through at the dusty hall below. "Footprints," he said.

Ntashia looked through the slats until she could also see the prints. "Those are our prints. My feet and yours."

"Good," said Garvey. "Maybe we'll be able to find our way out of here after all."

"Only if we can get down there. Can your American muscles bend these slats back?"

"There's only one way to find out." Garvey leaned over and pushed at the slats, but found they resisted his efforts. However, he didn't want to disappoint Ntashia, who had already expressed her confidence in his strength, so he didn't yet admit defeat. Instead he wedged his feet against a slat, and began pushing with his legs. Slowly, as he straightened his mighty thews, the slats bent away, finally leaving enough of a gap that he and Ntashia could slip through.

The Muvari warrioress wasted no time and dropped to the hall below, dust swirling about her feet as she landed. Garvey handed the suspensor disc down to her, and then followed.

"We still lack in climbing equipment," observed Ntashia. "But we may not need it now that we have this flying platform."

Garvey studied the footprints on the floor and patted the pouch on his belt, which contained about thirty silver-wrapped nutrition bars he had pilfered from the vault. "We do have a little food, let's follow our prints back to the ledge."

"The sinthral may be waiting for us..."

Garvey chewed on the inside of his cheek as he pondered this possibility. "Perhaps we can find those pneumatic trains that Sved was talking about."

"You think he was telling the truth?"

"I don't know. He may have been. He was going to kill us all along, there was no real reason to lie about it."

"Perhaps," answered Ntashia skeptically. "I remember the tunnel down which he said this new–matic transportation exists. If we back track, follow our footsteps, we should be able to find it."

They walked in silence for about ten minutes, each lost in their own thoughts. Finally Garvey broke the dreadful silence. "Were you married before?"

Ntashia chewed at her lower lip before answering. "You saw the image of me with another man."

"Yes, and then I saw that your left ear had been pierced—yet you wore no ring."

"My husband, Ranath Teig was killed in a Galbran raid. Now perhaps you understand why Omonyi berated me so harshly when I let you fight alongside the women. Each male is valuable to the tribe, and already with his other wives Ranath had created many children so that through them our tribe might live on."

"And you have no children?"

"We were married for just a short time before his death, and I was not able to conceive."

"I see," said Garvey, who contemplated this information for a moment.

"I did not want to tell you," she said softly. "I was afraid that you might value me less if you knew I had once belonged to another man."

"It was in an honorable state. I certainly do not think any less of you, though I admit to being jealous when I saw the image flash from that truth teller column."

Ntashia smiled faintly. "Jealousy, perhaps that bodes well for your feelings for me."

"Perhaps," admitted Garvey. "If I were not constantly fending off death from around every corner, I'd have a hard time shaking your image from my thoughts."

"Oh, how sweet," the voice came deep, gravelly, and derisively, echoing from the walls. Garvey and Ntashia whirled to find a figure clad only in a crimson cloth that was wrapped about his loins. His narrow chest was puffed up as large as it would go, which was ridiculously small compared to Garvey's healthy physique.

"Sved," hissed Garvey. "I was hoping we'd seen the last of you."

"And I you," answered the apparition, his opaline eyes swimming with malice. "When I kill something, it should do me the courtesy of staying dead.

Unless you two are apparitions like me, and I detect that you are not, you should be dead by means of asphyxiation."

"Leave us alone, or we'll burn your entire city to the ground!" snarled Ntashia.

Sved ignored this threat. "Next time I kill you I'll not be so kind. Perhaps I'll arrange for something more painful than asphyxiation—perhaps some sort of slow, torturous death."

Garvey saw that they had arrived at the dark tunnel which, Sved had earlier informed them, led to the pneumatic train. It seemed to Garvey as though Sved were trying to distract them from noticing the entrance. It was a futile effort.

Ntashia swung around to regard Sved's flickering image with a cold smile. "I believe that we must say goodbye now. If I remember correctly you called this next area the dead zone, and apparently you don't have the power to follow where we plan to go."

Sved glowered, his opaline eyes dangerous. "Perhaps not, but you will be seeing me again. On that you can count."

With those final words Sved's hologram sputtered and disappeared into the thin air from whence it had sprung.

"Good riddance," muttered Garvey with a sly smile breaking his lips.

The pitch darkness quickly enveloped them as they broached the dark portal and passed into its night-cloaked halls. Once again, Garvey used his Clip Pad, its cells newly recharged from the illumination of Caladrex, to light the way. In this green glow they stepped across cracked and uneven tiles and leaped great fissures that would have swallowed them up had they been traveling blindly.

An earthquake had obviously devastated this portion of the city and they passed through a massive metropolis that lay in utter ruin, its shiny spires cracked and tumbled, and its once glistening domes shattered like eggshells and laying amid tons of crushing stone that had split off from the vast cavern ceiling above and dropped upon the city.

They passed dark warrens and splitting stairs that led upward into the man-made obelisks of the city, or downward into its steaming bowels. Dark doorways stared menacingly, and the blackness pressed all around. Finally, the heaving and cracked boulevard gave way to a narrow tunnel, and they left the over-arching dome behind, the green glow of the Clip Pad still guiding their way.

"Are we even going in the right direction?" asked Ntashia.

An insidious chill crept up from beneath as they descended further into the tunnel. They felt the chill against their face, but the miraculous properties of their Caladrexian armor kept the cold away from their bodies, so that they were still comfortably warm.

"I don't know," admitted Garvey. "When Sved told us about the train he said to just follow the tunnel. He didn't say anything about an entire ruined city. We might have passed right by and not even known it."

"Maybe we should go back," she pressed, some sixth sense making her uneasy.

Garvey seemed oblivious to her discomfort as he raised the Clip Pad above his head, letting its feeble green rays seep down the polished black stone of the corridor. A brass plaque mounted on the wall was scribed with several incomprehensible runes, and an unmistakable arrow that pointed in the direction they were traveling.

"Let's go a little further," urged Garvey. "Something is down here."

The flesh crawled on the back of Ntashia's slender neck. "It's just a matter of whether what we find will kill us or not."

A sudden sputter of sound sent Ntashia whirling around on the balls of her feet, her blade sliding cleanly from her scabbard in the same smooth motion. She cleaved the air behind her, slicing through the hazy image of Sved. For a moment the image disappeared then reformed, grainy and entirely faded out below the torso.

"What troubles you, travelers? Perhaps you are lost?"

Garvey viewed the poor clarity of the hologram with a wry smile. "You don't seem to be coming in so clearly, Sved. We can't understand what you are saying."

Of course, Garvey could hear Sved clearly—but he wanted to see if he could toy with Sved, just as the hologram had toyed with them since their first encounter.

Sved's voice boomed through the corridor, this time fuzzed by the crackle of distortion. "I say, are you lost?"

Garvey kept a confident face, not wanting to betray their uncertainty. "Does it look like we're lost to you?"

"It was a miscalculation on my part," admitted Sved, "to give you so much information about how to escape. I assumed that you would never be leaving the vault."

"So why are you here, ghost? You're incessant prattling is beginning to bother me," said Ntashia as she resheathed her blade.

"I'm here to warn you," answered Sved with a mocking lisp. "If you proceed further you'll both be dead by the end of the hour."

"But you've admitted yourself, that we are on the right track," pried Garvey. "Why lie to us now?"

"You've outwitted me at every turn," replied Sved, though the tone of his voice echoed nothing but supercilious disdain. "You've won the game, and the prize is yours."

Ntashia arched her thin brow over her left eye. "What prize is this?"

"The riches of Caladrex are yours for the taking. I will lead you to their hiding place."

"Forgive me if I don't fall for your lies a second time, ghost. But we'll be on our way now." Ntashia turned and joined Garvey who matched her stride for stride as they marched down the hallway.

Sved's voice bellowed out behind them, echoing and crackling. "I'll have the last laugh yet, you mongrels! I'll stand dancing on your bloody corpses, you fools! Do you know what it is to be eaten alive?"

The holograms voice faded behind them, and soon all they heard was the sound of their own hollow footsteps.

"Do you think we've seen the last of him?" asked Garvey.

Ntashia shook her head. "When I bring the Muvari back to loot Caladrex, I'll see that we exorcise that ghost."

"He's nothing but a machine, like any of the Ancients' other technological devices."

"A machine can be broken," said Ntashia. "Can't it, American?"

Mischief sparkled in her violet eyes, and Garvey wanted to take her in his arms and kiss away the smirk on her lips.

"Look," cried Ntashia. "Is this the train?"

The tunnel opened up before them into a pillared hall with broad platforms, and an arched ceiling that reached further than the Clip Pad's weak light could penetrate. Running through the hall was a rail raised on pillars, a series of six train cars astride the rail.

Garvey mounted the broad marble stairs to the first platform, heedless of the bones and fresh feces that littered the hall. "On my planet they call this a monorail."

Ntashia called to him in a low voice. "Garvey."

"I wonder if we can get it running."

Ntashia repeated her call. "Garvey!"

"What?" He turned to find Ntashia halfway up the stairs, her back facing him, long braids spilling down the gleaming mesh of her armor, and the muscles of her bare calves taut and ready for action. Her sword was unsheathed and held firmly in her right hand.

Beyond her three saber-toothed tigers stalked from the darkness, to mount the stairs on padding feet that scarcely made a sound. Each of the creatures weighed in excess of a half-ton, their massive muscles rippling beneath their tawny hides. Each of the creatures possessed four eyes, two in the front, and one on each side of their feral skulls. Worse yet, a pair of suckered tentacles emerged from each shoulder. They undulated wildly, some reaching forward as if to test the distance between them and their wary prey.

"Vackri," whispered Ntashia, identifying the beasts, which had found them. "Perhaps Sved was right. He will be dancing over our bloody corpses."

Chapter Fifteen:
Temple of the Vackri

March 7, 2007 8:30 A.M.– The White House

President Welch took another look at the ultimatum delivered by courier from the Chinese embassy that morning, her stomach twisting into knots as she reread words that she had already committed to memory.

Though her tenure as President had consisted of only six months in office, she had been through crisis after crisis—narrowly averting one tragedy only to face another.

The fight against terrorism had been an expensive one for the American people, and already it had cost the life of her predecessor. As Vice President, and at 67 years in age, she had moved into the position with more than a few trepidations, but despite her detractors cries—that she was just another film actor trying her hand at politics—the former sex symbol had proved them wrong with her conservative straightforward, nononsense political style, rallying the citizens of the United States citizens behind her.

She reached out and hit the intercom on her desk, which rested in the plush sanctum of the oval office. "Get me the Secretary of Defense, the Homeland Security Director, and the Director of NASA for a meeting in my office."

Her secretary replied. "When would you like me to schedule this, Mrs. President?"

"I want them all on planes within the half hour."

March 7, 2007, U.S. Mars Base

Hank Giffen set aside the burned remains of the signal booster for the jammer, and sighed. The electronics were scorched and the wiring shorted. It had blown out when they first plugged it into the jamming system.

Unfortunately, it was a piece of electronics vital to the functioning of the signal jammer. Despite wrapping his considerable brain power around the dilemma he could not figure out a way to fix the component. NASA had miswired it, and now all they could do was wait for a replacement.

It wasn't the first mistake NASA had made, Giffen reflected as he turned to his computer screen and scrolled through the telemetry programming they had downloaded from the hulk of the Mars Climate Orbiter. He once again pinpointed the telltale code line that had caused the crash of the spacecraft.

"It's only taken me a year, but I've found the problem. I'm sure of it. The fuel to thrust ratios are entered into the programming incorrectly in the landing sequence. It only takes a few decimal places of error to put Garvey too far out of orbit to have enough fuel for a proper landing."

Thomas Bradley absently passed an electric razor over his face a few times, trimming away a five o'clock shadow. "Do you think Stechter had anything to do with it? We know that he lied to us about not finding the Mars Climate Orbiter. There's no way he could have missed it. The search pattern he followed took him right over the spot where you found it, and the metal detectors in the rover are sensitive enough to pick up something that size from three miles away."

Melhoff scratched at a beard that spilled halfway down his chest, and began to unwrap a protein bar. "We know that Stechter's always had a yen for glory. It doesn't seem out of character for him to lie about Garvey's landing so that he could be considered the first one to land on Mars."

"But do you think he's low enough to tamper with the coding to cause the crash?" asked Bradley.

"I don't see how he would have had the opportunity or even the expertise to pull it off. He's a pilot like you and Garvey—not a mathematician or an engineer. Bison was the lead on the coding. Everything was triple, and quadruple checked by him before getting an okay."

"Bison," muttered Bradley. "Reginald Bison." He snapped his fingers. "He's the guy that Stechter hit in the face the day that Garvey launched for Mars."

"Well, they could hardly be in cahoots, then," figured Melhoff.

"Unless they were in cahoots, and had some sort of falling out," said Bradley.

Melhoff screwed up his furry face as he considered this possibility. "My heads starting to hurt; enough with all these conspiracy theories."

"Have you got anything better to do, besides another hand of solitaire?" asked Giffen. "Originally, we were supposed to be here for two years—I'm sure I don't have to remind you how long we've been abandoned up here."

Bradley's face fell for at least the hundredth time that morning as he thought about his wife and family whom he hadn't seen for five long years. His kids were growing up without him. The astronauts to Mars had been forgotten in the turmoil of the fight against terrorism, and an assassinated president. No relief mission had ever come, and they'd been forced to raid the Mars Climate Orbiter for food and supplies to survive. On top of that they were missing the critical power amplification unit for jamming the Chinese transmissions. To sum it up, their mission was a complete failure.

Meanwhile, regular relief missions came to the Chinese base, and they had built a complex communications system fully capable of directing nuclear weapons platforms on orbiting satellites around Earth. Bradley had sued time and again for permission to launch an attack on the Chinese base, or at least to take out their transmission capabilities—but his requests had gone ignored and the Chinese had increased to a dozen in strength.

Of the three U.S. astronauts Thomas Bradley was the only one trained for combat. Giffen had no taste for it, and preferred to procrastinate the day of reckoning. Melhoff was an enthusiastic volunteer if the time ever came, but the odds were astronomically against them now.

Bradley kept close tabs on the progress of the Chinese, and they had installed a sophisticated array of motion sensors to detect any U.S. incursion closer than half a mile in distance.

To keep his mind occupied with something other than the mindnumbing games of solitaire that Melhoff seemed to play over and over, Bradley had been working on some ideas for cracking the Chinese perimeter defenses—but the chances were slight that three could prevail against a dozen better equipped and trained enemies. He smiled as he remembered the boot camp training that he and Garvey had endured so many years ago. He wished that Garvey was here now to give him a hand, but no trace of him had ever been found besides some blood in the Orbiter.

With nothing better to do, Giffen had run a DNA test on the crimson droplets and compared them to Garvey's DNA sequence on file in the NASA computers. They had matched, of course, and that had been the end of that investigation. No further clues had surfaced that might point to where

Garvey's body lay. Perhaps, thought, Bradley, Arnold Stechter had disposed of it somehow—or perhaps Garvey's body lay somewhere undiscovered, hidden beneath the shifting Martian sands.

"Anyone up for a game of Gin Rummy?" called Melhoff.

Bradley raised his hand, hoping to ward away the melancholy that was once again besetting him. "Deal me in."

"Hold up," said Giffen, "We're getting an encrypted transmission."

Giffen switched on the decoding box, which ungarbled the transmission.

"NASA control, calling Mars Base," came Allan Rigby's squeaky voice.

Giffen switched into encryption mode. "This is Hank Giffen at Mars Base. You calling to check in on our botany project?"

"Negative," answered Allan momentarily. "Are all three of you there?"

"That's affirmative. What's going on?"

"I'll let the president explain it. She would like to speak with you."

Melhoff's eyes popped open and he glanced over at Bradley. "Do you think she's wearing that little get-up from One Million BC?"

President Welch's voice came over the loud speaker. "I heard that, and if you three can pull off what I'm about to ask, I might even change into that outfit for you."

Melhoff's face turned crimson. "Sorry, Mrs. President, I didn't know you could hear me."

"Apology accepted, and I hope that you three will accept the sincere apologies of the United States. Mr. Stanton, the Director of NASA, has informed me that you've been stranded on Mars for five years serving your country. I've ordered a relief ship to take off for Mars at the next available window. I was unaware that we had astronauts on Mars, and it was a fact that my predecessor neglected to mention to me."

Bradley Thomas broke in. "Mrs. President, I greatly appreciate you sending a ship to retrieve us. I miss my family horribly, but I must ask you about the Chinese base here on Mars. At the very minimum we need replacement equipment so that we can jam their transmissions. They have the capabilities of launching nuclear missiles from earth-orbiting platforms. Nothing's stopping them."

"That's precisely the reason I became aware of your existence. Gentleman, the United States has received an ultimatum from China, and I'm afraid we don't have the luxury of waiting for jamming equipment to arrive on Mars."

"Can you tell me what this ultimatum entails?" asked Bradley.

"What I'm telling you can't be relayed back to anyone at NASA. This is top secret information."

"We understand."

"The Chinese letter basically outlines an extortion plan for ten billion in high tech military hardware and financial aid."

"This is a one time deal?"

"No, it's a yearly deal. Basically it amounts to annual tribute. No doubt, we'd be financing our own downfall."

"And if we don't?"

"They begin launching missiles at key U.S. cities—one at a time until we agree to their terms."

"What does Russia have to say about this?" asked Melhoff.

"I've been in communication with the Russian President and they have received a similar ultimatum. The Russian's have no presence on Mars, so it's all up to us."

"What do you want us to do?" asked Bradley.

"I'm ordering an attack on the Chinese base. The first objective is to destroy their communications equipment. The second objective is to kill their astronauts."

"We'll do it," said Bradley. "Can I ask you something personal?"

"You may…"

"If I don't make it back, will you personally relay a message to my family for me?"

"I will."

"Tell them I love them."

Mars, 47,000 B.C.— The Lost City of Caladrex

Tentacles snaking outward, the vackri slunk between great pillars, across the dusty monorail platform, and toward the stair on which Ntashia stood. The three great vackri closed the distance between them and their prey, saliva drooling from their fanged jowls, the eyes at the side of their head taking in their surroundings while the forward pair of eyes fixed on the Muvari warrior who stood at bay—afraid that a hasty retreat might provoke a charge by these beasts that the inhabitants of Caladrex had once worshipped.

Slowly, so as not to irritate the vackri into an early attack, Garvey reached back and unslung the rifle forged by the lost weaponsmiths of Caladrex. His breathing was slow and shallow as he leveled the rifle, aiming between the forward eyes of the vackri that padded up the cracked steps toward Ntashia's armored form.

A pair of tentacles, emerging from the left shoulder, snaked out toward her. Her sword blade rasped against her sheath as she slowly withdrew it—forfeiting the idea of using her rifle in such close quarters.

The tentacles reached out as if to touch her.

"Garvey!" she whispered, but before the sound of his name died on her lips, her companion eased back on the trigger of his rifle, and the weapon hummed in his hand as a beam of plasma burst from the muzzle.

The beam sliced through the broad chest of the vackri, and the beast opened its jaws wide in a piercing scream. It took another step toward Ntashia, and Garvey pulled back the trigger three more times, opening smoking wounds in the fur-covered hide of the vackri.

The beast took another step forward and pitched onto its face, writhing in pain. But even as it entered its death throes, the tentacles wrapped around Ntashia, lifting her into the air and thrashing her around as though she were a rag doll.

At the sound of the dying vackri's scream, the other two vackri bounded across the platform and up the broad steps—each a half-ton of snarling death, with Garvey fixed in their sight. They came with amazing speed, and Garvey held down the trigger of his rifle so that it spat crimson bolts like a machine gun threw lead. They leaped simultaneously when they reached the platform upon which Garvey stood. Bolts of plasma seared the air, ricocheting from pillars and lighting the shadowed recesses of the great hall.

The searing missiles sliced apart one of the vackri, so that it fell at Garvey's feet, a smoking pile of writhing flesh, its horrible screams rending the astronaut's ears. The second vackri somehow escaped the flashing bolts of plasma, and reached out a massive paw—razor claws extended to take Garvey's head from his body. As the beast came hurtling through the air toward him, Garvey defensively raised his rifle and the vackri's swipe bent the gun, sending its mangled remains spinning over the edge of the loading platform, and into the dark recesses of the trench below.

The paw continued in its path and struck Garvey full on the chest. Razor talons snapped and broke against his newly acquired Caladrexian armor, but the force of the blow picked Garvey up and hurled him ten feet through the air. The earthling landed heavily, but leaped to his feet, gasping for the breath that had been hammered from his lungs.

The vackri gave him no respite, fixing him with his baleful glare for only a moment before launching himself across the intervening space for a second attack. Without the amazing Caladrexian firearm technology at his disposal, Garvey was forced to resort to his sword and he swung it free to meet the charge of one-thousand pounds of homicidal beast.

Ntashia's teeth rattled as the tentacles of the vackri whipped her body about. The flailing motions of the tentacles several times brought her within a hair's breadth of dashing her brains out against a pillar. It took every bit of strength, will, and concentration for her to hang onto her sword—but she still clutched it tightly in a white-knuckled grip.

The whipping of her body and limbs hadn't yet given her the opportunity to bring the sword into play without fear of striking her own flailing body. But now, as the tentacles slowed their shaking movement and reflexively tightened around her body in an effort to crush the life out of her, she saw her chance. She pulled back her sword arm and sent it plunging forward, the honed edge of the blade slicing through a tentacle in a gout of greenish ichor.

The remaining tentacle constricted tightly around her narrow waist, and blackness appeared around the edges of her vision. The sword blade fell from her numbing fingers and clattered against the platform as the great coils slowly squeezed, her ribs creaking and groaning from the pressure. It was only a matter of moments, she realized, before her ribs gave way beneath the pulverizing force of those tentacles, and her insides turned to jelly.

Garvey struck the vackri as he unsheathed his sword and the incredible blade sliced through the breastbone of the beast, cleaving it wide open and rupturing the great aorta that beat within. Then the full weight of the dead vackri fell upon Garvey, smothering him in fur and flesh that was sticky with green ichor.

On Earth Garvey would have been unable to extricate himself from beneath the body that pinned him to the ground, but on Mars, and in its lighter gravity he had a chance. After a few moments of struggle he pulled his limbs into a position where he could push against the monstrous weight, and with muscle-straining effort he managed to free himself from the bloody mass.

He staggered to his feet, calling Ntashia's name. Only when he had wiped the vackri's blood from his eyes did he see her hanging numbly from the still-moving coils of a dead vackri, the scales undulating as they exerted yet more pressure on Ntashia's body.

With a cry Garvey leaped forward, and in one brutal stroke severed the tentacle. Ntashia fell to the ground, the now-lifeless tentacle loosening around her body. Without pausing to wipe his blade, Garvey shoved it back into its sheath, blood clotting at the hilt. He dragged Ntashia free from the tentacles and crouched over her still body. No breath passed her lips or lifted her breast.

Garvey gave out an anguished cry as he put his finger to the hollow of her throat beneath the left of her jaw. He was relieved to find that a pulse still beat strongly. His CPR training flooded back to him, and he tilted back her head, pinching her nose as he put his lips to hers. He breathed three times, and suddenly her eyes fluttered open with a gasp as her natural breathing reflex took over once again.

The astronaut sank down against a pillar, his prodigious strength draining from him as he realized how near he had been to losing Ntashia—and how dear that she was to him. How foolish he had been to stubbornly cling to that bit of imagined independence—and to spurn Ntashia's expression of love for him.

Ntashia slowly sat upright. "Are you alright, American?"

Garvey laughed weakly, thinking that he should have been the one asking her the question. "I am now."

"What happened?" she asked blankly, regarding the carnage that surrounded them.

"I thought that I lost you," he said.

A faint smile touched Ntashia's exquisite lips. "How could you lose me if you never had me?"

For a moment this comment threw Garvey, but then he comprehended her meaning. Though it was obvious that they shared a mutual attraction, he had yet to express a commitment to her. How could she truly have ever been his if he had made no commitment to her and her to him?

Garvey's heart leaped in his chest as he spoke the words—almost more strain than his body could take after the vicious battle he had endured. "If you would still have me, I would like to take you as my wife."

No expression passed Ntashia's face. "You would take me in an honorable Muvari marriage ceremony?"

"If you accept my proposal."

A broad smile lit Ntashia's beautiful face and she took Garvey in her slender arms. "Then we must return to Ledgrim as soon as possible to make our vows."

Garvey suddenly recalled the Muvari tradition of multiple wives in order to more quickly populate a tribe with far fewer males than females. "Ummm, Ntashia?"

"Yes?"

"The Council of Elders isn't going to force me to marry anyone else, are they?"

"As a part of the Muvari Tribe it will be your responsibility," she said soberly, "but you need not hurry. For the time, I'd like to keep you all to myself."

As much as the thought of marriage scared Garvey, the thought of being married to more than one woman terrified him. "That's the way that I'd prefer it," he agreed.

With a little coaxing Ntashia's memory of the conflict with the vackris returned, and she drew out the double-pronged blade she had stolen from the altar of the vackri. "We must take the adrenal gland of the vackri," she said.

"So you still think that they grant a long life?"

"Not an eternal one, but a youthful one," she replied. "The slaying of a vackri is a great deed. I will live in high honor to be married to such a great warrior as you."

Garvey shrugged. "Well, as you pointed out. I still have a lot to learn about using a sword."

"I am considered to be quite expert with the blade," she said. "And once we are married, I will teach you every skill of the sword that I know."

The astronaut nodded, then furrowed his brow. "If the males of the Muvari tribe are not allowed to become warriors because of their scarcity—how is it that I can have honor for being a great warrior, when only the women are allowed to become warriors?"

"Once," answered Ntashia as she cut into the corpse of a vackri, "our tribe had an equal number of males and females. A man took only one wife, and he did the fighting. So in our tradition we honor many great male warriors. In order to survive the Muvari Tribe has been forced to adopt new rules of conduct for the male and the female. As an outsider, about to join the tribe, you have already proved yourself a formidable warrior. You may be able to receive a special dispensation from the Elder Council that allows you to continue in your role as a warrior and protector of the tribe. Only in extraordinary circumstances would this dispensation ever be granted to a native son of the Muvari Tribe."

Garvey reflected as Ntashia removed the adrenal gland from the vackri and carefully sealed the dripping pulp in a watertight pouch they had obtained from the storehouse in the City of Caladrex. "I thank God we were kidnapped by the Galbran."

Ntashia lowered an eyebrow. "Why is that?"

"If it hadn't been for them I never would have found my way into your heart. You nearly put a spear in me when we first met. Because we were both captured together I got the chance to change your opinion of me."

Ntashia cleaned her knife and then kissed Garvey hotly on the lips. Garvey grinned as they parted. "I like that."

A coy expression crossed Ntashia's face. "There will be that…and more on our wedding night."

"It will take a steel will for me to wait so long," said Garvey.

"I'm sure you'll be up to the task. After all, it is an honorable Muvari wedding to which we agreed."

"That we did," sighed Garvey. "That we did."

With a length of pipe that Garvey pilfered from some rubbish alongside the platform, he pried open the double doors of the monorail and they entered the glowing interior of the car.

"This thing has still got power," commented Garvey. "That's a good sign."

"Just so long as Sved doesn't show his face again."

"I've had about enough of him, myself. But at least we've gotten past the things he threatened were going to be feeding on our entrails."

"The vackri," stated Ntashia as she poked among the corpses that littered the train car.

"That's how I interpreted it," said Garvey. He pressed a button at the front of the car and double doors slid open, giving them egress to another car ahead. "We'll keep working our way to the front of the train. Maybe we can get into the engineer's car."

Indeed, the lead car opened easily to their prying hands. The skeletal form of an engineer, moldering cap still in place, still sat in his armchair. The copilot's seat lay empty and covered with a thick layer of dust. Garvey stood and looked through the thick plate-glass shields at the single rail extending into the darkness of the tunnel ahead. The control board was a flat panel that glowed with symbols that seemed arcane and magical to Garvey and Ntashia.

Garvey hesitated.

"What's wrong?" asked Ntashia, fully confident that Garvey could somehow figure out the controls as he had done with the floating disc that they still carried.

"If I could read these symbols it might make things a lot easier."

"Or they just might confuse you," suggested Ntashia.

Garvey hit a couple of symbols, and other than a hiss of air ejected from the engine somewhere nothing happened. He depressed a third symbol and suddenly the train was sucked into the tunnel ahead. Ntashia and Garvey tumbled over backward, returning to their feet only when the train had gained some equilibrium.

A headlight flashed on, flooding the tunnel ahead as though it were daylight, revealing the ridged contours of the tunnel—like the ribs of a whale's belly. They twisted and turned, following the rail at incredible speed, so that the struts of the tunnel flickered by like cards in a shuffling deck. Broad train stations opened up to one side or the other, but disappeared as quickly as they appeared—receding and swallowed up in the greedy darkness behind.

"Do you know how to stop this thing?" asked Ntashia.

Garvey only shook his head. "Buckle yourself into that seat."

Ntashia sat down in the chair and lifted the straps and cankered buckles. "You mean these things?"

The astronaut leaned over Ntashia and helped her arrange the straps and buckles. "Yes, they help keep you in your seat in case of an abrupt stop."

"I thought that you didn't know how to stop it."

Garvey prodded the skeleton of the engineer aside so that it dropped to the floor. He took his place in the rotting seat. "It may stop itself."

The minutes rolled past, the tunnel becoming a haze in their blurring vision. As he watched the rail appearing in the headlights, it occurred to Garvey that the rail ahead was cracked. By the time that he willed his arm to move forward and press a button...any button, it was too late. The train vaulted from the broken rail, and continued straight into a train station as the broken and crumbling rail curved off to the left.

Metal screeched and sparks flew. A pillar leaped up before them and tumbled into sections falling over the top of the monorail cars, and shattering the windshield into a thousand shining shards. Garvey and Ntashia threw their arms over their eyes as a glittering avalanche of broken glass rolled through the interior of the car.

Finally the train screeched to a halt, accordioned, and lying jumbled like fallen dominoes. Garvey shook away the glass shards from his hair.

"Are you alive?"

"My ribs hurt," said Ntashia, "but other than that I'm just fine."

"Do your ribs hurt from the accident or our encounter with the vackri?"

She unbuckled herself, bending low in the caved compartment as she brushed the glass away from her stunning form. "Definitely the vackri."

A ten-ton block of stone pillar sat where the windshield used to be, but there was a small opening still, and Garvey squeezed through this and stepped out onto the broken tiles of the station. The train cars behind were broken and crushed, some of them on fire- ignited by the intense friction of the crash.

Garvey reached in and helped Ntashia step through the narrow gap. She slipped through much more easily than Garvey, and joined him amidst the devastation.

They picked their way through the great stone blocks that had once comprised pillars, and heard the earth groaning above them.

"The ceiling is about to give way!" shouted Ntashia.

Together they ran toward a set of ascending stairs, vaulting up the moss-grown and jumbled steps. They found themselves in a tunnel choked with debris and rubble from some previous cave-in, but a brilliant light seeped through a narrow fissure—offering them hope of escape.

Garvey raised his arms to shield his eyes from the intense glare, then remembered to pull down the visor he wore on his helmet. It quickly polarized to compensate against the intense illumination.

Ntashia did likewise, and they pushed through the fissure as the train station collapsed behind them, dust billowing through to envelope them in a choking cloud. They went down to their knees, coughing and hacking. Finally, when the dust settled a brilliant light reflected from their armor and they raised their heads to see a valley covered with glittering diamonds, each refracting and magnifying the sunlight to a blinding brilliance.

"The valley of Idor," breathed Garvey in awe.

Covered in a layer of dust, Ntashia spat out some blackened saliva, and stood. "I've been to the Southwest corner of this valley. From there I can guide us to the Muvari outpost above the Rift, and then back to Ledgrim."

She started to pick a path through the coruscating diamonds when Garvey called her back. "If you're in as much as a hurry as I am, I have a better idea."

He threw down the floating disc and stepped onto it. Hatches opened up in its face and the coils snaked up over his feet and secured him tightly as the control paddle rose. "If you don't mind holding on, we can save a lot of time."

"Ah hah," said Ntashia. "I'm not used to the luxuries of the Ancient's technology." She stepped onto the disc and wrapped her arms tightly around

Garvey's waist. "This ought to impress the Elders of the tribe."

"When we show up on a floating disc?"

Ntashia nodded. "The Elders haven't been very happy with me since my husband was killed. They said I shouldn't have allowed him to pick up a weapon to defend against the Galbran—and that because of me five women lost a husband."

"Maybe they'll find some forgiveness in their hearts once you tell them the location of Caladrex."

The disc picked them up, and they scudded across glittering fields of sparkling diamonds. To Garvey such a wealth of gemstones was nearly beyond comprehension. Investors would have fallen out of their seats to fund NASA could he have brought home pictures of such a valley.

For half of an hour the disc carried them over rugged acres of immeasurable wealth, and then the valley turned south and they found a jagged and treacherous trail that wound through and climbed over thrusting knobs of stone. Today, however, they were flying and they skimmed a hundred feet over the trail, and followed its winding course up the side of the valley. They dared not fly lower because of the black-barked trees that spread gnarled and leafless limbs into the bloody sky. Sometimes these shrouded the trail, their suckered branches waving in a non-existent breeze.

"Those trees are moving!" said Garvey.

"Just the branches," informed Ntashia. "Their sticky pods catch unwary insects and small birds and slowly digest them. They do this to augment the feeble nutrition that they derive from the sterile soil."

"If we were climbing that trail on foot could the branches reach down and pluck us up for dinner?"

"Of course not," said Ntashia with a smile, "The branches can only move slightly, but we would be foolish to fly to close to the Ascarna Tree.

Winged Muvari have crashed into the Ascarna and their bodies sucked dry of their life fluids by the time we could reach them."

This seemed a sobering thought to Garvey, and now he devoted more careful attention the flying of the disc, and less to the terrain below—anxious to leave the gaunt black trees behind them. Finally the skeletal trunks of the Ascarna faded into the distance as they topped the last rise of the valley and zoomed across a barren wastelands of shattered rock and cracked earth.

The sun blazed overhead, and the only thing that relieved the heat was the winds that battered them. The air was dry and Garvey thought he scented a sweet perfume carried on the air currents.

"What scent is that?" he asked.

Ntashia renewed her grip around his waist and pressed herself tightly against Garvey as the disc carried them at blazing speeds across the desert. "Those are the cacti blossoms. They bloom violet, and turn scarlet before withering."

Garvey lowered the disc so that they buzzed across the ground at about twenty feet. Here he could easily see the waxen-skinned and yellow stalks of barbed vegetation that took root in the parched soil. "Are we still heading in the right direction?"

"Just set your course for the double peaks, and you can't go wrong."

The astronaut had no difficulty locating the double towers of stone that poked like two skeletal fingers into the sky, and he adjusted the direction of the disc so that they headed straight for it. He estimated they had perhaps a hundred leagues to travel before they reached those twin towers. "Where is the Muvari outpost?"

"It built atop the higher peak on the left side. A narrow and easily guarded trail winds up to it from the rugged lands below."

"How are its defenses against flying Galbran?"

"Its walls are built with arrow slits for just that reason."

It was tedious and difficult for Ntashia to hang onto Garvey during the long journey to the outpost, and they stopped a half dozen times, taking reprieve among the shadows of monstrous boulders. Though they were making incredible time, Garvey's feet were cramping as he guided the disc—much as a snowboarder would guide his snowboard—and Ntashia had to stand very still so as not to throw off the balance of the disc as they flew.

So Garvey rested his aching feet while Ntashia stretched her lithe muscles, which were stiff from inaction.

Garvey watched red-throated snakes slip in and out of the shadowed rocks, their copper scales glistening and spiked tails dripping venom. Finally the travelers' muscles felt up to the task again, they mounted the disc and resumed their flight.

Dusk was falling, the flaming sun slipping beneath the horizon, but still stretching its bloody fingers into the sky, as they reached the tortured and tumultuous lands that surrounded the double peaks. They floated across valleys, chasms, rifts, and rope bridges that wavered in the thick green vapors that bubbled from the miasma below.

What had seemed a narrow finger jutting into the sky a hundred leagues away, now blotted out their forward vision with its sheer and weathered face.

"Land at the base of the peak," urged Ntashia. "We'll speak with the guards at the bottom of the trail, so they can send up a warning to the outpost above that we are not enemies."

"If they've been vigilant in the outpost," replied Garvey, "they have doubtless seen us coming."

"Doubtless," agreed Ntashia as the disc slowed and Garvey brought it to a gentle stop on a narrow trail that cut between two great boulders on its way toward the base of the peak.

Ntashia gratefully stepped off the disc and stretched her legs, and Garvey withdrew his aching arches from the coils that bound him. He slung the disc over his back, and joined Ntashia as she trudged up the trail, her footsteps crunching on loose gravel. In a few minutes they came to the base of the great stone peak, the path passing by a stone bench cut into the rock beneath a stone overhang.

Ntashia's violet eyes narrowed. "That's strange. There are no guards on duty."

Garvey strode to the bench and noticed a fine spray of liquid, which had dried to a dull purple. "This looks like blood to me."

The Muvari warrioress took only a moment to examine the markings. "It's blood, alright. This doesn't bode well."

"I guess we'd better check the outpost, and hope that the Muvari are still holding the fort."

Ntashia unslung her Caladrex-forged rifle, and after a moment found the trigger. "Let's take the path. I'm afraid that we'd be a napping skelk if we used that disc again."

"What's a skelk?" asked Garvey as he began to follow her up the path, which wound around the peak.

"A rat-like creature that tends to take a nap as soon as he finishes his meal—no matter how poorly—picked the spot is."

"If we get pinned down on the path, we can always resort to the disc if we need it."

Ntashia nodded, but Garvey could see that her mind was elsewhere. Her eyes were hard and her face tight. She held the rifle forward, keenly watching the trail ahead. The climb was long and as they rose higher their view expanded to take in the surrounding land hanging with thick green vapor. Its heaving landscape was a far cry from the flat and parched country they had crossed from the Valley Idor. A man could hardly find room to lie flat in this terrain.

They climbed five-hundred feet into the sky, but met no opposition as they circled the peak time and again. Finally they emerged onto a jagged plateau, and climbed a set of rough-hewn steps to find a stronghold wedged between two cleft promontories. The stronghold itself was carved from a combination of living stone, and heavy blocks of granite cut from that self same peak, and fashioned into a squat building that bristled with shielded crenellations and arrow slits.

A great bronze door cast with the symbol of once-powerful Gredgehold Muvari family stood wide open, the strange bird—carved long ago on the portal—clutching at brass spears and spattered with violet blood.

Ntashia's purple eyes narrowed and she pressed her lips together as she steeled herself for the sight of what was to come. Sword in hand she wheeled around the corner and into the broad stone-tiled foyer—her eyes adjusting to the comparatively dim light. Her feet stepped over dark purple bloodstains and against the walls she found three slumped Muvari women warriors. Garvey followed and surveyed the grim sight, while Ntashia knelt and examined the wounds that had killed the defenders of Gredgehold.

Some of the wounds had been caused by sword blade, others were cauterized holes that only could have been made by an energy weapon pilfered from the cities of the ancients.

"The Warlord Shaxia did this—may her liver be eaten by a hobranx," murmured Ntashia. "Only her torrack warriors have such weapons."

"I thought that the Muvari paid tribute to her, and were still on peaceful terms."

"Perhaps word of Lana's raid on one of her weapons caches reached her, and this is retaliation. Lana said you freed her from the stasis loop, but that the torracks did see you make your escape. It's likely that the Warlord has put together the clues and correctly figured that it was the Muvari who made the raid."

"Can you tell how long these Muvari have been dead?"

"Maybe three days."

"And how many Muvari did Ledgrim generally keep posted here?"

"As many as twenty…as few as a dozen," recalled Ntashia.

Garvey passed by Ntashia and delved farther into the dim halls of Gredgehold, unaware of the small oblong object pasted to the wall about shin level, and of the beam of ultra-violet light through which he passed.

The hall came to a T and Garvey slipped through the melted remains of a portcullis—the twisted and dripping bars, solidified now, evidence of the incredible weaponry that had been brought to bear against the Muvari stronghold.

Behind him, barring the other corridor, was the puddled remains of a second portcullis—stumps of iron protruding from the floor and from the ceiling. Ntashia followed and they found several more bodies strewn about the outpost keep. Life had long since left them all.

They explored the grisly remains of the battle and finally found the lean forms of three slain torracks among the dead on the upper parapets of the fortress.

"That clinches it," said Garvey. "It was the Warlord who did this."

Ntashia nodded somberly as she watched the last bloody finger of sunlight slide below the horizon, and the broad canopy of stars seemed to unroll in the heavens. She had never entertained any doubt that it was aught other than the Warlord Shaxia. "I personally knew many of these warriors—they were my sword sisters."

"I'm sorry," said Garvey. "I should have realized that coming from a tight-knit society like Ledgrim that you would know many of the dead."

"It's not your fault. It's a fact of life on Mars; kill or be killed. Life is often short, and sometimes brutal. How many score Galbran did we behead as they tried to emerge from their cavern?"

"Four or five, probably," figured Garvey with a shrug.

"Do Galbrans mourn their dead?"

"I don't know—but like you said, it is kill or be killed."

"It is, and I'd personally like to see Shaxia's head on the tip of a spear."

Phobos and Deimos glowered in the sky, and for a moment Garvey saw their rays reflected in the sky—glittering movement that traveled in their direction at tremendous speed. Then the forms materialized as Garvey scryed the darkness—fleeting shadows that rode the night like an ocean wave, mounted on shining metallic discs that propelled them through the air with reckless abandon.

"The torracks have returned," said Garvey as his steel rasped from his sheath. "If it's vengeance that you want, now is your chance!"

Chapter Sixteen:
Defense of Gredgehold

March 8, 2007– The Surface of Mars

The double moons shone brightly in the clear sky—so brightly that Bradley Thomas could see the volcano Olympus Mons, and the smoke that spiraled from its glowing maw. Far away, limned in the hellish glow stood the Chinese base camp, and now Bradley looked over the silent encampment from the very spot where he had first spied upon the enemy astronauts.

Shadows lay thick upon the ground, but Bradley knew that a sophisticated sensor array guarded the perimeter of the base and that if he triggered a motion detector or interrupted the beam of an electric eye that the Chinese would immediately be alerted to his presence, and that the American chances for a successful surprise attack would virtually be eliminated.

Bradley lowered a converted Night Owl infrared monocular to the clear glass of his helmet and searched the terrain ahead. The Night Owl sent out a beam of infrared light, which would effectively light his way in the darkest of nights, but he thumbed the infrared beam off and scanned the horizon through the lens. With the infrared light extinguished he normally would see nothing, but the special lens illuminated the Chinese detection system, picking up a series of infrared beams that criss-crossed the landscape.

Bradley spoke into his intercom, addressing Melhoff and Giffen who lurked in the darkness behind him. "Are you both seeing the security beams?"

The two of them also surveyed the rocky hillside and depression with their monoculars.

"Affirmative," answered Melhoff.

Giffen set up a small mechanical unit with rotating antennae on a nearby boulder, and patted it affectionately. "This will bombard the motion detectors with high frequency sound, rendering them ineffective until we slip through the net. The detectors will be unable to detect any change in the bounce of their own sound chirps because they'll be inundated with rapid fire chirps from this baby."

Bradley locked the Night Owl lens into place on his helmet, and took hold of his Swiss built assault rifle fully loaded with a double clip of cartridges. "Good. Step carefully gentleman, and may God be with us all tonight."

"They'll be a good chance that we'll be meeting him tonight," rumbled Melhoff.

"Except for Giffen," chuckled Bradley. "If he doesn't live through the night, he's going to meet Science."

In the face of death, Giffen didn't seem to find this too amusing.

"Hah, very clever," he muttered unenthusiastically.

They crept down the slope of the bowl-like depression, carefully stepping over or ducking under beams of infrared light as they scuttled from boulder to boulder. Bradley took the point, the muzzle of his assault rifle covering the shadows that filled the creases between the domes—domes that glowed with the fiery light of Olympus Mons.

The primary objective of their raid was to disable the Chinese communication array so that they no longer possessed the capability of controlling the orbital nukes around Earth. The second objective was to destroy the Chinese base and China's foothold on Mars. During the planning phase of this mission Bradley put on a bold face with Melhoff and Giffen, but the truth was that he didn't like their chances of succeeding at the second objective. The odds were far too long.

They crept into the shadows beneath the tower and communications array. Bradley stood guard while Giffen and Melhoff cracked open an electronics box bolted to the aluminum frame of the tower.

Melhoff unscrewed the faceplate with a power screwdriver, the screws tumbling to the ground in the low gravity as he let them fall. Giffen was ready with a set of insulated wire cutters, and he went to work as soon as Melhoff pulled the steel plate away. In less than a minute the communications array was severed from the control dome of the Chinese base.

"How long before they notice that we've cut off their communications?" asked Melhoff.

Giffen carefully replaced the cutters in his pack and snapped it closed. "Could be an hour…or they could be noticing it right now."

"And when they do, complete Hell is going to break loose," muttered Melhoff.

"Weapons locked and loaded," ordered Bradley. "We're going in."

Pale-faced, and breathing shallowly Giffen fumbled with his assault rifle as he took the safety off. Giffen and Melhoff's NASA curriculum hadn't included much in the way of weapons training. Bradley had taken them out into the dunes to show them the ropes. They were competent, they knew their weapons, but they were a long way from being hardened warriors. Still, they were game, and that was what counted most now. Bradley hadn't told them they were all going on a suicide mission.

A pang of conscience hit Bradley hard, stopping him in his tracks. Was it absolutely necessary that all three of them died? He raised his left hand in a signal for them to stop.

"What's up?" asked Melhoff.

"There has been a change in plan. We won't be assaulting the Chinese domes together. You two have five minutes to get out of this crater before I start the attack."

"Are you insane?" asked Melhoff. "You can't take out a dozen men by yourself. It's suicide!"

"It is suicide," admitted Bradley, "but it's better that just one of us die than all three. I've got enough firepower to take this place apart by myself. You two get clear. I'll cover you."

Sweat streamed down Giffen's ashen face, his teeth still chattering, but he was clearly relieved to be absolved of his part of the attack. "God bless you, Bradley. I'll always remember this."

"Just say a prayer for me," asked Bradley Thomas.

Giffen nodded fervently. "I'll do that."

Melhoff shook his furry head inside his helmet. "I can't let you do this alone. I'm staying with you. That will leave Giffen to hold down the base until relief arrives."

"I can do this as well myself. I guarantee you that at the very least this transmitter will be blown to so many pieces that it will take another rocket trip from China before it's repairable. In the meantime the relief mission will be here from the United States with a brand new signal amplification unit so we can jam any Chinese transmissions."

Melhoff gripped Bradley by the hand and forearm. "You're a good man.

I'll tell your family that you died a hero."

Bradley felt tears welling in his eyes as his thoughts drifted back to his children. "Thanks. Now get going and let me do this."

Giffen turned and began trotting toward the perimeter, locking his Night Owl monocular into place on his helmet so he could avoid the web of infrared beams. Melhoff hesitated.

"You sure about this?"

"It's gotta be done," growled Bradley. "Now get out of here. That's an order!"

"Give them hell!"

Bradley didn't wait for Giffen and Melhoff to reach the perimeter of the encampment. Instead he leaped upward, taking advantage of the weak Martian gravity to propel himself to the lowest cross beam of the transmission tower. His gloved hands caught hold, and he hoisted himself onto the beam. In the next moments he clambered up the network of cross beams until he was perched a hundred-sixty feet in the air, and with an eagle's eye view of the encampment.

The pouch at his side held a half dozen fragmentation grenades—every bit of explosive power that they had brought with them from earth; three grenades were fixed with rocket propellant for firing, the other two were pin activated. He pressed one of the three rocket propelled grenades into the launcher mounted beneath the barrel of his Swiss SG551. Another he lodged firmly beneath the transmitter mechanism beneath which he crouched. He tied a nylon line from the pin and snapped it to a triangular clip on the back of his suit, allowing for about five feet of slack—it was a suicide trigger to ensure that his mission was a success, even if the Chinese should shoot him from his perch.

Now he crouched with his back against a girder, his assault rifle cradled in his lap. With infrared beam on, he watched the glow of Melhoff and Giffen's bodies as they picked their way through a tangled field of infrared beams, making their way to the slope at the outer edge of the crater.

He turned and watched the airlocks of the domes below. Suddenly, the airlock of the fourth dome hissed open and Bradley saw the glow of a human outline stepping from the closet-sized chamber and onto the dry Martian landscape. Bradley didn't know whether the Chinese astronaut came armed to check for intruders or if he was merely coming to check on the disruption of their communications lines. He couldn't afford to care.

With a snap Bradley brought his rifle up to his eye and adjusted upward to allow for the descending arc of the grenade. He pulled back the trigger and the pop of the launcher echoed in the confines of the crater.

The grenade hit bullseye inside the airlock just before the door slipped shut and a moment later the roof of the fourth dome blew apart in a frenzy of glittering metal plates and licking flame. The oxygen inside the dome fed the fire, fierce flame guttering through the hole, and dark smoke mingling in the dusty sky.

Bradley heard Melhoff's voice in his ear. "What's going on back there?"

"We've been discovered. Make a run for it. I'll cover your backs."

Giffen and Melhoff scrambled forward disregarding the infrared beams, which they were cutting through. An alarm went off somewhere in the complex, and Bradley slammed a second grenade into his launcher, watching the various airlock exits like a hawk.

When the Chinese finally came it wasn't by the dome airlocks, and it took a long moments for Bradley to spot them swarming up from an access hatch hidden in the earth directly below him, at the very base of the communications tower in which he crouched.

Bradley turned sharply, swinging his rifle so that it pointed downward. As he twisted, the Night Owl monocular hit against a beam, knocked loose, and clattered downward, ricocheting from cross member to cross member. Even without the Night Owl, he could still see the enemy, their forms illuminated by the double moons—six of them armed with Chinese-made machine guns. A spatter of light rippled across them as one of the Chinese opened up on the dark figures of Giffen and Melhoff scrambling up over the lip of the depression. Bullets threw up gouts of dust from the earth and ricocheted from nearby rocks, but the two American astronauts scrambled to safety, thankfully throwing themselves down on the earth once they made it over the rim.

The other Chinese astronauts looked upward, alerted by the clatter of the falling monocular. Bradley pointed down through the maze of interlacing cross beams and fired the grenade launcher. Smoke trailed from the grenade as it plunged between the beams and then struck Chih-Hao Fung in the shoulder, blowing him into three pieces. Shrapnel cut through the oxygen suits of three other astronauts, and sent them all tumbling before the force of the explosion. The northwest leg of the tower blew free of its concrete mooring and the tower creaked, swaying beneath Bradley's feet.

Bradley let go of his assault rifle, which dropped to the length of his shoulder strap as he reached out to get a grip on the shaky tower. No sooner did he get hold of a beam than the tower moaned and began to topple. Slowly gaining speed, the tower fell, aluminum breaking and bending as Bradley rode it to the ground. At the last moment he leaped free of the falling behemoth, impacting the ground with gut-wrenching force, and rolling free as a cloud of dirt billowed from beneath the fallen tower.

For a moment Bradley came to his knees, hoping to gain some greater distance between himself and the tower. He had attached a guy line to the planted grenade in case he was shot from the tower by the Chinese, the idea being that when he fell the line would pull the grenade pin and make a mangled mess of the transmitter in the tower. Now he found himself in the unlikely situation of still being alive, and having already pulled the pin.

Before he could get to his feet the grenade went off, a spike of yellow flame that pushed a dust cloud before it. Bradley felt a whoosh of hot air just before a piece of the grenade's shrapnel whirled through the dust and hit his helmet, slicing his cheek and shattering his face plate.

Oxygen gushed out from his suit and he took one last breath of air as bits of glass trickled down his chest.

He squinted his eyes against the billowing dirt and plunged into the midst of its dark turmoil, holding tightly to his SG551. Maybe he could hold his breath for a minute or two. Then it would be over; his mission done. At least he could take satisfaction in the destruction of the transmitter array. He may not have completely succeeded in accomplishing the second objective, but the first had been a smashing success.

Mars, 47,000 B.C.– The Muvari Keep of Gredgehold

Ntashia knelt on the parapet of Gredgehold and threw the redlens plasma rifle to her shoulder. She fired it as if it were a crossbow, hitting the foremost of the torracks square in the chest and burning a hole all the way through his body. For a moment the torrack stood astride his anti-gravity disc, still not realizing that he was a dead man. Then he crumpled and, his feet still bound to the disc, he veered off course, blazing an erratic trail through the sky and into a craggy cliff side.

Garvey snatched up a crossbow from the dead hands of a Muvari warrior and fitted a quarrel from her quiver. He easily pulled back the cable and carefully drew a bead upon the host of incoming torracks.

Though a powerful weapon by medieval standards, the crossbow wasn't on the same level as the rifle that Ntashia was using. While Garvey waited for the torracks to come within range Ntashia burned two more of them from their metallic perches.

Finally Garvey fired. The torrack saw the bolt coming and twisted his thin torso so that his disc began to veer away, but his action came too late and the bolt caught him through the thigh. Screaming and clutching in vain, the torrack lost the delicate control required to fly the disc, and he went spiraling into the dark oblivion of night, his cries echoing against the somber walls of Gredgehold long after he was lost from sight.

Garvey slapped a second quarrel into the crossbow and brought it to bear just as a torrack zoomed toward him, leaning and swinging a wicked scythe. As the American astronaut fell back to avoid the blade he fired his crossbow, burying a quarrel to the feathers in the torrack's narrow chest.

The scythe struck the breastwork behind Garvey's head and shattered, then the disc spun out of control, cartwheeling it and its unfortunate rider across the top of Gredgehold before coming to a halt in an ignominious heap against the far parapet.

During this close call Garvey lost hold of his crossbow, and now he frantically groped for it as silver discs flashed through the air overhead, some dragging entangling nets between them, others sweeping scythes.

Ntashia switched the setting on her rifle and pulled back the trigger as a net whistled through the air toward her. Bolts of plasma slashed through the air, tumbling rider and disc smoking from the sky. Though the torracks that pulled the net were dead, the net came on, wrapping Ntashia up and rolling her across the rooftop as riderless anti-gravity discs clattered about her, and torrack bodies fell in seared heaps.

The stench of burning flesh caught in the wind as Ntashia futilely struggled against the net which enfolded her. She was hopelessly snared, her rifle lost somewhere in the tangled folds. With great effort she worked her hand around to her side and found the sacrificial dagger, which she had taken from the altar in the lost City of Caladrex.

Garvey saw Ntashia picked up by the net and tumbled across the roof. He abandoned the idea of using his crossbow and leapt up, unsheathing his sword as he bounded across the dark stones to Ntashia's side. Anti-gravity discs zoomed overhead, and Garvey lashed out with his Caladrexian forged-steel, slicing through the poles of sweeping scythes, and shearing antigravity discs in two with the marvelous blade.

In a few moments he reached Ntashia and found her sawing through her bonds with the sacrificial knife. It was forged of a similar metal as their swords, and the tough metal-woven strands of the net parted easily.

"Hold on," said Garvey as he joined the effort. He carefully drew the tip of his sword across the strands of the net and they popped apart, springing from the blade as though it were an intense flame. Still, many folds enwrapped Ntashia and it would be more than the work of a few moments to free her.

"Go on," urged Ntashia. "If you stay to free me they'll capture you. Follow them and rescue me from the Warlord when you have a better chance."

"I can't leave you to them," grunted Garvey stubbornly as he continued to work at the net.

"It's too late, anyhow," a baritone voice informed them from behind.

Garvey slowly turned and found a cadre of purple-skinned torracks standing behind them, plasma rifles drawn, their gaping muzzles yawning like black holes. Garvey's eyes scanned the sweat-slicked torsos of the genetically bred warriors, and went to the hollow face of the black-bearded sergeant, whose dark eyes looked mercilessly upon his two captives.

"Give up your weapons now," demanded the sergeant, "or you'll be incinerated by a dozen plasma beams. You have five seconds to decide."

It was really no choice at all; Garvey threw down his sword and a half dozen torracks rushed forward, binding his hands behind his back.

They stripped the armor and weapons from both Garvey and Ntashia and threw the two prisoners half-naked in the center of a great net, which they spread across the rooftop.

The sergeant stood before them, appraising them critically. "I see you both have had the good fortune to stumble across some of the treasures of the Ancient Ones. The Warlord Shaxia will be very interested in speaking with you both. She might be lenient if you disclose just where you came across your armor and weapons."

He turned his attention to Garvey, studying him more closely than made him comfortable. "And you appear to be a functional male. The Warlord always has a great interest in such as you. I may even receive a bonus for tonight's efforts."

"Glad I could be of help," answered Garvey unenthusiastically. An idea occurred to him. "If you found the location of a city of the Ancient Ones would the Warlord Shaxia give you even greater honor?"

Ntashia shot Garvey a hard glance, not sure what he was planning.

"Oh, you'd better believe it. My designation is Number Seven. If I were to come back to her with a location filled with technology of the Old Ones she would likely designate me Number One or Number Two."

"What if we showed you where the city is? Could you let us go free in exchange?"

Number Seven frowned. "You tempt me, but the penalty for losing a prisoner is greater than the reward if I found a city of the Old Ones."

"What penalty is that?" asked Ntashia.

"I would lose my head, Muvari. Just as you will if you keep asking questions." Number Seven turned and shouted out an order to the remaining twelve of what had begun as a cadre of twenty-two. "Take the prisoners up. We fly to Braxenridge!"

Two ends of the net were each tied to an anti-gravity disc, and when they carried their riders aloft, the net folded around the forms of Garvey and Ntashia. They had, perhaps, enough room that they might have climbed the folded net and leaped out the sides or top, but that would result only in a fatal fall—for in moments they were swinging through the night, a dozen discs flashing in the light of the double moons as their riders flew to Braxenridge; the city ruled by the Warlord Shaxia.

The shadowed landscape opened up before them on their pendulous flight—rock and rill giving way to the terrifying depths of the steaming Rift. This they crossed, and they flew over thick forest land, the violet moon-washed leaves fluttering as they passed. They climbed higher, leaving the whispering voices of the leaves behind as they headed toward a rocky butte at the center of the vast forest.

As they drew closer Garvey and Ntashia could make out the pitch outline of a massive castle rising from the butte; built atop the sheer faces of ancient cliffs, the jagged crenellations girding the wall tops and Deimos standing behind, its yellow light like a beacon to the returning torracks.

The soldiers flew their captives up and over the dark walls of Braxenridge, executing a number of sharp turns through the twisting alleys, and taking a perverse pride in narrowly missing the bulbous roofs and sharp spires as the net and its captives swung perilously close.

Ntashia and Garvey threw their weight to various sides of the net as they tried to reduce the momentum that might take them crashing into the side of a stone wall or beaten copper roof and crush them to an oozing pulp.

"Apparently they've forgotten how badly they wanted to question us," said Ntashia through grimaced teeth.

Garvey threw his weight to the right as they swung within a hair's breadth of a cupola crawling with crimson ivy. He wished he had a knife to cut through the net so that he and Ntashia might make a leap to one of those sloping roofs, but he had nothing left but flesh and sinew—and the net resisted his mighty efforts to pull apart the filaments. His palms showed bloody red lines where the net cut into his flesh. It was useless.

Now the discs rocketed upward with the net in tow, the stonework masonry of the castle's largest tower looming before them as they climbed to the top. The torracks dropped the net roughly to the flat roof of the tower, sending Garvey and Ntashia sprawling, only to be further entangled in the net.

Before they could make any effort to disentangle themselves from their prison a dozen torracks sprang forward from the crenels at the edges of the tower, thrusting their spears through the gaps in the net so that the steel points pricked the prisoners' skin.

"Don't move, skelks—unless you want a spear point through your heart!"

Garvey hissed as a point jabbed into his forearm. "I'm not moving, idiot!"

The silver discs of their captors flitted through the moonlight and hovered to a landing. Coils snaked back into their hatches, releasing the feet of the riders, and Number Seven strode across the rooftop shouting orders.

"Don't kill them! The Warlord will want to question these!"

The torracks fell back, apparently acquiescing to Number Seven's superior rank.

"You nearly splattered us against the side of a building three or four times," said Ntashia angrily as she struggled to pull herself free of the net. "And now you are worried about keeping us alive for questioning?"

Number Seven laughed heartily. "We've negotiated those city corridors a thousand times. You were in no real danger!"

"I, somehow, doubt that," muttered Ntashia, recalling how close they had come to meeting a wall head on.

The tall, lean bodies of the torracks surrounded the two prisoners, and at spear point they marched into the bowels of the tower, a trap door clanking open as two guards cranked a double chain onto a large spool.

The torracks' march was strangely synchronous—the group falling into step without so much as a word from Number Seven. No orders were needed, but yet they knew exactly what was expected of them.

Garvey felt like a midget among the host of purple-skinned bodies that uniformly reached the height of seven feet tall. His wide shoulders, and thick chest drew a sharp contrast to the narrow-bodied, lean-armed torracks that looked positively fragile when compared to a physique used to the pressures of Earth's gravity. If it weren't for the spear points that hovered about them Garvey would have taken a chance on battling his way free…despite the outrageous odds.

They descended through high-ceilinged halls and antechambers decorated with shield, sword, and scythe, and followed broad steps that circled around the inside of the tower until they entered through a vast portal, the great doors of ascarna wood thrown wide open. Flanking the opening were two identical statues of a beautiful woman, granite thighs set wide, and sword upraised in victory, a shield resting against her booted leg, and a mass of hair falling from beneath a carven helmet that concealed all but a magnificent set of bee-stung lips.

They crushed the vermilion carpet beneath their feet as they stepped into the great hall filled with blazing light from hovering glow lamps stolen from the technology hordes of the Ancients. The ceiling soared overhead, supported by great black beams of close-grained timber, and tapestries depicting the greatness of the Warlord Shaxia fell thick along the walls.

All about the room, gathered in knots, supplicants from many tribes knelt with their offerings. Two spear-bearing women stood directly before the gold and silver throne dressed in glittering bangles and ruby-studded bandeaux.

Their skin was dusky, and their eyes dark as they surveyed the groveling subjects that fell before the might of the Warlord.

Astride the throne, bare legs thrown over the cushioned armrest, and supple body reclined with head supported on crooked elbow was the Warlord Shaxia. Upon arrival of Garvey and Ntashia the bored expression passed from her face and she sat upright on her great throne, leaning forward with interest as she motioned a slender finger toward Garvey.

Her voice was husky as she spoke, her full lips pursing as she examined the astronaut. "Bring the man here so I may take a closer look."

Raven hair glowed with purple highlights beneath the lamps of the Ancients as the Warlord Shaxia stood, her silken skirt falling high on her thighs, and her yellow eyes glowing like embers.

Number Seven ushered Garvey forward and the astronaut moved only with a backward glance at Ntashia who shrugged slightly, unsure of what this meant to their chances of survival. Like Ntashia, Garvey was bound hand and foot, and he moved forward with a series of shuffling steps, Number Seven's spear point pricking him beneath the shoulder blades the entire time.

Shaxia circled Garvey, licking her lips. "An interesting specimen; far too squat, but I've never seen limbs and torso built so powerfully."

"Are you fully functional?" she asked.

Garvey didn't understand what she was asking. "I suppose so."

"He supposes so!" laughed Shaxia boisterously. "Well, I suppose I will just have to find out for myself later on this evening."

Shaxia's spear bearers glowered sullenly, and Garvey raised an eyebrow as the connotations of the warlord's question dawned on him. He remembered that the same question had been put to him by Lana, when ascertaining if he would be of value to the Muvari Tribe. The torracks, she had informed him, were genetic aberrations designed by the Warlord Shaxia to be warriors only—and not equipped for reproduction.

Garvey glanced at Ntashia and could see her purple eyes seething with anger. Her arms strained at her bonds, but she did not have the strength to work her way free.

Number Seven glanced backward and as if reading his mind several torracks bearing the equipment stripped from Garvey and Ntashia came forward, and bending low, deposited it at the Warlord's sandaled and manicured feet for her examination. They scuttled backward ten feet, faces in the carpet before uprighting themselves.

"Ah, Number Seven!" cooed Shaxia, "you bring me gifts from the treasuries of the Ancients! Tell me, where did you find these?"

She picked up the redlens plasma rifle first, studying it with great admiration.

"This man and the woman were carrying these when we captured them at the Muvari outpost of Gredgehold."

"Really!" She turned to Garvey. "Where did you find these?"

"We stole them from the Galbran," lied Garvey.

"The Galbran!" shrieked Shaxia. "Those hideous, malformed lumps of skelk dung aren't smart enough to have uncovered these!"

Garvey shrugged as if it made no difference to him what she believed. "So I thought myself, but there they were when we were escaping from their lair."

"Their lair, you say?" Shaxia's yellow eyes burned suspiciously. "What were you doing in their lair?"

"Trying to avoid becoming a meal, mostly. Ntashia and I were captured in a Galbran raid on Ledgrim. We were lucky enough to escape from their larder."

"You lie!" hissed Shaxia. "Your story becomes more unbelievable all the time."

She turned her glare on Ntashia. "You were there when you found these weapons and armor?"

"Yes," answered Ntashia simply, but hatred burned in her eyes.

"And where did you find them?"

"In the lair of the Galbran," said Ntashia emphatically.

Shaxia turned her bare back on her captives, and with a toss of her hand climbed the steps back to her throne. "We shall see soon enough. Take the woman for interrogation. Fit the man with a subjugation collar, then chain him in my bedchamber."

Chapter Seventeen:
Fugitives of Braxenridge

March 8, 2007– Mars, Chinese Base

Bradley's lungs screamed for air, but he knew that to give in and take a breath of Mars's nitrogen-thick atmosphere would mean only death. As he struggled through the billowing smoke and scathing clouds of sand thrown up by his own grenades, a moment of clarity came to him.

Blackness crept in around the edges of his sand-flung vision, and he sank to his knees, his fingers fumbling for the sheathed knife on his left leg. He found the knife and yanked it free. Bradley knew that his oxygen supply was being pumped in from a tank built into the back of his containment suit. This oxygen, however, was pouring out the gaping hole in the faceplate of his helmet, and being replaced by nitrogen faster than it could be pumped.

Bradley stuck his knife in the sand between his knees and with numb fingers he pried loose the helmet and tossed the useless thing aside. Now, with a bit of increased mobility he reached behind his head, between his shoulders and found the thick, corrugated rubber tube that fed him the vital oxygen he needed so badly. With his other hand, he took hold of his knife and cut the hose, which he wrapped around the side of his cheek and clamped between his teeth.

He took a deep breath of the life-giving oxygen and exhaled through his nose repeating the process for about a minute until he regained his equilibrium. The sand was settling now, but as Bradley rose a thick haze still hung in the air. He knew that he had to find the hatch through which the Chinese astronauts had exited at the base of the now-toppled communications tower. If he could make his way inside the complex he might have a chance of finishing off the Chinese. If he didn't, chances are they would form a retaliatory party and go after Giffen and Melhoff, and he didn't give his fellow astronauts much chance against a bloodthirsty killer like Xio Cheng.

Sucking on his air tube, Bradley made his way through the smoldering wreckage, and climbed through a screen of twisted metal to find the still open hatch that led down into a dark access tunnel. He pushed aside the broken and bloody body of a Chinese astronaut and lowered himself down the aluminum rungs into the cool air below.

Dim lighting strips illuminated his way, and Bradley could see that the tunnel was constructed with material salvaged from a one-way relief mission that had arrived from China about a year ago. Panels from the ship were bent and reformed to construct the arcing walls of the corridor, and then welded to seal in the atmosphere.

There was nothing but nitrogen in the air now, though, and Bradley continued to breath through his tube as he negotiated the corridor, passing beneath the earth until he reached the end of the tunnel. An airtight hatch was situated in the ceiling above, and Bradley worked the wheel until he heard the hiss of escaping atmosphere.

He lifted his Swiss SG551 and used his earthly muscles to propel himself up through the hatch in one mighty bound. The oxygen gushed out behind him as he landed inside a small room, and found himself surrounded by bristling machine guns.

Xio Cheng's thin lips moved beneath his drooping mustache as his bony finger tightened on the trigger of his gun. "So, finally, the Americans come—skulking like dogs in the night!"

In addition to Xio, behind the machine guns Bradley recognized the sallow faces of Dong-Soo Hwon, and Kien Kuong—both highly regarded astronauts and pilots—and the fighter pilot Yew Lun, who had caused a collision with a U.S. spy plane in international territory about eight years prior.

Bradley let his left hand drift to the grenade at his belt, his right hand firmly holding the gravity-lightened machine gun aloft. "Drop your weapons and I'll let you live!"

"You'll let us live?" mocked Yew Lun, his sharp features tightening with a predatory fierceness.

"In case your eyesight is as poor as your intelligence, let me remind you that you are outnumbered four guns to one," said Xio. "And there is nowhere for you to disappear like that astronaut Stechter!"

Bradley didn't know what Xio Cheng was getting at, but he chalked it up to the Chinese astronaut's thick accent. "No one's disappearing, Xio. And let's get this straight. I have no illusions about living through this. All four of you are going to die, and so am I! The only way that won't happen is if you all lay your weapons down right now."

Mars 47,000 B.C– The Castle of the Warlord Shaxia

Ntashia grimaced as the torracks tightened the metal halo around her head. Already her slim wrists were strapped to a metal chair, and her torso cinched to the skeletal chair back via a leather strap passing just below her breasts. The two torracks that assisted in her preparation for interrogation were older—some of the lucky few that outlived their maximum efficacy as warriors and were assigned to some other post as a reward for their long service. Still, they were engineered to be warriors, and they didn't have the brain power for the more delicate operations involved in using a device that had obviously been pilfered from the Ancients.

Number 283 turned to his fellow torrack as they looked at the jumble of cords, which needed to be connected to the halo that hovered around Ntashia's forehead. The halo periodically flashed beams of light at her skull as if probing for weaknesses.

"We must go interrupt Sar Savaht so that he can properly perform the ritual."

The second torrack nodded effusively and they scuttled through a steel doorway, leaving Ntashia in the encroaching gloom that filled each corner of the barely-lit chamber in which they had her imprisoned. She didn't know what had befallen Garvey. The torracks had separated them immediately after they had been taken from the throne room. She had seen the lust sparking in Shaxia's eyes and she had only too strong of an idea of how the Warlord might utilize Garvey.

It burned Ntashia's blood to imagine how Shaxia might use her betrothed, and she only wished that she could find a way out of her own predicament so that she could track down and rescue Garvey. For ten minutes Ntashia seethed helplessly, then the torracks returned with a wizened old man who was not one of Shaxia's genetically altered warriors.

"We need you to perform the ritual," said 283.

"Yes, yes," muttered Sar Savaht to himself as he carefully examined each mass of connectors before plugging them into an elliptical console in front of the torracks. He waved his hands a couple of times in nonsensical gestures as if to appease the torrack's desire for a ritual, and then turned to gaze briefly upon Ntashia.

"Such a beautiful young girl," he muttered. "It's a shame that Shaxia has taken a disliking to you. This machine will extract whatever memories Shaxia is trying to find. Unfortunately, it is quite painful. Perhaps, it is not too late to tell Shaxia what she needs to know?"

Ntashia shook her head emphatically. "The future of my tribe depends upon this secret. It would be better if I die than my lips utter what I have found. Is there no way to defeat this machine?"

Sar Savaht shook his head sadly. "I am afraid not, my dear young lady. This is a device of the Ancients that probes the neural pathways and deciphers the magnetic resonations, uncovering the memories stored there. It is quite fool proof... unless you have had some exposure to other memory devices of the Ancients? Sometimes those inadvertently block the same neural pathways which are used by this very device."

Ntashia shook her head. "You seem like a kindly man. Is there nothing you can do to save me?"

The scientist frowned, his rheumy eyes drooping. "I am afraid not. Long ago I made a deal with the devil. Shaxia is my master and in return I am allowed to explore the scientific mysteries of the Ancients. Sadly, I have no real power here."

Sar Savaht turned and shuffled out the door leaving the two gleeful torracks, who grinned maliciously as they set the dials on the elliptical console.

"This will be quite painful," 283 assured Ntashia, his beady eye glowing with a dangerous fervor.

Garvey's hands and legs were chained. The thick metal collar around his neck served as more than just a leash, but it was also a technology of the Ancients—used to painfully remind prisoners and servants of their proper place.

A lean torrack with burn scars deforming his face inspected the last lock after he snapped the final shackle into place. The other four torracks lowered their weapons as the locksmith backed away, apparently satisfied that Garvey could pose no threat now.

A fifth guard entered the room bearing an arm load of Ntashia and Garvey's stripped weapons and armor, and crossed the fur-strewn floor to carefully place them in the far corner of the vast bedchamber near a rack of spears and swords and a large gong that hung with a leather-wrapped mallet.

Garvey eyed the pile covetously, wishing that he could find someway to reach them. The burned locksmith followed his gaze, and grinned foully as he pressed a pyramid-shaped device in his hand.

Immediately, pain poured from the collar that Garvey wore, spreading down his nerves like fire until his entire body was burning with a torture so incredible that the astronaut could not even force himself to take a breath of air. Finally, when Garvey thought his body would explode into scraps of flesh, the locksmith eased his thumb away from the pyramidal device and the pain ceased—leaving the American bathed in sweat and gasping for air.

"You'd best be advised, slave," warned the locksmith, "to obey the Warlord's wishes implicitly. For this will be constantly in her hand should you fail to please her."

Garvey couldn't manage a reply, but he got the picture vividly. Should the locksmith have continued the pain for just a few moments more he would have lapsed into unconsciousness. If the pain had continued for much longer beyond that he would have expired, his seized lungs unable to take another breath.

The torracks departed the bedchamber leaving Garvey alone to ponder on his predicament. Obviously Shaxia was used to having her way with male prisoners. These restraint devices, he was sure, hadn't been installed solely for his benefit. They had been put into use many times before. He found that his chains allowed him enough slack to roam the large bed to which he was shackled, but they did not allow him any farther.

The locksmith had set the pyramid on an ornate table of chiseled wood beside the single entrance. Garvey figured that if he could reach this and destroy it he might have a better chance fending off Shaxia's advances. The chains however held him fast to the bed, and the table was a good thirty feet away.

Straining his earth-borne muscles he pressed both legs against the wall in back of the bed, and pulled against the lock. The chain, the lock, and the stanchion in the wall all held tight, showing no signs of giving.

Though there were various weapons in racks and adorning the walls around the room, none were close enough that Garvey might lay a hold of them and beat against his shackles. He hated to admit it, but he was at

Shaxia's mercy.

Now he turned his attention to the bed, wondering if there might be something here that he could turn to his advantage. The bed was constructed from a great iron frame, its legs bolted firmly to the floor. Above the floor, on this frame lay great mattresses stuffed with feathers, covered with silken sheets and animal skins, and strewn with crimson-tasseled cushions.

Garvey took one of these sheets and began twisting it into a long rope, tying it with torn strips so that it would not unwind. When he finished he tied a noose on one end, and dragged himself to the end of the bed. He certainly possessed little enough in the way of lariat skills, but that wasn't going to stop him from trying.

His makeshift rope was just long enough to reach the table by the door, but he cast it a number of times—unable to land the noose about the pyramidal control device that lay on its polished surface. With the chains weighing down his limbs it was difficult to make a decent cast, and the rope tended to fall short of the target.

He was about to make another attempt when he heard footsteps down the hall. He thrust the rope coil beneath an overlarge cushion and backed away so that he was no longer sitting at the edge of the bed. No sooner had he settled back when the Warlord Shaxia threw open the door to her chamber, flanked by her duo of dusky-skinned female bodyguards.

Shaxia plucked up the pyramid of which Garvey had been so desperately trying to get a hold. "This produces the most hideous pain known to Martian," she said. "Displease me and you shall feel that pain time and again. Please me and perhaps I will let you live to further serve me."

"No pressure," muttered Garvey.

Shaxia tossed the pyramid to her left hand guard, a sloe-eyed woman who studied Garvey darkly as she caressed the device. "My handmaid, Thracia, will administer the pain if she perceives that I am threatened in the slightest."

The Warlord drew nearer, her bosom heaving as she lifted a mass of raven hair. She leaned over and began to crawl across the bed toward Garvey, the pale threads of many a scar crossing the supple skin of her body, and yellow eyes burning hot.

Despite the woman's great beauty, Garvey felt a wave of revulsion pass through him. Her physical appearance was deception—beneath the stunning façade was a monster ravenous with power, greed, and bloodlust.

Garvey leaned back, thrusting his hands beneath the strewn cushions.

"Ah," said Shaxia, taking this as an act of submission. "Where should I start?" She placed a hand on Garvey's thigh, moving yet closer until he could feel her hot breath on his body.

Number 283 adjusted the dial on the ancient mind reading device and watched the muddle of imagery that swirled on the holographic projector. "Begin the probe 462!"

With bland expression, the torrack studied the dials in front of him. "The probe has already begun."

"Then why aren't we seeing her memory paths? You'd better go fetch Sar Savaht. Perhaps the ritual was done improperly."

The torrack leaped to his feet and ran out the door of the dim chamber, while the other tugged nervously at his thin beard, helplessly watching the dials of the ancient device spin out of control.

Ntashia writhed beneath her halo, flashing lights spinning forth and probing her skull, attempting to plumb the neural pathways. Though her thoughts were fragmented and disjointed, Ntashia fought the machine, her shackled arms straining against their imprisonment, and her mind screaming for relief.

Her braids flailed as her head vibrated beneath the intense pressures exerted by the neural probes. Still, the three-dimensional holograph showed nothing but a garble of conflicting images; fleeting depictions that swirled and twisted surreally, and fell into a vortex of jumbled scenes.

Ntashia's body shook and spasmed, the chair rattling and the lynch pin that held her right hand shackled, jumping up and down. For one moment it leaped high and Ntashia forced her arm to move upward, slamming the manacles open and sending the loose pin flying across the room.

With every bit of concentration that she could muster she reached up and tore the halo from her head, hurling it across the room so that it shattered, exploding into a shower of sparks and flashing light. Ntashia reached across and freed her left arm, and then with trembling limbs she lurched to her feet.

As soon as torrack 283 looked up from his instrumentation his hand went to the dagger at his side, but Ntashia was already leaping over the console. Her bodyweight tipped him backward in his chair and his skull connected hard with the stone floor, Ntashia riding him all the way.

The torrack went limp, his mouth wide open as violet blood trickled along the grout lines of the floor. Shaky and queasy, Ntashia rose to her feet over the dead body of her inquisitor. She bent and pried the torrack's fingers loose from the hilt of his knife and took it for her own.

As if exhibiting anger at Ntashia's escape the equipment behind her let out a continuous high-pitched squeal. She ignored the noise and stumbled to the door, then broke into an unsteady gait as she negotiated the long and shadow-spun hallway beyond. When they had brought her to interrogation she had paid close attention to the twists and turns of the halls and stairways. Now she retraced those steps in the hopes of returning to the throne room of the Warlord Shaxia. She recalled the corridor where she and Garvey had been separated, and down which passage they had dragged the American. Maybe, just maybe she would be in time to avert the warlord's lecherous plan.

At first the hallways were empty and she encountered no opposition, but as she climbed higher in the vast tower and drew closer to the throne room the patrols of torracks became more frequent, and more difficult to avoid. To escape the attention of an oncoming patrol she slipped into a narrow alcove and pressed deep into the shadows.

The designers of the tower meant this alcove, and the matching alcove on the opposite side of the hall, to be a defensive position in case the enemy breached the outer walls and were climbing higher into the tower. Now, the alcove was empty and Ntashia used it to her advantage, slipping into the cool umbra that cloaked her still-trembling limbs. She clutched her dagger tightly as the footsteps sounded louder in the hall, and watched a squad of six torracks march by, oblivious to her presence.

She waited until the sound of their steps receded and then ducked back into the hallway. Finally she reached the four-way intersection where she and Garvey had been torn apart, and she marked the broken tooth on the gargoyle over one of the arches before plunging into the carpeted corridor. Without detour the hall ran directly to a thick portal equipped with a massive brass handle and lock. The casing of the doorway was thick with scrolled woodwork.

Ntashia paused then carefully checked the door handle to see if the portal was locked. The door latch held firmly. She leaned against the cool stone of the wall, and considered her next course of action, when the sound of a terrible struggle within the locked room came to her ears.

The Warlord Shaxia crept nearer, her breath coming in soft pants of anticipated pleasure. Thracia stood by in her glittering bodice, watching intently with the pyramidal pain device gleaming in her open palm. Braza bared a dagger and perched herself on the edge of the bed.

Shaxia's palm slid higher on his leg and Garvey pulled the coiled rope from its hiding place beneath the cushions. Before Shaxia or Thracia could react he looped the noose around the Warlord's neck and cinched it tight. In the same movement he yanked the rope with all his Earthling strength and hurled Shaxia from the bed. Shaxia struck Thracia hard and they went down in a tangle of flailing limbs, the metallic pyramid clanking as it cart-wheeled across the stone floor and came to rest upon a striped skin of purple and gold.

While the warlord disentangled herself from her handmaiden Garvey turned to see Braza lunging at him with upraised dagger, her lips pulled back in a snarl that revealed the white teeth beneath. Garvey snapped out with the chain that bound his right arm, so that the links undulated forward and took Braza in the side of the face. She cried out and fell to the bedside, clutching at her cheek, her dagger temporarily abandoned among the scented pillows of the bed.

Garvey reached out and snatched this blade up, turning his attention back to the tangle of bodies on the opposite side of the bed. Shaxia's lithe form was stretched out, her hand reaching for the pyramid.

The astronaut knew that his chains would not allow him enough slack to reach her before she recovered the control device, so he lifted his arm and hurled the dagger.

Shaxia glanced up and saw the blade whirling toward her. With battle-honed reflexes she cast up her left arm and deflected the point of the blade with the metallic bracer that she wore on her wrist. Her dark hair writhed about her as she rolled across the skins and plucked up the pyramid.

"You'll die for that, you insolent slug!" She pressed a geometric outline on the pyramid and sudden, horrendous pain poured into Garvey's body. His back arched as he fell spasming into the sheets, unable to lift a finger of his own accord as indescribable pain burned through each fiber of his body. His very eyes seemed afire, as though they might incinerate in his skull—and he prayed for a quick and merciful death.

Ntashia thrust the point of her purloined dagger into the keyhole and kicked the pommel. It knocked the blade deep into the lock, and she twisted the hilt as she put her shoulder against the door. Metal ground against crumbling stone and Ntashia forced her way inside the room to find Garvey's form convulsing on a wide cushion-strewn bed, his trembling lips unable to form the scream of pain that caught in his throat.

Her eyes quickly took in the kneeling form of Braza, clutching at her injured face, the exposed figure of the Warlord Shaxia, dark hair swaying as she worked the device in her hand, and her handmaiden, Thracia, who was still on her hands and knees, regaining her feet.

Ntashia was weaponless, her dagger hopelessly entrenched in the lock, but as she glanced around at the accoutrements of the bedchamber she could see plenty of weapons at hand.

Shaxia whirled at Ntashia's unexpected entrance. "Thracia, summon the guards!"

Thracia stumbled to her feet and across the room to the great gong that hung on a wooden frame. Ntashia took this opportunity to whirl and grab a scimitar from the wall on her right. The Warlord Shaxia, also, wasted no time in arming herself, and she slipped a round shield studded with spikes onto her right arm, and hoisted a wicked sickle with the left.

She rolled the pyramid across the carpeted floors, and to Thracia's sandaled feet as her handmaiden picked up the mallet and struck the gong, the shivering tones echoing through the tower.

Again and again Thracia struck as Shaxia advanced upon the Muvari intruder, her wary eyes burning yellow while she sized up her opponent. As the air vibrated with the clashing of the gong, their sword blades licked out like adders then sprang apart. Again and again they met in a deadly dance. One would feint and glide in for the kill while the other would dance away and launch a counterstroke, only to have their blade parried in the nick of time.

As Garvey slowly gained his addled senses, still rendered helpless by the pain wracking his body, he saw the splendid figures of the two warriors in their dance of death. Ntashia fought in a whirl of pale braids, while the raven nimbus of the Warlord Shaxia's hair floated about her head and shoulders. Both women possessed incredible skill, and their swordplay baffled the eye. Thus far Garvey had relied on sheer strength and speed to see him through his many violent encounters on Mars, but these two fought with such subtlety that he doubted his ability to last even a minute against either of them in a fair sword fight. These were a far cry from the untutored and unskilled Galbran hordes, which he had faced.

Ntashia's purple eyes were complete concentration as she faced the most skilled swordswoman on Mars. The Warlord Shaxia was famed for her ability to face and kill three or four foes at a time, and Ntashia found herself consistently on the defensive. The attacks came so swiftly and so unexpectedly that she scarcely had time to fend off one before the blade retreated and flickered toward her again.

She fought with skill and not a little desperation, marshalling all her knowledge and prowess to fend against the whispering attacks that hissed through the air. Ntashia realized that the Warlord was driving her back toward the gong, and Shaxia's handmaid, Thracia, who still held the mallet in her hands.

Shaxia pressed so hard that Ntashia was forced to take a series of quick steps backward to avoid the Warlord's slithering blade, and she knew that as soon as she was in range Thracia would strike her down with a blow from behind. At the last moment, Ntashia retreated with an extra bit of unexpected speed and with scarcely a glance behind she lashed out behind herself, catching the unready Thracia in the side of the head.

As Thracia's form crumpled against the gong, muting its riotous quaverings, Ntashia found herself amid a web of Shaxia's deadly blade. Shaxia's sword, the Muvari could see, was forged of the ancients, and it was rapidly destroying the scimitar, which Ntashia had snatched down from the wall. Even now the blade of the scimitar was scored with many a notch where she had parried Shaxia's superior sword. At any moment the scimitar would be shattered and she would be defenseless against the warlord's attacks.

With locked and seizing muscles screaming out in protestation, Garvey pulled himself along the bed to the length of his chains. He lay on his chest, stretching out his quivering arm toward the pile of Shaxia's discarded clothing at the foot of the bed. Finally his fingers fell upon the glittering band of a jeweled girdle, and with intense effort he dragged it toward him, and fumbled among the straps and pouches. The sound of steel upon steel fell upon his ears as he searched, but in a few moments his numbed fingers fell upon a brass key.

As Ntashia twisted aside from a well-aimed sword thrust her foot struck against a pile near the base of the gong. A quick glance disclosed that the pile consisted of the armor and weapons that had been stripped from she and Garvey upon their capture by Shaxia's torracks. Their Caladrexian forged swords lay glittering at the top.

Going into a crouch, Ntashia hurled her scimitar upward toward Shaxia's chin. The Warlord fell back two steps to avoid being sliced open by the whirling blade, but still it caught her on the cheek, cutting a narrow furrow of violet. Ntashia used her brief respite to retrieve the straight blade at her feet.

Before she could rise, Shaxia was upon her, angrily driving her back down with a furious blow. Ntashia raised her blade and parried, the Caladrexian steel cutting through Shaxia's sword so that it shattered into three pieces. Rising in a storm of scattering metal, Ntashia swung upward, the tip of her sword blade glancing along Shaxia's left rib cage and sending her reeling to the ground.

Ntashia's lithe figure loomed over the fallen body of Shaxia who raised only the shattered hilt of her sword as a pitiful defense. As the Muvari lifted her sword to smite the Warlord with a final deadly blow, she heard Garvey's chains rattle as the unlocked shackles fell from his limbs. Then she was perplexed to see a flicker of a smile cross Shaxia's lips.

While Garvey had freed himself from his chains Thracia rose staggeringly from her crumpled heap at the base of the gong, and blood streaming down her face, sneaked up behind Ntashia. Garvey tried to cry out, but his vocal cords were still paralyzed from the torture he had undergone.

As soon as the last shackle fell from his ankle Garvey coiled his legs beneath him and once more defied Martian gravity as he hurled himself across the intervening space between him and Shaxia's handmaiden. He hurtled by Ntashia, and bore Thracia to the ground as if he were a 350-pound linebacker sacking a quarterback, the handle of Thracia's mallet beating futilely against his broad back.

Garvey rose on his left arm, and struck her with his right fist. Thracia's head snapped and her eyes rolled back into her skull as she lapsed into unconsciousness.

With a groan Garvey rolled from Thracia's body and onto the fur-covered floor, this brief bit of exertion sapping his shallow reserves of strength and energy. Now Ntashia turned back to finish her quarry and found Shaxia scrambling toward the door on hands and knees. Before Ntashia could intercept her, the Warlord regained her feet and sprinted into the hall.

Ntashia moved to follow, but when she reached the portal she quickly changed her mind. A tide of torracks surged down the hallway, pausing only as they met the retreating Shaxia. Bolstered by these reinforcements the Warlord halted her flight and paused to remove a sword from the wall. Newly armed, she shouted orders to the torracks, who came pouring down the hall—lean bodies glistening and blades flashing as war cries howled from their green-tinged lips.

Chapter Eighteen:
The Laboratory of Sar Savaht

August 23, 2000– Mars U.S. Space Station

Sweat poured down Arnold Stechter's face as he looked into the cold, dark eyes of Xio Cheng. Cheng aimed his rifle, licking his thin lips and the edges of his drooping mustache as he pulled back the trigger to execute the hapless American astronaut.

He fired a three-round burst with his Chinese assault rifle, and the bullets punched through Stechter's space suit, oxygen atmosphere bursting out in milky trails. Suddenly Arnold Stechter's body seemed to fold in on itself as though he were an origami man, and in a blink of the eye he was gone—leaving nothing but whitish wisps of vapor behind.

The seven-millimeter bullets from the rifle punched through the far wall of the dome. Cheng rapidly blinked his eyes as if to clear the hallucination away, then craned his neck, searching the room for some sign of his quarry. There was little place to hide in the close confines. Cheng searched every inch of the place, finally getting down on his hands and knees to see if there was some sort of trap door in the floor of the dome, through which Stechter might have escaped.

Sweat dripped from his brow, across his narrow lips and down his razor chin. There was no sign of the American astronaut, and for the life of him he could not figure out where Stechter had gone.

Mars 47,000 B.C– The Bed Chamber of the Warlord Shaxia

As the screaming tide of torracks rushed down the hall Ntashia spun away from the door and to a rack of weapons. To face such incredible numbers by herself would bring sure doom unless she could find some way to even the odds, and here were the prime picks of the Ancients' technology troves. She plucked up a silvered rifle of black gunmetal and hastily found a button beneath a ring guard. She thrust the gaping snout of the rifle down the hallway and depressed the button. Flame rolled down the hallway, filling every square inch. The torrack's cries of horror were extinguished as the intense heat cascaded over them. Sweat poured down Ntashia's body as the incinerating heat reflected from the stone walls. The flame died, leaving fifty feet of nothing but blowing ashes eddying in the heat. Just beyond the blackened corridor, melted shields still dripping from the walls, the Warlord Shaxia glared from hooded eyes.

Shaxia didn't spend time bemoaning the loss of forty of her torracks; they were nothing but numbers to her, but her pride had been stung by her defeat at the Muvari's hands. To assuage that sting she would readily sacrifice a hundred…even a thousand of her neutered soldiers.

"Squad Seven," she hissed.

The soldiers of Squad Seven shouldered to the front of the pack and presented themselves to their warlord—ten proud torracks in oiled harnesses adorned with buckles of silver and gold. Shaxia knew that she was sending them to their death, but she didn't blink as she gave the order.

"Captain, I want your squad to charge my chambers. Send your men one at a time and at five second intervals."

The captain crossed his right arm and clasped his left shoulder in a salute, nodding his head in deference. "It will be done!"

Shaxia knew from experience that the weapons of the Ancients often held a limited amount of charges. Some could be used only once or twice before they became useless pieces of shiny metal, and others fired up to a hundred or more times. Only the scientist Sar Savaht had any success at predicting how many times a weapon might fire, and this due to his extensive studies of the Ancients' technologies.

The first torrack drew his blade and upon the command of his captain he charged down the hallway. He nearly reached the doorway at the end when the second soldier started his headlong sprint toward death.

Ntashia, crouched low at the edge of the doorframe, fired the rifle and flame blossomed from its dark maw, consuming the two soldiers and casting them instantly into an outline of hazy ash that drifted to the floor.

The third torrack charged across the hot floor, flinging himself through the char still hanging in the air. When he got within ten feet of the doorway, Ntashia fired again instantly cremating the soldier in mid stride. They came one after the other, giving no chance for respite, and steadily draining the charges in Ntashia's flamethrower.

While Ntashia kept the torracks at bay, Garvey took the time to clothe his still trembling limbs with the armor he had taken from the ancient vault in the City of Caladrex. Once he had pulled on the sparkling mesh he belted on his sword and hoisted Ntashia's plasma rifle. He staggered across the room and joined Ntashia at the doorway, lowering the snout of the rifle.

Already Ntashia had cremated two full squads of torracks, and a third was working up their courage to make a suicide charge down the hallway.

"They're sitting just out of range of my weapon and sending torracks down the hallway one at a time," said Ntashia.

"That Shaxia is as clever as the Devil himself," answered Garvey, "but this ought to throw her for a loop. These plasma rifles shoot for miles."

The holographic construct, Sved, had promised them a thousand shots from the rifle. Now was a good time to find out if he had been telling the truth or telling another of his clever lies. Ntashia cleared the way with another incinerating blast of heat and Garvey opened up with the plasma rifle. Rapid-fire beams lanced down the hallway, single shots slicing through seven or eight torracks at a time.

Shaxia scrambled into the safety of a niche as a beam burned across her shoulder blade. In under a minute's time Garvey burned through half of his magazine, and the corridor was carpeted with the smoldering bodies of nearly a hundred torracks. Only a few survived, lurching into the safety of a niche or ducking around the wall at the end of the corridor.

"Get your armor on," said Garvey. "I'll keep watch here."

Ntashia nodded and after leaning her flamethrower against the wall retreated to the pile of armor near the base of the gong. In a few minutes time she attired herself in the Caladrexian garb while Garvey held vigil at the door.

The stench of burnt flesh wafted down the corridor, but all was quiet except for the occasional groan of the dying. A torrack leaned from around the corner of the hallway a good hundred feet away. His rifle chirped and hazy blue beams flashed, slicing a trio of holes through the door to Shaxia's bedchamber.

Garvey hissed. It had only been a matter of time before Shaxia's torracks pulled out the ancient weaponry from some cache within the tower. He fired back, sending plasma bolts ricocheting off the stone wall, inches away from the torrack firing upon him. The torrack ducked his head back behind the wall, and Garvey waited and watched. Soon gunmen were popping out from both sides of the hallway and firing.

Here, however, Garvey had the advantage. He had spent a number of years in the Navy with his buddy, Thomas Bradley, and he had extensive training with the rifle. The torracks, although quite good, were working with a technology quite alien to them, and their aim wasn't quite on par with that of the astronaut—just as Garvey's swordsmanship wasn't nearly on par with theirs.

Garvey sighted in and waited, dropping gunmen time after time, but as soon as he killed one a hand would reach out and drag the weapon back to safety. Shortly another torrack would pop around the corner firing the ancient weapon.

Attired in glittering armor, Ntashia joined him at the edge of the portal as a series of plasma bolts singed the air and scattered against the far wall of the bedchamber.

"We're pinned down," she said. "It's only a matter of time before she gets us. If she's patient enough she could even starve us out."

"Shaxia doesn't strike me as being that patient," said Garvey. "For some reason I get the idea that when she wants something she wants it now."

Ntashia remembered the lustful glow in Shaxia's yellow eyes as she had gazed upon Garvey.

The American interrupted her train of thought. "By the way, thanks for rescuing me."

"I was only returning the favor," she said with a coy smile.

Garvey jerked his rifle back inside the portal as the heat of a plasma bolt seared the knuckle on his middle finger. "Is there no other way out of here?"

Ntashia glanced about the tapestried walls of the room. "Nothing obvious." She sprang to her feet and went about the chamber tearing the drapes, and revealing the barren walls behind them. Finally the brick walls lay exposed, but the tapestries had concealed no other egress from the room and they were still penned inside.

Garvey let loose with a burst that spattered plasma down the corridor and sent the shooting torracks back behind the cover of their walls. For a brief moment he thought he saw the voluptuous figure of the Warlord Shaxia move in the shadows of an alcove halfway down the hall. He swung his rifle in her direction, but saw too late what she was intending.

Shaxia lifted an arm and sent a small golden device bouncing down the hallway in his direction. Garvey couldn't be sure what it was, but his experience with Navy grenade drills spurred him to action. As it bounced toward the portal Garvey rolled away and kicked the door shut. The device rebounded from the door and settled to a rattling halts about two feet away.

Three golden prongs snapped outward revealing a central eye inside, and unleashed the awesome power contained within. A great flash of white light burst forth. Garvey blinked as the door disappeared, and a globe of light, extending to about ten feet in diameter, devoured everything it touched. Ceiling, wall and floor dissolved into nothingness, and then the bubble of null-space disappeared, leaving only smooth, arced surfaces where it had been.

The power of this ancient grenade was mind-boggling to Garvey. Now he could see into the corridors of both the floor above and below him. Likewise, the torracks were stunned by the awesome sight—none before having witnessed the use of such a device by the Warlord Shaxia.

Garvey pulled back the trigger of his rifle, bolts of plasma screaming forth and scathing the walls across the open pit created by the grenade. He hoped that Shaxia didn't have too many more of those grenades up her sleeve. Only his instinctive reaction of closing the door had saved their lives. But perhaps Shaxia had miscalculated by using so much power against them. Perhaps she had inadvertently created an escape route for him and Ntashia.

Garvey leaped into the pit, and dropped fifteen feet to the floor of the tower level below them. "Come on!" he shouted to Ntashia.

She wasted no time following him, but landed a little hard, rolling into the far wall. Garvey fired up into the level above, randomly scattering plasma bolts, hoping to discourage any return fire—or further grenades.

Ntashia stumbled to her feet and they made good time down the dark hallway, soon leaving behind the gaping hole in the ceiling through which they had jumped.

They passed by many an intersecting corridor, their unmapped flight carrying them down a narrow and spiraling staircase lit by an occasional torch-filled sconce. They heard no immediate sounds of pursuit, and soon the only noise that came to their ears was the tread of their feet and their hearts beating heavily. Finally they were halted by a door of red stone that rose to seven feet in height. Two similar Martian symbols were engraved in silver upon the bloodstone face of the portal.

"What are these?" asked Garvey.

"Initials," replied Ntashia grimly, her face and figure half hidden in shadows. "I think we've stumbled upon the abode of Sar Savaht."

The name meant nothing to Garvey. "Who is Sar Savaht?"

"Shaxia's resident scientist. He studies all the technologies of the ancients that Shaxia unearths and tells her how to use them."

"Is he dangerous?"

"Not physically," said Ntashia, "but the man's a genius, so don't think that we'll be able to outsmart him."

Garvey retreated up the stairs and recovered a torch from a cankered cresset anchored to the wall. In a moment he once again stood by Ntashia, and lifted the torch, letting its wavering light play across the speckled red surface of the bloodstone door.

"There's no handle," he said quietly.

"How would a genius open a door with no handle?" asked Ntashia.

"I don't know what a genius would do, but I would push," answered Garvey.

He put his hand about where the handle would be and pressed. Nothing happened.

"So, American, do you have any other brilliant ideas?"

"Not yet," admitted Garvey as he ran his hand across the smooth, cold surface of the door.

Ntashia leaned against the wall, the torchlight glistening against her armor. She hoisted the flamethrower she had so effectively used in the corridor outside Shaxia's chamber. "I'll watch the stairs. You work on the doorway."

Garvey continued to pass his palm across the stone, halting as he felt a series of tiny impressions. He lifted the torch to find those depressions, but could see nothing marking the smooth stone where his hand had felt the irregularities. The torch flared as he pulled it away, and once again groped in darkness until he found the depressions. This time he kept his fingers near each of those three divots as he brought the torch forward.

Still the torchlight revealed nothing, but Garvey slipped his fingers into the divots, reassuring himself that they did indeed exist. For some reason his eyes and his fingers were telling two different stories. Suddenly, as his fingers rested in the trio of depressions, the portal began to slide open, grinding backward for about three feet until it revealed a gap on either side through which a man might pass.

Ntashia heard the rumble of the door opening, and grinned broadly as she saw that Garvey had succeeded. "How did you figure it out?"

"Ah," answered Garvey. "You just have to think like a genius…which isn't so hard for someone of my superior intellect."

Ntashia caught the self-deprecating tone in his voice. "You may be no Sar Savaht in the mental department, but you're much more handsome than he is."

"Oh really?" said Garvey. "So this Sar Savaht, is he a good looking fellow?"

"Some woman might consider him very attractive…" teased Ntashia as she remembered the wizened body and wrinkled face with cloudy eyes that somehow took every scientific fact into focus.

Garvey slipped into the thick darkness, and Ntashia quietly followed, still watching their rear as she slipped through the inky shadows of the portal. The astronaut's torchlight revealed yet another set of stairs, the flights set side by side, and switching back and forth at a steep angle of descent.

"Perhaps we should retrace our steps," suggested Garvey.

Ntashia shook her head. "We run a greater risk of running into a patrol of torracks. Let's keep on going."

Garvey responded by pushing the stone portal back so that it locked into place with a satisfying click. Their footsteps echoed hollowly as they descended the steps, the air thick with dust, and fist-sized spiders scuttling for the safety of their webs.

With a grimace Garvey skewered a fat spider on the tip of his blade. "These things remind me way too much of the sinthral." He flicked it away and let the still-wriggling spider fall down into the dark shaft between the flights of unrailed stairs.

Ntashia shuddered as she remembered her close encounter with death by the sinthral known as Shavrena. "I hope we never see her again."

She hadn't said, but Garvey knew to whom she was referring. "She ought to be dead. I don't see how anything could survive a free fall to the bottom of the Rift."

The Muvari warrior took some satisfaction from this. "That was some battle."

"I've had nothing but a string of close calls ever since I met you."

"It's not me," she rectified. "It's Mars. Life on Earth sounds like a somewhat staid and unexciting existence."

"Perhaps one doesn't appreciate life as much until he finds it in constant danger," replied Garvey. He stopped at the bottom of the steps, a neon green light emitting from a hovering globe washing over his body as he stood in front of a blank wall.

Ntashia stopped beside him and surveyed the dark cul-de-sac in which they found themselves. "Are we really at a dead end?"

"Why put a light at a dead end? There's got to be some sort of door hidden around here." Garvey fell to examining the brick walls that were thick with layers of cobweb and grime.

"Look at the floor," said Ntashia. "There's a path."

Garvey turned his eyes toward the floor, and indeed a path had been worn in the dust, and led directly to the east wall about ten feet off.

This also appeared to be a blank wall, but the footsteps proceeded directly to it. He reached out to touch the wall and found that his hand passed through as though it did not exist.

"Take my hand." He reached out and Ntashia raised an eyebrow as she took it in a firm grip. Sword in right fist, Garvey plunged through the wall and was swallowed up whole. Ntashia's arm was sucked in up to the elbow, but she could still feel Garvey's hand holding hers. She lowered her head and followed him through the illusory brick and mortar, and suddenly found herself in a vast laboratory jumbled with strange and exotic machines that only could have been built by the Ancients of Mars.

Crystal coils gleamed with fiery light and shining metal canisters thick with wires and glowing symbols cluttered the floor. Long tables of wood filled the room, their tops scattered with ancient weapons, and devices—many of which were opened up, the pieces laid out carefully and numbered with diagram-scrawled vellum sheets held down by various knick-knacks of brass and carven stone.

Garvey looked back and saw a great metallic door sitting just above the illusionary wall, great pistons waiting to lower it into place. He passed his hand across a glowing sensor mounted in the wall, and the pistons hissed, pushing the door firmly into the wall, where it locked into place with immense bolts the size of Garvey's arm.

A haze of ozone gathered thick in the air over the hum of the ancient machinery that cluttered the laboratory. Garvey saw an old man wending his way toward them through a maze of glistening engines. His form was bent and his eyes foggy, his steps stilted by the ravages of age.

"Sar Savaht," murmured Ntashia.

"So, I'm more handsome than this guy?"

Ntashia flashed him a smile. "It's too close to call."

Sar Savaht came closer, and then a sudden realization dawned upon him as his feeble eyesight finally focused in on his visitors. "You are not Shaxia! You are the woman whom she ordered interrogated."

Garvey lifted his sword blade. "Unless you want me to hew you down, I'd suggest that you keep quiet about it."

A faint smile formed on the man's lips. "Aye, I'll keep quiet enough. I'm actually glad that you managed to escape…so much senseless death and torture, I am pleased when someone manages to slip through Shaxia's grasp."

"So, you're not going to trigger an alarm?" asked Ntashia.

Sar Savaht waved his hand in a futile gesture. "If Shaxia knows that you have escaped she will find you soon enough. In the meantime you shall have a brief respite here. This is one of the last places that she is likely to look. Shaxia knows that I like my privacy when conducting experiments."

"Oh, she knows that we're missing," replied Garvey with a nod.

"Make yourself at home," said Sar Savaht. "I'm going to continue with my experiment."

"What experiment is that?" asked Garvey, suspicious that the scientist might be using his experiment as a pretext to slip away and warn Shaxia.

"If you two promise not to touch anything you are welcome to observe." He turned and began to wind his way back toward a large circular device around which stood three cylindrical chambers. He passed by these chambers and stood at a large crystal lens set into the top of a gleaming metallic canister. With gnarled fingers he carefully adjusted a vast array of dials, then settled in over the crystal, intently watching its face.

Garvey searched the hazy room for some sort of escape route and found several darkened archways nearly hidden in the shadows of looming pieces of ancient machinery. Ntashia, for the moment, took more interest in the images that swirled past in the crystal as Sar Savaht twiddled a peculiarly shaped knob.

"What does this machine do?"

Sar Savaht answered in an absent-minded fashion, his mind clearly on the images that he was viewing. "The Ancients seeded Mars with a number of artificially created time-space anomalies called stasis fields. By using this machine I am able to peer through those anomalies and see events in the past, present, and future. It is quite a fascinating study. Did you know that in thirty thousand years seismic and volcanic activity will destroy that atmosphere and that all life on Mars will die?"

"Is that how it happened?" asked Garvey. Talk of the stasis loop had suddenly piqued his interest. This was the device with which the Warlord Shaxia had caught Lana, as she raided one of the Warlord's technology troves, and had kept her in limbo until that fated day Garvey dragged his broken body from the wreckage of the Mars Climate Orbiter and fell into the buried chamber of an ancient Martian structure.

"Yes, yes," muttered Sar Savaht as the crystal lens revealed the image of a desolate Martian landscape.

Garvey started, and then jabbed a finger toward the lens. "That outcropping of rock! It looks a lot like the outcropping where I crash-landed my spaceship."

The scientist raised a furry eyebrow and cast a sidelong glance in Garvey's direction. "You don't appear to be from Phobos. The Karpathesians are generally slighter and taller than the average Martian due to the reduced gravity of the moon. This, of course, is subdued somewhat by the effect of their breeding with concubines kidnapped from the Martian surface—but you are rather short for even a Martian male."

"That's because he's from a planet called Earth," said Ntashia proudly—as though she were exhibiting something in a kindergartner's show and tell.

Sar Savaht didn't accept this pronunciation at face value, but neither did he scoff. "What planet is this Earth?"

"You're aware of the concept of a solar system?" asked Garvey.

"Of course, of course—the sun and the solar bodies that revolve in its gravitational field."

"Earth is the third planet from the sun, and, of course, Mars is the fourth."

Sar Savaht rubbed at his prominent chin. "Fascinating. Earth is a larger planet with a higher gravitational pull than Mars. That might account for your diminished height and more powerful musculature."

"It might," said Garvey.

"On the other hand it is possible that you are merely a genetic aberration that developed here on Mars."

"Perhaps I can prove to you otherwise."

"How so?" asked the scientist. "I suppose if we had the time I could run a battery of tests and compare your genetic building blocks, but at best we have two or three hours before the Warlord Shaxia discovers your presence. That would hardly be sufficient for my needs."

Garvey shook his head. "The view from this anomaly should be sufficient. If you are able to move forward far enough in time perhaps you'll be able to see me landing on Mars."

This seemed to intrigue Sar Savaht. "You do not jest with me? I am an old man and my heart cannot take false promises of scientific discovery. How is that you came to Mars in the future, and now are existing in the present?"

"I stumbled into a stasis loop and was thrown back with the woman who was caught in the loop."

"Ah yes. Shaxia had me trap several of her technology troves with stasis loops, which are based on the space-time anomaly. But the stasis loop requires a bit of onsite machinery to maintain. It would be extraordinary that the machinery would stay functional for such a long period of time, and the functions would have to be reset for the anomaly to cast you back in time."

"I don't know the science of it," admitted Garvey. "I can just tell you what happened. I landed a bit east of the promontory. Hopefully, you will be able to see me land."

"Is it is possible that seismic activity moved a part of the trove to this area?" muttered Sar Savaht to himself. "I can move the anomaly to the East. This device allows me some limited control."

"How far forward in time can you see?"

"Time is but an illusion, young man. It is a reckoning developed by our finite minds to mark the passage of events."

"Does that mean that you can?" asked Ntashia.

"Of course, I can." The scientist's gnarled fingers adroitly adjusted the dials and the three of them watched as windstorms swept the plains, the outcrop of rock eroding as time past until it finally took the shape that Garvey fully recognized. Then there was a flash in the sky, a fleeting impression of a metallic shape—and then it was gone.

Sar Savaht adjusted the mechanism and brought the image back, watching more slowly. Garvey felt the tension rising in his body as he relived the moments that life–altering crash. But this time he watched it from outside as the Orbiter plunged perilously fast through the atmosphere, heat flaying from its sides and rockets flaring until the fuel was gone and the craft plummeted like a stone.

Garvey braced himself as the Orbiter struck Mars, crumpling like a tin can; milky trails of oxygen hissing out into the dead atmosphere, the scathing sand carrying it away like straw before a hurricane. Long moments later a hunched figure dragged itself from the wreckage hopping on one leg, the storm winds carrying him sidelong as he struggled with the heavy equipment he bore.

Garvey realized he was looking at himself, and a strange thought struck him. "If I was dragged through a stasis loop back in time, is it possible to reach out through one of these anomalies and drag someone back through time?"

"Why, yes. Look at the enclosed cylinders around us. The ancients did precisely such a thing. In fact, an elite few predicted the cataclysm that would befall Mars, and escaped to the past to live out the rest of their lives."

"What if you were to reach out through this anomaly and grab me as I left my spacecraft? What would happen to me then?"

"Why you would appear in one of these chambers."

"And I would forget everything that happened to me? My history would change?"

"It would be an interesting case study if I had the time," sighed Sar Savaht, "though I hardly think it would change the outcome of your future. You would still be in Shaxia's power, and subject to her whims. Likely you would end up in her bed as is her wont with many functional male captives."

Garvey shrugged. "I wouldn't change things even if it meant I could go free. If you grabbed me after the crash landing I never would have met Ntashia."

Ntashia smiled, pleased with this response.

"I am curious, though," said Garvey. "Did any other visitors come to Mars?"

"Were you expecting more ships from Earth?" asked Sar Savaht.

"We were trying to establish an outpost before our enemies could do the same. I wondered if we were successful."

Once again Sar Savaht fell to rubbing his prominent chin as he pondered the thought. "It may be difficult to track the event down. You understand that I'm working with a limited number of anomalies, perhaps three score, over the face of the entire planet. Unless you could give me a precise location to direct one of those anomalies I'm afraid it might take years to answer your question."

Garvey produced his Clip Pad and punched up a schematic for the U.S. base on Mars, which he was to have established. "I can give you the precise coordinates. I doubt any succeeding missions changed the location."

Sar Savaht got a glint in his eye as he looked over the coordinates and translated the longitude and latitude into a system with which he was more familiar. "Very interesting, Earth man. Very interesting."

Once the coordinates were converted Sar Savaht punched in the location on a holographic screen, and the singularity began to move, slowly at first but gaining speed until it whizzed across the craggy and sand-locked surface of a dead Mars. As it reached the basin where Garvey had hoped to construct the base from light weight metallic panels collapsed and stored in the Mars

Climate Orbiter, the singularity slowed and stopped, time once again resuming its accelerated forward march.

Before their amazed eyes they saw a knobby-tired buggy gleam silver as it arrived and disgorged a single passenger. The images moved quickly, stuttering through time at a pace the eye could barely follow, but for Garvey it was impossible to mistake the American flag fluttering out front of a dome that grew up from the nothingness.

A hundred times the harsh glare of the sun gave way to the silvery light of the double moons of Phobos and Deimos. Strange figures lurked in the night then daylight dawned and the panels of the dome disappeared leaving a windswept skeletal husk that protruded from the drifting sands.

"Wait!" cried Garvey. "What happened?"

"Details are often difficult to discern at such a speed. If you want an explanation for the fall of your outpost perhaps we'd better decelerate the speed of the anomaly."

"I do want to know what happened," agreed the astronaut.

"Your time here may be running short," warned Sar Savaht, "perhaps you'd best plan your escape now."

Garvey glanced at Ntashia, and she gazed coolly back. "Take as much time as you need. If this were the future of the Muvari I would want to see what happened."

Sar Savaht subtly worked the controls, slowing the molecular reverberation of the anomaly so that they watched the visual echo at a speed their eyes could more easily comprehend. He moved the anomaly in closer until it rested within the oxygen dome, and they saw the American astronaut that manned the outpost.

"Arnold Stechter," breathed Garvey. All his dislike for the arrogant astronaut was forgotten as he viewed his space-faring comrade through the distance of forty seven thousand years. He felt a wash of admiration and pride that NASA had finally succeeded at putting a base on Mars.

Ntashia studied the sharp, but handsome features of the blonde astronaut. "You know this man?"

"He was one of the astronauts that I trained with," said Garvey.

"He is also shorter than the Muvari men," she observed, "and more muscular."

"Also a product of the Earthling gravity," observed Sar Savaht with interest. "I notice that a great effort is made to keep a controlled atmosphere within his abode. How is the Martian air at that point in time?"

"It's almost all nitrogen," said Garvey. "There's not enough oxygen for any human or animal life to survive without some sort of artificial means."

"Fascinating," muttered Sar Savaht.

The days accelerated past on the crystal view screen as Arnold Stechter cycled through his daily schedule. This repetitive routine continued until Garvey caught sight of a second astronaut stepping into the dome.

"Slow this down!" cried Garvey. "I need to find out who that is."

With a slight adjustment the scientist complied, and Garvey watched in horror as the malicious visage of Xio Cheng swam into view, lips pulled back over his sharp incisors, and mustache drooping across the sneering corners as he pulled back the trigger of his Chinese-made assault rifle. There was a flash of Arnold Stechter's panic-stricken face as he crawled backward, unable to escape his inevitable doom.

"Can you pull him out with your anomaly?" asked Garvey urgently, forgetting that Sar Savaht could go back and replay the scene over and over at will.

"The blonde-haired man?" asked Savaht.

"Yes, if you don't, he's a dead man."

"By transporting him into the heart of the Warlord Shaxia's stronghold I may only be prolonging his life for a matter of a few hours," warned Sar Savaht.

"Then you can do it?"

"I know that the ancients did such things, but I've never tried it myself. Still, I am curious to see if it works. You do understand that your friend may not even survive the transport?"

"He's as good as dead already. He's got nothing to lose."

The images in the crystal spattered a crimson haze as Cheng's gun flamed and stuttered hot lead. Arnold Stechter twitched and wallowed in his own blood as death overtook him.

"Is it too late?" asked Ntashia.

"No, no," answered Sar Savaht. "Time is not immutable. That much I have come to realize."

He adjusted the anomaly, reversing the spatial echo so that it traveled back in time, but a few minutes. Once again Xio Cheng strode through the door, a sneer on his thin lips. Sar Savaht triggered an array of dials and quickly adjusted them, blue energy crackling along great coils and resistors. "I've got him!"

A great moan echoed through the laboratory as Sar Savaht threw a great lever. Rampant energy made their hair rise upon their heads as the very air became supercharged with cascading power. Forty seven thousand years away Xio Cheng pulled back the trigger of his rifle, and Arnold Stechter's space-suited form blinked from view, leaving a bewildered Chinese astronaut behind.

The moan rose into a howl and eerie lights played inside the tube at the far right corner of the apparatus.

"He appears to be caught in mid-transition," said a puzzled Sar Savaht. He made some more adjustments, the great coils unleashing lightening flashes of unbridled power that whirled dangerously about them.

Suddenly, amid coruscating flashes of energy, a form began to take shape in the tube. The shape coalesced and became solid, and Arnold Stechter sat huddled in the corner, his NASA space suit melted and smoking about him. For a moment Stechter face registered only shock and bewilderment, then he stood, ripping off his dripping helmet and hurtling it against the clear tube that confined him.

His earthly strength shattered the translucent material and he leaped through bellowing in rage, landing catlike among the shards. Wild eyes darted to and fro and then they fell upon Garvey.

"You!" he shrieked with an accusatory voice. "What have you done to me?"

Garvey tried to interject with some sort of explanation, but Stechter was waiting for no answers. He launched himself toward Garvey, tackling him and bearing him through a tower of crystal distillation beakers.

The two tumbled head over heels, and when they rose amid the shattered ruins blood was flowing.

Stechter's voice quavered as he jabbed an accusatory finger at Garvey. "You! You're in league with the Chinese!"

Chapter Nineteen:
Through the Portals of Time

Mars 47,000 B.C– The Workshop of Sar Savaht

"Take it easy, Arnold," warned Garvey as he shook the shards of glass from his body. "Let me explain what's going on here."

"His transition through the anomaly may have induced some paranoid reaction," speculated Sar Savaht.

"No," sighed Garvey. "He always thought that I was out to get him."

Stechter cast about for some sort of weapon and settled on an iron bar that protruded as a lever from a nearby piece of machinery. "It's time that you and I had it out once and for all. You've been nothing but a hindrance to me— stealing my mission, my fame, and stealing my glory. I don't know where you've brought me, but it's over as of now!"

Arnold Stechter swung the bar with both hands and it whistled through the air. Garvey pushed back with the tips of his toes, and somersaulted backward through the Martian gravity—just avoiding the end of the bar. He landed awkwardly, but quickly regained his balance as Stechter, swearing furiously, closed the gap between them.

"I thought that they were friends," mused Sar Savaht.

"So did I," said an equally puzzled Ntashia as she pulled her sword blade from its sheath and began to advance.

Garvey ducked and the pipe slammed into a console, leaving a two-inch indentation. He didn't want to hurt Stechter, but at the rate things were going it didn't look like he had much choice in the matter. That pipe had come awfully close to braining him. He reached down to the hilt of his sword, about to pull it free of its scabbard when Stechter staggered backward. The length of pipe fell, clattering against the stone floor as he let it drop from his fingers. Then he slipped to the floor against a cankered hydraulic press, cradling his head between his hands, and drawing his knees up toward his chest.

"I'm sorry, I'm sorry," he said over and over, rocking back and forth as he repeated the words. "I didn't mean to kill you. I just wanted to be first."

Hand still on the hilt of his sword, Garvey cautiously approached Stechter who continued to repeat the mantra.

"I just wanted to be first. I just wanted to be first."

"You didn't kill me," said Garvey. "You missed with the pipe. I'm still here, no harm done."

Stechter gazed wild-eyed from between trembling fingers. "Of course, I missed with the pipe," he choked. "I can't kill you twice. You're already dead!"

Garvey shook his head in bewilderment. "What are you talking about?"

Ntashia surveyed the new American with a critical eye. "Was he always like this?"

"No," admitted Garvey. "He wasn't always the nicest person, but he wasn't insane. For some reason he seems to think that he's killed me."

Sar Savaht paused to pluck up a quill and excitedly scrawled some notes on a wavy piece of parchment. "It's quite possible that he's suffering from some psychosis created by a shift in chemical levels while he was pulled through the time-space anomaly."

"Maybe you're right," said Garvey soberly. "There is something wrong with him. He seems severely disoriented."

The scientist started a second column on his parchment. "Tell me, Garvey, how did you feel after you exited the stasis loop with the Muvari woman that you freed?"

It didn't take Garvey much effort to recall the feeling of weakness and disorientation that he had experienced. "I passed out during the transfer, and didn't feel too healthy when I woke up."

"It is very possible that your friend is undergoing a more severe reaction. If he is lucky his condition will prove to be as temporary as yours."

"And if it isn't?" asked Ntashia.

"Then he may be a gibbering idiot for the rest of his life," answered Sar Savaht matter-of-factly.

Ntashia listened to Arnold Stechter ramble on. "He thinks that he killed you, Garvey!"

"I already explained to him that he missed with the pipe, but he doesn't seem to comprehending that."

"No. He thinks that he killed you some other time. He thinks that he killed you while you were trying to land your spacecraft on Mars!"

A cold chill ran down Garvey's back. Was it possible that Arnold Stechter had been responsible for the trajectory miscalculations that had caused his crash on Mars? His eyes shifted from Ntashia's violet gaze to the huddled form of his fellow astronaut, who continued to stutter words from between trembling lips. The words spoke of treachery, treason and guilt, and cold realization washed over Garvey.

His crash had been no accident, but a planned act of sabotage by Stechter and the trajectory programmer, Reginald Bison. On the day of the launch Bison decided that Stechter wasn't offering enough recompense for his complicity in the plot. When Bison tried to extort Stechter, he got angry and gave Bison a broken jaw, after which he was expelled from the Cape Canaveral launch site that fateful December eleventh. The story was all there—in fragmented pieces babbling forth from Stechter's mouth, and it didn't take a rocket scientist to put two and two together.

Eventually Stechter's torrent of words slowed then ceased entirely. The darting eyes calmed, the twitching of his limbs ceased, and finally his face took on the composure of resumed sanity.

"Slay the treacherous skelk," exclaimed Ntashia. "He put a knife in your back once and he won't hesitate to do it again."

Garvey suspected that Ntashia was right, but he couldn't bring himself to do the deed. Stechter was his only connection with Earth, and despite his betrayal Garvey still felt a certain brotherhood with the astronaut. "I can't do it. Not now, not after I just saved his life."

"But he tried to kill you again with a length of bar just a moment ago. To leave him alive is a mistake."

"Perhaps," admitted Garvey, "but the Warlord Shaxia may well rectify my mistake for me. We'd best concentrate on figuring a way out of here before it's too late. I've wasted too much of our time saving somebody that it turns out wasn't worth saving."

Arnold Stechter spoke, his voice no longer quavering and unbalanced as he carefully hoisted himself to his feet. "I don't blame you for feeling that way—I probably deserve to die."

Garvey viewed the recovering astronaut narrowly. "You're feeling a bit more stable now?"

Stechter nodded. "But all the more ashamed. I owe you an apology for what I've done—but I don't think there's anything I could do or say to make up for it."

"Probably not," agreed Garvey, "but you can start by arming yourself and getting ready to fight."

"So, you are going to kill me," said Arnold.

"Not me," answered Garvey. "I don't have time to explain it all now, but we've got a bunch of angry seven-foot tall warriors looking for us. Right now we're intruding on their territory, and they won't hesitate to kill any one they happen to find."

"Just where are we, and how did I get here? One minute I thought that I was dead, and the next minute I show up here. I thought that maybe I'd arrived in hell."

Garvey found a short sword among a host of implements leaning in a corner and tossed the still-scabbarded weapon to Stechter. "Put this on."

"A sword? Don't you have anything a little more modern?"

"It's 47,000 years before we were even born, so we can't be too choosy."

"What are you talking about? Aren't you going to tell me how I got here?"

"You wouldn't believe me if I did."

Arnold Stechter took a long look around the laboratory, taking in the alien machinery that surrounded him. "You're probably right."

The anomaly device was still running and Sar Savaht bent over the crystal screen watching time running forward. "There is more!" he mumbled to himself.

Garvey turned to see what Sar Savaht was talking about when Stechter spoke again. "You don't know how glad I am that you're alive. I thought I'd killed you, and the guilt was eating me up."

A great reverberation at the doorway drowned out Garvey's reply. Sar Savaht looked up distractedly from the images that had him enraptured. "It appears that the Warlord Shaxia has finally tracked you fugitives down. That's her torracks at the door now. Perhaps you'd best formulate a plan for escape."

"Are there any other exits?" asked Ntashia.

The scientist shook his head, his thoughts elsewhere. "No, I'm afraid not. There's only one way in and only one way out. That door is quite sturdy, however. It will take them at least five or six minutes to cut through it with even a heavy plasma weapon."

Garvey chewed on the inside of his cheek as he concentrated. "We've still got a plasma rifle and an extra power pack."

"That's a start," agreed Sar Savaht with an impassive shrug. "But they've got access to the weapons of the Ancients also. I suspect that they won't waste any time bringing them to bear. Shaxia's torracks number in the thousands and they have you effectively trapped. Unless you get creative I think that your fate is a foregone conclusion."

Sar Savaht related this in a matter of fact manner, as though he were disinterested in the outcome. He watched the crystal. "They're rebuilding your atmosphere dome."

"They who?" asked Garvey.

"Some other travelers, perhaps also from Earth. They are wearing similar protective garb to that your friend was wearing when he arrived."

He motioned toward the broken cylindrical chamber and the helmet that lay outside. Stechter began removing the melted remains of his NASA space suit, tossing the pieces into a haphazard pile. Garvey leaned over the crystal, and saw three astronauts assembling various panels on the looted dome and tightly sealing them against the outside atmosphere. He could plainly see the American flag on their suits, though the names inscribed ontheir helmets moved by too quickly for him to make out.

Prepared to sell her life dearly, Ntashia ensconced herself behind a bank of machinery and rested her rifle across the top, aiming it in the direction of the door so that the moment the torracks opened the portal she could begin firing. Stechter belted his short sword around his waist, and looked around the room in a bewildered fashion.

Garvey watched as the dome was assembled and saw that soon the three astronauts moved about inside, unencumbered by their atmospheric suits. "Send us there!" he said suddenly.

Sar Savaht looked up with an expression of wry amusement crossing his wrinkled face. "I wondered if you were going to think of a creative solution."

"You've got to do it now, before too much time passes—while they've got a dome erected and it still holds oxygen."

The scientist pressed a button and the scene stopped, two astronauts frozen in mid-action. "There's no time to waste. If the torracks come through during the transfer they might easily disrupt the process. They have no respect for science unless they think that it can kill them somehow."

As Garvey called to Ntashia and Stechter the great door began to hiss, its metal skin glowing red as a multitude of plasma beams heated it from the other side, smoke rolling forth in dark billows.

"Sar Savaht is going to send us into the future with the anomaly machine. This way we've got a chance to live."

Ntashia frowned at the scientist. "Why can't you send us through another anomaly that is tuned to our own time, but a different location?"

"I could," admitted Sar Savaht, "but it would take quite a bit of time to tune into the proper space-time frame. I believe you have only a few moments left."

Ntashia hesitated. She held information vital to the survival of the Muvari people. If she were transported forward in time she would have no way of communicating the whereabouts of Caladrex and its troves of technology. The information that would allow her people to resist the tyranny of the Warlord Shaxia would be lost to them forever.

Sar Savaht stepped forward and began fitting them each with a belt, which was equipped with a small metallic box.

"What are these?" asked Arnold. "You're not expecting me to get back into that thing again are you?"

"These are, as best as my research indicates, anomaly recall devices. If there is a hang up in the neutrino flow of the anomaly, instead of dispersing your body across thousands of centuries it recalls you back.

You first traveled without the benefit of this device, so it was fortunate for you that you did not encounter any such impasse. As far as getting back into that device, I was meaning to get to that…"

"Get to what?" asked Garvey.

"Well, your blonde-haired friend here shattered one of the transference chambers with his helm when he arrived. That leaves only two functioning chambers, which means that two of you go first, and the third must follow behind. The problem is there may not be enough time to successfully transfer the first two of you, let alone the third, before the torracks start mucking up my laboratory."

"So the last person to go will probably be killed by the torracks."

"I'd estimate the odds of such an occurrence at being a nine in ten chance," agreed Sar Savaht.

Stechter's face tightened as he tried to comprehend all that was going on around him. He had been thrust from one deadly situation to another, with scarcely the ability to understand what was happening to him.

"So this machine will send us somewhere safe?"

"That's the plan," said Garvey.

Stechter face softened as he came to a decision. "The two of you go first. If there's time, I will follow."

"You sure about that?" asked Garvey.

"I've never been more sure of anything," said the man who had caused Garvey's crash landing. "I owe you. This is the least I can do to repay you."

Garvey reached out and clasped Stechter's hand. "Perhaps I'll see you on the other side."

"Perhaps," said Stechter.

Garvey stepped up into the transference chamber, but Ntashia paused on the platform.

"I can't go, Garvey. I've got to stay and tell my people where Caladrex is located."

"If you stay you'll be too dead to tell anybody about it. I'm sorry, but there's nothing we can do to tell them now—unless Sar Savaht can relay the message."

Sar Savaht shook his head. "That's not a secret that you can entrust with me. I've sold my soul to delve the secrets of the ancients—and I'd do it again. Tell me though, perhaps my altruism will win me over—or perhaps not."

"Mayhap it is a secret that best stay with me," replied Ntashia shrewdly.

She stepped into the transference chamber, and the crystal doors swung shut, locking both she and Garvey inside the tubes—and eliminating any chance of changing their minds. Ntashia glanced to the great metal door and watched it melting away, pooling in great molten puddles, and trickling silver streams that meandered through the mortared hollows between the stones of the floor.

The tremendous coils of the machinery began to hum, and once again crackled with rampant power. A great pain seized her body, intense and excruciating to the point she thought her mind would explode, but then as suddenly as the pain took hold of her it began to drain away, her mental faculties slipping away with it.

Blue light strobed within the chambers and the bodies of Ntashia and Garvey disappeared leaving only a curling whisper of smoke behind.

Arnold Stechter blinked, not certain whether or not he should believe his own eyes. He turned back to the door and saw that half of it had melted away, revealing a horde of towering, blue-skinned warriors. Bolts of energy skimmed through the doorway, slicing through machines and skipping off reflective surfaces. A fluorescing bolt hit a power cable over Stechter's head, cutting it in two, so that it curled downward, sparking and spitting.

Stechter leaped away, sparks still smoldering on his arm.

"Hurry!" called Sar Savaht. He motioned him toward the smoking chamber, which had moments before contained Ntashia's lithe form.

The astronaut staggered through a storm of flashing bolts and into the still-warm chamber. Sar Savaht passed his hand over a sensor and the crystal door locked tightly over Stechter. The coils flashed lightning and a horrible hum grew in Stechter's head until it became a banshee, screaming to be let loose. Blue light flashed in his skull, and his mind plunged through a swirling vortex of space and time.

A plasma bolt struck the transference chamber and it burst asunder. Sar Savaht wheeled from the console and shook a gnarled fist at the torracks. "You blithering idiots! This is irreplaceable technology. I'll see that the Warlord has your heads for that!"

March 8, 2007– U.S. Mars Base

With a whoosh the airlock door opened and Brendan Melhoff and Frank Giffen stumbled inside. They unclamped their bubble helmets and tossed them away, revealing their sweat-drenched hair and haunted faces.

Melhoff grabbed a towel and wiped his brow, his furry expression twisting in doubt. "We shouldn't have left him there to fight alone. We just shouldn't have."

Giffen's bare head gleamed in the low light of the dome. "You heard what he said. There was no point in all three of us dying."

"Maybe, maybe not," glowered Melhoff through his bristling beard, "but I can't help but feel like I've been a coward, and deserted him."

"There's nothing we can do now," said Giffen as he sat himself in front a row of electronic devices. "Except keep a close eye on the perimeter sensors in case…"

He ceased speaking as the receiver squawked wildly with strange energy. For ten seconds the needle of every sensor pegged to the far right and stood there, unmoving. Energy crackled within the dome and the hair on Giffen's arm and Melhoff's head stood on end. A rush of air ruffled the papers within the dome and an electric scent came to their nostrils.

Two shapes began unfolding from the thin air at the middle of the dome, and a moment later two figures sat sprawled and dazed on the floor.

The man's hair was sandy blonde, and his eyes steel gray. He wore a strange reflective armor that reminded Melhoff of the chain mail that medieval knights had worn, and a sword was belted at his side. His forearms were lean and muscular, and covered with scars and still healing cuts.

The woman attracted Melhoff's gaze like a magnet. Not because of her sudden appearance, but because of her stunning, exotic beauty. Her pale blonde hair possessed a hint of purple in the strands and was braided into a dozen tails that fell about her shoulders. Her eyes were a luminous violet color and of a piercing quality that made him shiver, and her skin coloring possessed a hint of green melanin. She wore glistening, pliable armor similar to the man, and also possessed a sword at her waist. On her back rested a rifle that was unlike any that he had ever seen.

Giffen's gaze rested longer upon the man's handsome visage—sun darkened, and covered with a deep stubble that made his face difficult to place. Finally Giffen jumped to his feet, giving a shout of recognition.

"Garvey Dire!"

Still dazed from his journey through time and space, Garvey turned at the sound of his name and studied the sharp nose and regular features of the man who had addressed him. Finally the face filtered through the foggy reaches of his memory and back to Cape Canaveral. "Hank Giffen. It's good to see you."

Giffen rushed over and offered Garvey a hand, helping him back to his feet. "Where did you come from?"

"That's a long and bizarre story."

As Garvey blinked trying to correct the blurry vision that still assailed him, Melhoff stepped forward and extended a hand to Ntashia who, after a wary moment, finally accepted the proffered help to her feet.

"I don't understand," said Melhoff. "I guess that somehow you managed to survive your crash landing and survive here on the planet, but where have you been—and who is this woman?"

"This is Ntashia, my fiancée. I smuggled her on board the Orbiter."

Giffen took this opportunity to examine Ntashia more closely. She was certainly beautiful, but there was something alien in those sloe eyes, and that greenish skin color. Her frame was impossibly thin, but still full-figured and fleshed out with long, lithe muscles. "I don't believe it," he said finally. "There's no way that the Orbiter could have supported two adults for the entire journey."

"You're right," said Garvey, "she's a native Martian from 49,000 years ago."

Both Giffen and Melhoff remained tongue-tied, unsure of how to respond to such a preposterous claim—but unable to think of any logical explanation to explain her presence.

"I didn't say that it was going to be easy to swallow," said Garvey after enduring enough of the uncomfortable silence.

"What are your names?" asked Ntashia of the two astronauts.

They quickly introduced themselves, and Ntashia practiced saying their foreign sounding names. Her mental link with Garvey in the hot spring cave after their encounter with the sinthral had imbued her with an understanding of English, just as Garvey's initial encounter with Lana had imparted the ability for him to speak and understand the Martian language.

"Are you both American men, like Garvey?" she asked.

Melhoff smiled in spite of himself, finding himself already enthralled by her charms and the quaint way she spoke the English language. "Why, yes, we are."

"I thought that I saw three of you," questioned Garvey. "Wasn't there somebody else with you?"

Giffen and Melhoff's expressions turned grim, and finally Giffen spoke. "Thomas Bradley came with us, but I'm afraid that we may have just lost him."

At the sound of his close friend's name Garvey felt an elation creeping over him, but that was quickly dashed by the dark words that followed. "What happened? Where is he?"

"China successfully established a Mars base about five miles from here in a large basin. They are capable of sending transmissions to control orbital nukes over earth and have threatened to use them unless the U.S. ponies up a large amount of cash. Our jamming equipment here is short a few fried-out components, so the President ordered an assault on the Chinese base camp."

"And Bradley went?"

"We all went," said Melhoff. "We disabled the transmission equipment and Bradley ordered us back to base camp, so he could go it alone."

For a moment Garvey wanted to lash out at them for abandoning Bradley, but he quickly realized that was a waste of energy. "How long ago was this?"

"We were back at camp for just a few minutes when you and Ntashia appeared."

"How long does it take to do the five miles to the Chinese camp?"

"Only a few minutes. We found Arnold Stechter's buggy stashed in a cave not far from here, and have been using it to get around. It's parked outside. We never did find hide nor hair of Stechter, himself. It was as though he disappeared off the face of the planet."

Garvey motioned to Melhoff. "Give me your suit. I'm going to see if Bradley needs any help."

"It may be too late to do anything," warned Giffen. "If the Chinese are still alive they'll be sure to see you coming."

"Give your suit to Ntashia," ordered Garvey. "She'll be backing me up."

March 8, 2007– Chinese Mars Base

Bradley Thomas stared into the face of doom, his hand holding down the mantle of his grenade, while the snouts of three automatic rifles pointed in his direction. Just one bullet could put a hole in the dome large enough to effectively suck out all the oxygen that was so carefully preserved inside those sealed walls. Would those same walls be able to withstand an exploding grenade? Bradley doubted it. The grenade's shrapnel would pepper the walls with so many holes it would leak oxygen like a sieve.

"Is this what they call a Mexican stand off?" asked Xio Cheng, his thin lips barely moving as he spoke.

"There's no stand off," Bradley repeated. "We either all live or we all die. You make the call. If you lay your weapons down, I won't blow you all to kingdom come. If one of you pulls the trigger I let go of the mantle of this grenade. The pin's already pulled, and as soon as my fingers loosen this thing will blow us all into a million pieces."

Sweat dripped down Xio Cheng's forehead as he contemplated the next course of action. He didn't want to die, but neither could he let this American dog get the best of him. "I have another solution, American."

"What's that, Cheng?" Bradley figured that he had the luxury of time. He had nothing to lose but his life.

"You put the pin back in your grenade and we pay you a million dollars. You go home a rich man."

Bradley shook his head at the feeble attempt to bribe him. "Like I'd ever see that million dollars. You're going to have to try harder than that."

"We'll pay you now," said Cheng. "Not in Chinese money, but ten million dollars worth of diamonds."

"And you just happened to bring ten million dollars worth of diamonds with you into space? I find that story just as unlikely."

"We didn't bring them with us," said Cheng. "We found them in a valley some distance from here— a valley covered with diamonds."

"An intriguing story," nodded Bradley, "but all the diamonds on Mars couldn't bribe me."

"And why is it that you pretend to be so noble, American?"

"Your country is holding the threat of nuclear annihilation over the United States. My wife and kids live in Fort Lauderdale, Florida. Do you think that a few shiny baubles are worth more to me than their lives?"

Xio Cheng shrugged. "Some men would knife their own mother for the wealth that I'm offering."

Ntashia started firing as soon as the dune buggy cleared the ridge. Garvey wrestled with the wheel as it bounced over the rocky slope, bright lances of plasma flashing from Ntashia's rifle as she leaned from the passenger's seat. They rolled through a dozen early warning systems, recklessly pounding across the bottom of the basin, and toward the smoking and charred tower and moon-glistened domes.

The bright lances of energy cut through the domes like a knife through soft flesh and hazy atmosphere sighed as it leaked away, mingling with the nitrogen thick air that blanketed the ancient planet.

Kien Kuong cried out as a plasma bolt cut through his body, and Dong Soo Hwon, standing next to him, started as his rifle was sliced in half by the same bolt. Kien Kuong crumpled, a cauterized hole in his midsection. A second bolt flashed through the upper part of the dome, leaving behind an entry and an exit hole.

Bradley didn't know what was happening, but he took advantage of the situation and dropped back through the hatch through which he had entered the dome. As he leapt he pulled the trigger and fired his Swiss SG551. Bullets spewed from its ugly maw, throwing Yew Lun up against the far wall of the dome, spattered with a half dozen crimson-leaking holes.

Xio Cheng swore foully and sent a hailstorm of bullets rattling around Bradley as he dropped below the level of the floor. Bullets clanked against the floor, and cut through his space suit, nicking flesh and his oxygen regulator, which hissed angrily as it spilled out its life-giving air.

Dust rolled into the light gravity atmosphere as Garvey braked to a hard stop in front of the central dome. He leaped from the vehicle as Ntashia rose and continued to rain plasma into the domes. In moments, the domes looked like lumps of Swiss cheese, and by the time Garvey tore through the riddled front hatch with his gloved hands Ntashia's rifle ran dry.

He found dead and dying astronauts lying broken against the wall or in steaming heaps, but he did not pause in his search. He burst through doorway after doorway, sword in hand, meeting no resistance. Somewhere outside he heard a machinegun stutter.

His sudden entrance into the third dome surprised Xio Cheng, who had been stalking toward an open floor hatch across the room. Garvey leaped into the air trying to close the distance between them, but Xio was quicker and he swung around and emptied his rifle clip into Garvey's chest.

The bullets cut through Garvey's borrowed suit and pounded against his chest, but he felt them as though they were only raindrops beating against his breast. The amazing shirt of Caladrexian mail dissipated the impact, and left him unharmed except for the hot lead that burned him as it rattled down his body.

The front of his suit was nothing but a ragged hole through which his miraculous armor glinted, but Garvey staggered up from where the barrage of bullets had thrown him, and he swung his blade in a cruel arc that separated Xio Cheng's head from his body. As Cheng's body crumpled, Garvey felt his lungs crying for oxygen. The atmosphere within the dome was fleeing, and his suit would no longer hold oxygen.

He ignored the pangs of deprivation and staggered to the edge of the hatch, in time to find Bradley Thomas sucking uselessly at a tube that no longer supplied oxygen. Thomas glanced up, bewildered as he saw the NASA issue helmet peering down from above.

"Melhoff?" he gasped. "Why did you come back?"

Garvey ripped loose his helmet and let it bounce to the floor. "No, it's me, buddy."

Bradley grinned widely, and let out a delirious laugh. "Garvey? Then I must already be dead."

"No, you're not going to die Bradley. You've got a wife and family to get home to." Garvey ripped off the arms of his suit and then his torso piece. He cut his own oxygen tube, gasped at its life giving air then passed the tank and tube down to Bradley.

With desperation Bradley sucked oxygen into his deflated lungs, and passed the tube back to Garvey. Garvey pulled Bradley from the hatch and into the gore-spattered room before taking another pull of oxygen.

"Come on," said Garvey between breaths. "The buggy is waiting outside."

Buddy breathing, they passed back through the carnage that Ntashia had wrought with her plasma rifle, and Bradley stared in amazement. They negotiated the torn and melted metal of the air lock doors, and out into the cold Martian night.

Dirt hung hazy in the air as they crossed toward the dune buggy. Garvey's heart began beating faster. Where was Ntashia? He glanced about, but didn't see her anywhere until they came closer to the jeep. Her suited body lay sitting against the knobby rear tire of the buggy. Bullet holes riddled the side panel of the buggy, and Ntashia's faceplate was shattered, violet blood trickling down her face where the glass had cut her cheek.

Her eyes were open, but she did not see. No breath passed her lips, and her body was still. Garvey broke away from Bradley, and cried out in a bellow of pain that expended every bit of oxygen stored within his lungs. He clutched Ntashia to him, lungs gasping futile paroxysms as shadowy death closed in and finally claimed him as its own.

Chapter Twenty:
At the Gates of Ledgrim

June 8, 2009– The White House Lawn

President Welch rose and crossed to the podium, her once raven hair, now silvery, flowing about her shoulders as she gracefully moved. She paused in front of the microphone, letting the gravity of the moment hold sway before she commenced.

"Citizens of the United States, we are gathered here today to honor brave men who left their families and loved ones to serve us. By their bold actions and their sacrifices they have created a safer world for us to live in. Today we honor five men. Two of these men died in the service of our country."

"Garvey Dire and Arnold Stechter gave their lives, as thousands of patriots have before them, to protect our way of life; to protect our God given freedoms and liberties. To three of these men we are awarding the Distinguished Service Cross; Brendan Melhoff, Hank Giffen, and Arnold Stechter—whose father will be accepting the award on his behalf."

A clean shaven Brendan Melhoff led the way along the podium to humbly accept the award, followed by Hank Giffen, also resplendent in military uniform, and then by Arnold Stechter's lean-faced father. As the three turned to leave the stage, President Welch whispered in Melhoff's ear.

"I hope you're not going to hold me to changing into my cave girl outfit."

Melhoff smiled as he departed the stage, letting his imagination run rampant.

"The final two awards are the highest that the U.S. government can bestow—The Congressional Medal of Honor, which is awarded only to one who distinguishes himself or herself conspicuously by gallantry and intrepidity at the risk of life above and beyond the call of duty in the service of the United States. I hereby present the Congressional Medal of Honor to Bradley Thomas and Garvey Dire."

"In the absence of any living relatives, Garvey Dire's posthumous award will be accepted in his behalf by his best friend and peer, Bradley Thomas."

Bradley rose and came to the podium, somberly accepting the award that President Welch pinned to the breast of his uniform. He turned the velvet-lined case that held Garvey's medal and watched the light play against the starred blue ribbon, and the gold eagle that crested the green-wreathed star and the profile at its center.

Then his eyes turned back to the seats along the podium where his raven-tressed wife, Sena, sat, glowing with pride, and his two daughters and oldest son, Bradley Jr., who likewise beamed in the reflected glory of this moment. And why not, he mused. It had been their sacrifice. For five years they had gone without a father, and for five years Sena had gone without a husband. It was they who deserved this medal.

And Garvey? Without Garvey's sudden arrival Xio Cheng would have shot him down while gasping for air in the tunnel below the room. Where the woman, Ntashia, had come from was equally as baffling. Melhoff and Giffen had told him that they had suddenly unfolded from thin air. As incredible as this seemed, Bradley was inclined to believe it.

For at that moment when Garvey clutched the fallen Ntashia to his chest, the two of them seemed to fold inward, collapsing into nothingness and disappearing in a blink of the eye. Where or how they had gone Bradley couldn't say. He knew only one thing—that in his time of need, his best friend had appeared and saved his life.

Mars 47,000 B.C.

Garvey awoke on a rocky promontory, the red sky overlooking, and with Ntashia tangled in his arms. His lungs took in the oxygen rich air as he struggled to a sitting position, his head pounding with horrible pain. With anxious movements he tore the shattered NASA helmet from Ntashia's head, and leaned over her violet-threaded lips. He murmured a prayer of thanks as he felt the dew of breath against his cheek.

He laid her carefully on the ground, her purple-tinged braids splaying on the rocks, and methodically he began to remove the bulky pieces of space suit from her body, freeing her from its confines. Once he removed the suit he found the belt that Sar Savaht had placed on them before sending them through the anomaly. He had told them that it was a recall device in case of some sort of neutrino impasse or disruption in the neutrino flow to the anomaly.

The metallic device attached to the belt was burned and charred as if it was shorted out. Garvey looked to his waist and found that the device was still smoking on his belt. He quickly removed the two belts and tossed them aside. Perhaps the torracks had burst into Sar Savaht's laboratory and destroyed the anomaly device, disrupting the neutrino flow and somehow snatched them back through time in some sort of delayed reaction.

Doubtless, Arnold Stechter was dead— slain in the conflict, or too late to pass through the anomaly. Whatever misdeeds he had committed during his life, he had in some measure redeemed himself by his brave offer to stay behind.

Garvey's headed throbbed fiercely as he staggered to the edge of the promontory. Each time he went through an anomaly the pain and disorientation seemed to be worse. It was no wonder that Stechter had, in his confusion, attacked Garvey after coming through the anomaly and into Sar Savaht's laboratory.

The displaced astronaut sat on a boulder at the edge of the plateau and looked out across a vast, and rocky plain scattered with black-limbed ascarni trees. Beyond he could see the double peaks of the Gredgehold outpost, and beyond that the steaming lip of the yawning Rift. As he watched he saw a host of silver flashes in the crimson sky—a swarm of them descending upon Gredgehold peak.

Garvey felt a hand upon his shoulder, and heard Ntashia's voice. He had been concentrating so intently on the fleeting silver in the sky that he had failed to hear her awake from her slumber. "It is the forces of the Warlord Shaxia. They are using Gredgehold as a base of operations. No doubt they will soon be launching an attack on Ledgrim."

"Then we've got to warn Ledgrim," said Garvey.

Ntashia nodded and took a seat on the boulder next to Garvey, resting her aching head on his broad shoulder. "You're right. We must. But the distance is long on foot, and I don't know that I have the strength for the hike, yet."

"Me, neither," said Garvey, wishing he had a monster ibuprofen to ease the feeling that his head might explode at any moment. "But I'm afraid that we're going to have to attempt it anyway."

"Just give me five minutes to get myself together," said Ntashia.

After sucking the juice from the pulpy flesh of a blue cacti, Ntashia and Garvey felt amazingly refreshed—due in part to the anti-inflammatory effects of the liquid, and the amazing boost of energy imparted by the indigo elixir.

Ntashia wiped a blue droplet from her lips. "Lost Muvari have lived for weeks on the pulp of the Kwadeu cacti."

"It tastes like ambrosia to me, but, of course, I was starving—so almost everything would taste like ambrosia."

With renewed vigor in their limbs they set out across the sun-seared plains, a brisk pace carrying them for miles through the rocky wastes. Strange two-headed snakes and six-legged lizards basked on rocks, and Ntashia constantly called out warnings to Garvey lest he blunder into a nest of foot-long hypervian lizard wasps, whose sting was deadly poison—or worse yet, if he encountered the lair of the hobranx, which snacked upon the hypervian lizard wasps as though they were buttered kernels of popcorn.

As night fell Garvey took down a three-foot long lizard with a shot from their plasma rifle, and Ntashia expertly started a fire in a rocky alcove by using a piece of flint-like rock and the thorns of a dead cacti as tinder.

They roasted the lizard in his skin over the fire, and to his chagrin Garvey had to admit that the meat tasted somewhat like chicken. The double moons illuminated the twin peaks, and fluttering wings passed their shadows across the luminescent faces of Phobos and Deimos—as well as silvery threads of light. Ntashia cast sand on the fire and extinguished the flames.

"Shaxia takes much risk by moving her armies at night. True, the Muvari are less likely to see the movement, but the pesthules are abroad in the dark. They strike with stealth and are afraid of no army."

"Is that why you extinguish the fire?"

"Though they do not like its light, the fire will serve as a beacon calling them to feed upon our blood. They seek out movement and light and pounce on their prey. Thus it is foolhardy to travel in the dark."

"These pesthules are only abroad at night?"

"They fear the light of the sun."

They slept that night under rotating watches, taking turns peering into the night with the Caladrexian rifle cradled in their arms. As the dim light of dawn broke they set out once again hoping that they might reach Ledgrim in time to thwart disaster.

As the sun reached its zenith they hiked to the smoking edge of the Rift, and perched on the edge, Garvey stared down the vertiginous walls, into its fetid bowels. No naked eye could hope to pierce the screen of clouds that lay across its hidden depths. "Where is Ledgrim from here?"

"The way is secret and difficult without wings, but the descent starts south of here near a finger of rock that protrudes out over the Rift."

They skirted along the jagged teeth that jutted from the cliffside and finally came to the jutting rock that Ntashia described. To Garvey it appeared as a skeletal hand pointing the way, misty spume curling around its tip.

Ntashia fearlessly wormed her way around a jagged spike of stone, clinging to miniscule crevices and cracks while Garvey watched with trepidation.

"Come on," she shouted.

Despite his reservations Garvey easily scrambled across the stone. His Earthly strength gave him an advantage in clinging to the rock, and his unnatural leaping ability made it easy for him to reach out of the way handholds that provided a superior perch.

On the far side of this stone spike a narrow ledge protruded, and a dark grotto pushed into the solid rock. Ntashia led the way into the darkness and Garvey followed closely, listening to her footsteps scuff the stone ahead. Her footsteps stopped and Garvey lifted his Clip Pad, letting the green light illuminate the grotto. A single iron door was set at the back, concealed by thick vines and moss.

Without hesitation, Ntashia crossed to the door and knocked six times. Garvey glanced upward and among the hanging vines he found the gleaming points of a hundred spears studding the ceiling surface—their blades pointed downward and stained with orange venom. Each of these javelins was pressed into a coiled spring, which was held into place by a narrow bar of beaten iron. If this bar was moved the spears would be released, plunging into whatever hapless victims were standing below.

Garvey's eyes followed the vine-draped bars and saw that they ran through a series of holes bored into the rock wall of the grotto. He suspected that a lever existed in the chamber beyond, which could unleash the storm of javelins.

"Who dares disturb the sacred grotto?"

"It is I, keeper of the holy shadow and spirit," answered Ntashia.

The lock rattled and the door scraped open, pushing the mass of foliage ahead of it. Garvey saw the handsome, bearded face of Clivok Shar, Lana's husband, emerge from the shadows. He embraced Ntashia with a cry of joy.

"We thought you dead! Eaten by the Galbrans. Lana will be overjoyed when she hears of your return."

Clivok Shar's face darkened when he saw Garvey in the grotto behind Ntashia. "I see that you bring the outlander with you also."

"We are promised to be joined when we return to Ledgrim."

Clivok Shar's face lightened some, and he responded gruffly. "The tribe will be pleased that you have found a husband to strengthen our people."

Garvey read a dislike in Clivok Shar's eyes, and he wondered if he knew of the mental bond that he and his wife, Lana, had shared that first few moments after he had passed through the anomaly of the stasis loop.

"Unfortunately," continued Ntashia, "we have little time to celebrate. "Garvey and I have been prisoners at the Warlord's castle. I have met her blade to blade, and we slew many of her torrack guards in our escape to warn you that Shaxia has taken Gredgehold. Even now her forces are gathering so that they might sweep down upon us and destroy Ledgrim."

Two Muvari warriors emerged from the chamber beyond, a deep-bosomed woman with dark purple hair and skin as pale as moonlight was the first through, followed by a slender brunette with wide-set eyes and a mole on her left collar bone.

The purple-haired Muvari spoke. "This is grim news indeed. We'd best relay it immediately."

"Yes, Cinyan—but we will keep our post. Ntashia and Garvey will take the spiral staircase and deliver the warning."

Garvey could see by the matching rings in their upper ears, Clivok wearing four, that Cinyan and the brunette warrior were two of his wives, apparently on duty here with him.

"Where is Lana on duty?" asked Ntashia.

"She is serving as front guard for Ledgrim. If the city is not warned she will be among the first to fall," answered Clivok Shar.

"You didn't happen to hear if a man named Cray Lith made it back to Ledgrim after escaping from the Galbran lair?" asked Garvey.

Now Clivok smiled. "He did, indeed. You and Ntashia are quite legendary among the Muvari now for your daring stand at the entrance to the Galbran lair—though no one dared hope that the two of you actually still lived."

Each of the Muvari and Garvey took turns clasping their left shoulders with their right hands and bowing in a gesture of respect and comradeship before he and Ntashia passed from the deadly antechamber and into the guardhouse beyond. It was furnished simply with four cots draped with tangled blankets, a barrel of water, dried provisions, a small table scattered with writing quills and gaming dice, and a goodly number of spears, axes, and sword blades barreled up for neat keeping.

On the far side of the room a narrow staircase spiraled down a natural chimney. The Muvari had laboriously carved out a staircase that circled the chimney, which descended for thousands of feet through the cliff wall. The steps were narrow and uneven; one misstep could result in plummeting down the open center of the shaft, so Garvey and Ntashia didn't rush their progress, descending singly as the stairs were rarely so wide as to permit them to walk side by side.

Occasionally a gust of wind caught in the mouth of the chimney far below, and the air swirled upward carrying bits of twigs and moss aloft for hundreds of feet. These breaths of fresh air were welcome relief to the stifling atmosphere that rose through the shaft. The temperature cooled as they descended and finally they emerged through a recessed portcullis in the mouth of the chimney and onto a broken ledge. The chain and gears of the portcullis clacked as the spiked gate descended behind them, and they followed a treacherous path, the broad mouth of the Rift gaping below them, its steamy clouds boiling and heaving as the earth rumbled below.

"How much further is Ledgrim?" asked Garvey as he picked his way along a rocky ridge that extended from the cliff side.

Ntashia motioned to a spot where the trail stopped against a rugged cliff wall. "We are nearly there."

They stopped at the wall and Garvey looked around at the sheer slopes on either side of them. "Where to now?"

"Inside," answered Ntashia as she picked up a stone and pounded it six times against the wall of the cliff. "This is what they call Fargate."

A minute later a response came in the form of two sharp clicks that reverberated through the cliff wall. Once again Ntashia struck the wall six times. One response came and Ntashia struck the wall seven more blows.

Where Garvey might have sworn there was no entrance a seam opened up in the solid rock of the wall, and a section of cliff slid back allowing Ntashia and Garvey to slide through into a lantern-lit hallway beyond. As soon as they entered three Muvari warriors, skin glistening with sweat, pushed the gate shut. These leather-harnessed women locked the gateway into place and wedged the iron tracks upon which the door rolled.

Garvey noticed that the women wore little in the way of clothing other than a narrow skirt about their waist and a cloth to bind their breasts. The leather harnesses were to support their weapons. He also noticed that the air was thick with steam, and that along the hallway vent holes plumed with moist air. A man, quite burly for a Martian, and wearing a thick mustache that spread its wings into heavy sideburns approached and carefully studied them, his hand resting upon the hilt of his rapier.

A light suddenly went on in the man's eyes "Ntashia Stridj and Garvey Dire! You both live!"

Garvey saw now that this was Cray Lith with whom they had escaped the lair of the Galbrans. He smiled broadly. "I'm glad to see that you made it home safe and sound!"

"Oh, a harrowing journey it was—but not half as harrowing as yours must have been. You two are legends here now. I've told your story many times, though I didn't dare hope that you both still lived."

The warriors suddenly gathered round at the sound of their names. "You are the ones who beheaded a thousand Galbrans!" exclaimed a blonde warrior with unusually broad shoulders, and green eyes.

"That may be a bit of an exaggeration," answered Garvey modestly.

"We thought you were dead!" offered a dark-haired warrior with a pale scar running from rib to thigh.

"Nearly so," admitted Ntashia. "But we have grave news of which we must warn you."

"Oh?" said Cray Lith, his brow furrowing.

"The Warlord Shaxia has overtaken Gredgehold and is gathering her forces to attack Ledgrim."

Cray snapped his fingers. "Sersi!"

"Yes, husband?"

"You are the fastest of all the Muvari fliers. Perhaps you should put on some wings and warn the main city?"

Sersi licked her dark lips in thought. "I think that would be the wisest course of action." She leaped to her feet and scrambled off into one of the side rooms, emerging moments later with her arms thrust into brown membranous wings. She took quick steps down the hallway, and then launched herself into the air, her wings taking her aloft. In seconds she hurtled around a wide corner hundreds of feet away, and was gone.

"Do you know from which direction the attack will come?" asked the gatekeeper.

Ntashia shook her head. "Only that the attack will come. I know not if Shaxia has discovered Fargate."

"Let us pray not," answered the gatekeeper. "If Shaxia penetrates the gate, our defenses here are weak. It is only I and my wives Belish, Maron, and Sersi who hold the gate. They are fierce warriors, but even in need I doubt if they would allow me to put my life in jeopardy."

"I wish we would have had time to mount an expedition to Caladrex for weapons," said Ntashia. "Shaxia has the technology of the ancients as well as thousands of torracks at her disposal. It will cost her dearly, but there's no question of what the outcome of this battle will be."

"Don't write our epitaph yet," said Garvey. "We do have our plasma rifle with a nearly full clip. Shaxia won't be expecting the Muvari to have more than a smattering of the Ancients' weapons and with only a few charges left. This rifle is fully charged. If we can get it into the right position we may be able to force her to reconsider her plans."

"Perhaps," said Ntashia, "but you're a better shot than I. I fire it like I would a crossbow, but my aim still lacks something."

Garvey watched another gout of steam billow from a vent and into the hallway. "Where does all the steam come from?"

"From the bottom of the Rift. Some of it funnels up through a series of natural caverns. It's sweltering during the summer, but during winter this is the ideal post to have."

Cray motioned to them. "Perhaps you would like some nourishment after your long journey? I've got some provisions in the dining chamber—some of the best mushrooms grown in the caverns of Ledgrim!"

"Yes, thank you," said Ntashia, who felt the pangs of hunger working in her belly.

Garvey enthusiastically joined in on a meal of dried meat and mammoth mushrooms glazed in some sort of citrus sauce. He was about to indulge in a second helping when the flapping of wings sounded down the corridor and Sersi returned from the main city, alighting softly on her feet.

"The attack has begun at the main gate," she reported. "All our warriors have been called out to fend off Shaxia's attack. The presence of Ntashia Stridj and Garvey Dire is requested immediately."

Ntashia snatched up her sword and strapped it to her waist. "The attack has begun sooner than I thought. We'd best make haste if we are going to get to the front lines."

Garvey wasn't so ready to rush off. "Did you see Shaxia's forces?"

Sersi nodded in the affirmative.

"How many torracks were there?"

"At least two hundred. They have already landed a force on the outside ledge and driven our warriors back within the gates."

Garvey frowned and ran a hand through his tousled hair. "That's not enough."

"You're right," answered Sersi eagerly, her dark eyes flashing. "Shaxia has severely underestimated us."

"No, that's not what he means," said Ntashia as her mind settled into the same track as Garvey's. "We saw at least a thousand troops fly past the moon a night ago and take up position at Gredgehold. Shaxia is holding some forces in reserve, but where are they?"

"The torracks at the front gate are a diversionary force," said Garvey. "The others will attack at another entrance after all the other Muvari soldiers have been pulled to the front gates."

"But they already have moved to the frong gate," cried Sersi.

As if to confirm Garvey's theory a scathing sound penetrated through the concealed rock portal. The cavern here rose up for forty feet, ladders running up the walls to various ledges, which contained peep holes and firing slits that were hidden on the outside by the crawling ivy that cascaded down the cliffside. Maron, a warrior with wide shoulders and a blond ponytail that fell halfway down her back turned her green eyes on the small group gathered below.

"They're outside," she stuttered.

"How many?" called the Gatekeeper.

"I couldn't count them all."

Garvey coiled his legs beneath him and leaped to a ledge fifteen feet up the cavern wall, then leaped to another ledge ten feet away. The gatekeeper and his wives gaped at his jumping ability, but Garvey had no time for their awestruck gazes and peered through a narrow slit and into the crimson sky beyond.

Against the bloody backdrop of the Martian skies hundreds of silver discs floated bearing torracks in gleaming leather harnesses, naked swords thrust through belts, and some bearing rifles, which they aimed squarely at the secret door. Beyond the silver discs came an army on fluttering wing studded with razor sharp blades. Garvey quickly figured that Shaxia's present army must be five or six hundred strong.

As he watched a signal flag came down from a captain standing center on a disc. A score of ancient weapons burst forth lighting up the cliffs in a strange aurora of blue and red. The stone door began to heat, and finally the very rock began to melt away, dripping down in sizzling rivulets.

Garvey could see that under the combined barrage the doorway would not stand for long. He grabbed hold of the redlens narrow beam plasma rifle of which the apparition Sved had extolled the virtues. There was one nearly-full power pack seated in its belly.

He lowered his visor, thrust the snout of the rifle through the loopholes and pulled the trigger back. Bright lances of plasma spurted from the rifle. Garvey could hardly miss in the enemy-thick skies. He swept fire across the ranks of the enemy, but concentrated on the plasma weapons that were burning at Fargate. Single bolts cut through, two, three and even four enemies at a time, so heavy were they in the air.

Torracks toppled by the score from their silver discs—cut through by searing plasma. Winged torracks death-dived, crashing into the cliff side or wheeling out of control into the Rift where the boiling clouds swallowed them up.

In a matter of minutes, hundreds of torracks died horrible deaths. Garvey fired so rapidly that the rifle barrel glowed red and melted into a lump. He shoved the molten weapon aside before it could burn his hands and he watched the confused hosts of Shaxia's army wheel in the sky, seared and smoldering bodies heaping the ground in broken piles beneath, and winged specks of wounded and disabled torracks spiraling into the oblivion of the Rift.

For a moment Garvey planned to follow his barrage with a series of crossbow bolts, but he realized that to start shooting quarrels so soon would tip his hand that he no longer had any of the ancient technology at his disposal. Shaxia would realize that she had nothing more to fear from the devastating energy weapons.

Garvey hoped that the torracks would reconsider their decision to attack Fargate and break rank, fleeing before the horrible power of the Ancients, and for a moment they wavered and swirled in panicked turmoil.

Then Garvey saw a statuesque figure, resplendent in ancient armor, whirring through the throng, lashing out with metal-tipped whip at anyone who lagged or disobeyed. When she struck the whip flashed with blue light and the offending torrack plummeted smoking from the sky.

Garvey instantly recognized this dark-haired figure as the Warlord Shaxia. She had come forth to rally her troops. Now with her heavy weaponry destroyed or lying in mangled heaps below she had a diminished capacity to melt away the rock gate. Apparently she decided upon some other plan because she flashed forward, the wind billowing her hair behind as she surfed the currents of air. As she neared Garvey saw that she held a flashing gold ball in her hand.

This ball was familiar to Garvey. He recognized this as the type of device that had turned walls, ceiling and floor into a hollow void in Shaxia's castle—and he knew that Shaxia planned to deal with Fargate in the same manner.

Each ledge held a barrel of crossbow quarrels and a stand of crossbows that could be fired through the loopholes. Shaxia had already called his bluff so Garvey snatched up the nearest of these crossbows, yanked back the cable, and quickly slipped a four-bladed bolt into the groove.

Shaxia skimmed closer on the anti-gravity disc, nearly to the gate now, drawing back the golden globe to hurl it. She was moving fast, so Garvey was forced to lead her with the crossbow. It was a difficult shot at best, and an impossible one at worst.

Garvey pulled the trigger and the cable snapped forward. The bolt struck Shaxia's breast over her heart and shivered into pieces on her mail. Before Garvey could reload his crossbow Shaxia sent the globe bouncing forward so that it settled at the base of the concealed gate.

"The gate is breached!" shouted Garvey. "Prepare to fight!"

Cray Lith drew his sword blade, but Sersi and Belish pushed him backward, blades flashing as they took the forward position. Maron slid down the long ladder and dropped to the floor, taking up position alongside of Ntashia—who watched and waited, her violet eyes grim.

Outside, the metal ball clicked, its arms opening up and a blue light growing from the central eye within. A flash of blinding light exploded forth, consuming everything within a ten-foot radius. Fargate was gone—a gaping hole and a pit with sloped sides as smooth as glass replaced what had been there moments before.

Cray Lith and his wives gaped in amazement, but Ntashia moved to the edge of the pit. She could see torracks swarming from the sky like hornets from a nest, the red sun gleaming from their discs as they surged forward at impossible speeds. With their sweeping scythes and tremendous speed Ntashia knew that their feeble defense would last for only moments before they were overwhelmed. Yet there was nothing else to do, but go forth and die bravely.

On the ledge above, Garvey could also see the torracks swarming toward the destroyed gate. He too saw the hopelessness of their situation, but an idea flashed into his head. A long metal ladder extended upward—from the ledge on which he stood to yet another loophole above.

Without pausing to think his plan through Garvey leaped upward ten feet to land midway upon the ladder. He coiled his legs and jumped again, to the very top of the ladder. Here the ladder was affixed with two bolts driven into the wall. Garvey rocked backward and used his legs to pry the ladder free from the stone wall. As he teetered high above the gate he threw his weight to the left and the ladder squealed as it bent downward, swinging Garvey across the mouth of the gate, and leaving the ladder crossing the gaping hole.

No sooner had Garvey let go of the ladder and dropped to the floor when the first wave of torracks plowed into the ladder. It was too late for them to slow their momentum and their anti-gravity discs disintegrated as they struck, bodies impacted and broke, falling with horrible cries into the dish-shaped pit below.

The slaughter continued until fully two score torracks fell torn and maimed into the pit beneath. Flaming wreckage scattered the chamber and howls of pain filled the air. Now came the winged torracks, some ably darting beneath the ladder as they entered the gate. Garvey, Ntashia, and Belish were there to meet them, hacking away wings and clogging the entrance so that Shaxia's remaining forces must proceed on foot across the blood-slickened mounds of their own dead.

But come they did, swarming across their brethren with war cries on their lips. Their treacherous footing put them at a disadvantage, which the Muvari exploited to its fullest, and for a moment it looked like they might be able to hold off the Warlord's forces. A score or more torracks went down to join their dead and dying brothers, when Sersi's scream caused them to pause from their slaying.

Ntashia cried aloud in horror as she watched chitinous black legs emerge from one of the steam vents. Sersi was caught in one fully regrown pincer, and Shavrena grinned maliciously. The skin of her torso was blistered from the intense heat she had endured by crawling through the steam caves, but still a smile rode her gray lips.

"What? Are you surprised to see me, worms?" She tightened her left pincer and cut Sersi's body in two. Sersi gave a final scream before dying.

Cray Lith snarled, rage contorting his face. He lifted a heavy blade and charged at the sinthral, but she lifted a spear and brought it down, pinning him, through the shoulder, to the stone floor.

"I thought you were dead!" gaped Ntashia.

"Nearly so," admitted Shavrena, her pointed ears pinning back against the sides of her skull as she viewed the carnage. "But you didn't reckon for my ability to stick to things. I managed to reach out a leg and catch hold of the cliff side—which is more than I can say for my unfortunate companions."

Garvey watched helplessly as the torracks crept in through the open gate. They were caught between two dangerous forces—either one of which might have been able to destroy them. He, Ntashia, the wide-shouldered Maron, and dark-haired Belish stood in a square, their backs facing inward as their enemies closed about them.

"You tracked us here?" asked Garvey in disbelief.

"Oh, no. I suspected I might find you somewhere in Ledgrim, but what a sweet surprise to find you so handy. My hunger for revenge has been insatiable."

"And that is why you've thrown in with the Warlord Shaxia?"

Another, familiar voice, injected itself into the conversation and Garvey saw Shaxia striding across the skulls of the dead as though she were walking on stones in a river. She came through the gate, her deadly whip smoking in her hand, her cold eyes feasting upon the carnage. "I made her an offer too sweet to refuse. Shavrena was my contingency plan in case something went awry—which it certainly did thanks to you two pesky gnats!"

Shavrena closed the distance, her long legs moving like black stilts over Cray's writhing body. "The Warlord Shaxia has promised me a steady supply of warm bodies on which my babies can feed. Plus she has made with me a blood oath that I can kill the two Muvari who slew my mate!"

"That's generous of Shaxia," replied Ntashia. "But how is she going to make good on her promise when she's dead?"

Before she finished speaking Ntashia plucked the slit-bladed sacrificial dagger she had recovered from the City of Caladrex from her waist and hurled it. Shaxia had not been expecting the sudden attack, but saw it coming out of the corner of her eye. She twisted her torso to make a narrower target and raised the metal bracer on her right wrist to block the darting blade.

The ancient sacrificial dagger whirled past her upraised arm, a hair's breadth away from being deflected by the bracer, and it struck the Warlord Shaxia in the breast. This time her ancient armor did not protect her from the blow. The sacrificial daggers of Vackri were forged of the finest alloys that Caladrexian technology had to offer, and the double prongs pierced Shaxia's armor and the cold heart that beat beneath.

Shaxia's yellow eyes grew wide as she clutched at the graven pommel, and then she collapsed, stone dead. The torracks gave out a cry of horror that filled the chamber, and some immediately fell back, scrambling toward the gaping hole of Fargate. While this indecision fell over the torracks Garvey leaped over Maron's head, and hurtled toward Shavrena.

She raised her spear and thrust it hard into Garvey's abdomen, but the Caladrexian armor shattered the tip of the spear. The impact of the blow spun him around in mid-air. As his body twirled he swung his sword, and the blade severed Shavrena's torso from her spiderous body. He crashed into the chitinous black plates of her bloated body as it collapsed, the great pincers snapping reflexively. As Garvey rose he chopped them into pieces, then mounted the great dark mound that had once been Shavrena.

"We have slain Shaxia and Shavrena!" he bellowed. "Does anyone else dare stand against us?"

This was mere bravado and bluff on Garvey's part. The torracks still numbered in the hundreds and only four still guarded the Fargate at Ledgrim. If the torracks so desired they could still take the gate and maybe even the city, depending on how well the Muvari had fared at the front gate.

Garvey waited for his challenge to be answered, but the heart had gone out of the torracks. They turned, fleeing through the gate, struggling through the mire of dead in their reckless flight. Once free of the gate they took to the air, spreading their dark wings over the Rift until they mingled with the rising steam and were lost from sight.

Maron and Belish found Cray, and cut the spear shaft before pulling the blade out his back. They feverishly worked over him to save his life, stanching the flow of blood with compresses and then making a poultice of the fennivrae leaf.

Garvey knelt down beside him, observing the pain that showed in his face. "Hang in there, Cray. If the poultice doesn't take, Lana Shar has a healing device, which does incredible things."

"We did it," gasped Cray. "We held the gate!"

"That we did, but at a heavy cost."

Garvey found Ntashia crouched over Shaxia's body. She pulled the double-blade free and wiped the violet blood away. She smiled faintly as she saw him approaching. "We're no longer in subjugation to the Warlord now. No more yearly tributes. No more fear."

"That was quite a throw," said Garvey.

"And you dealt Shavrena quite a blow. I was worried that if I didn't act quickly the sinthral would subjugate me with her mind again, and I would be unable to act at all."

"And you did about the only thing that might have possibly won the battle for us."

"So…" said Ntashia with a mischievous smile.

Garvey cocked his head sideways wondering what Ntashia was getting at. "What?"

"So are you still going to marry me, or were those just words that you spoke in the heat of the moment?"

Garvey pulled Ntashia to her feet and looked deeply into her fervent violet eyes. He easily swept her up in his arms, and after partaking of her sweet lips began to stride down the long hall toward Ledgrim.

"Where are you taking me?" laughed Ntashia.

"I won't wait any longer," said Garvey, his blood racing as he felt the warmth of her body against his. "I'm going to find a priest."

Books from Pulpwork Press:

Joel Jenkins
Dire Planet
Exiles of the Dire Planet
Into the Dire Planet
Devil Take the Hindmost

Derrick Ferguson
Derrick Ferguson's Movie Review Notebook
Return of Derrick Ferguson's Movie Review Notebook
Dillon and the Golden Bell
Diamondback: It Seemed Like a Good Idea at the Time

Josh Reynolds
Bury me Deep & Other Southern Folk Songs
Wake the Dead
Born Under a Bad Sign: The Ghost Breaker & Other Weird Heroes

For more information on these and other titles, or for online ordering visit us at **PulpWork.Com**.